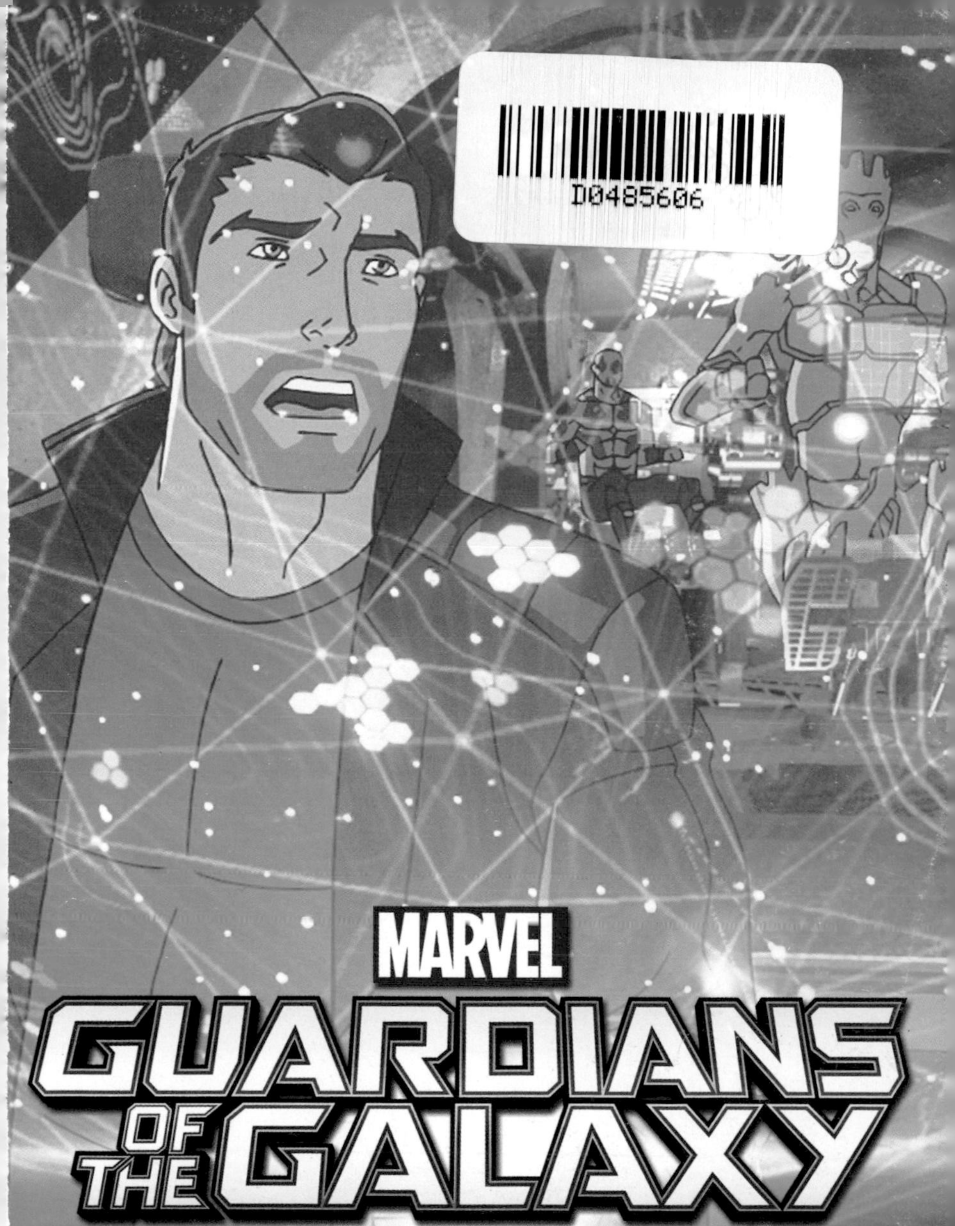

MARVEL

GUARDIANS
OF THE GALAXY

MARVEL UNIVERSE GUARDIANS OF THE GALAXY VOL. 2. Contains material originally published in magazine form as MARVEL UNIVERSE GUARDIANS OF THE GALAXY #5-8. First printing 2016. ISBN# 978-0-7851-9913-7. Published by MARVEL WORLDWIDE, INC., a subsidiary of MARVEL ENTERTAINMENT, LLC. OFFICE OF PUBLICATION: 135 West 50th Street, New York, NY 10020. Copyright © 2016 MARVEL No similarity between any of the names, characters, persons, and/or institutions in this magazine with those of any living or dead person or institution is intended, and any such similarity which may exist is purely coincidental. **Printed in the U.S.A.** ALAN FINE, President, Marvel Entertainment; DAN BUCKLEY, President, TV, Publishing & Brand Management; JOE QUESADA, Chief Creative Officer; TOM BREVOORT, SVP of Publishing; DAVID BOGART, SVP of Business Affairs & Operations, Publishing & Partnership; C.B. CEBULSKI, VP of Brand Management & Development, Asia; DAVID GABRIEL, SVP of Sales & Marketing, Publishing; JEFF YOUNGQUIST, VP of Production & Special Projects; DAN CARR, Executive Director of Publishing Technology; ALEX MORALES, Director of Publishing Operations; SUSAN CRESPI, Production Manager; STAN LEE, Chairman Emeritus. For information regarding advertising in Marvel Comics or on Marvel.com, please contact Vit DeBellis, Integrated Sales Manager, at vdebellis@marvel.com. For Marvel subscription inquiries, please call 888-511-5480. **Manufactured between 5/20/2016 and 6/27/2016 by SHERIDAN, CHELSEA, MI, USA.**

10 9 8 7 6 5 4 3 2 1

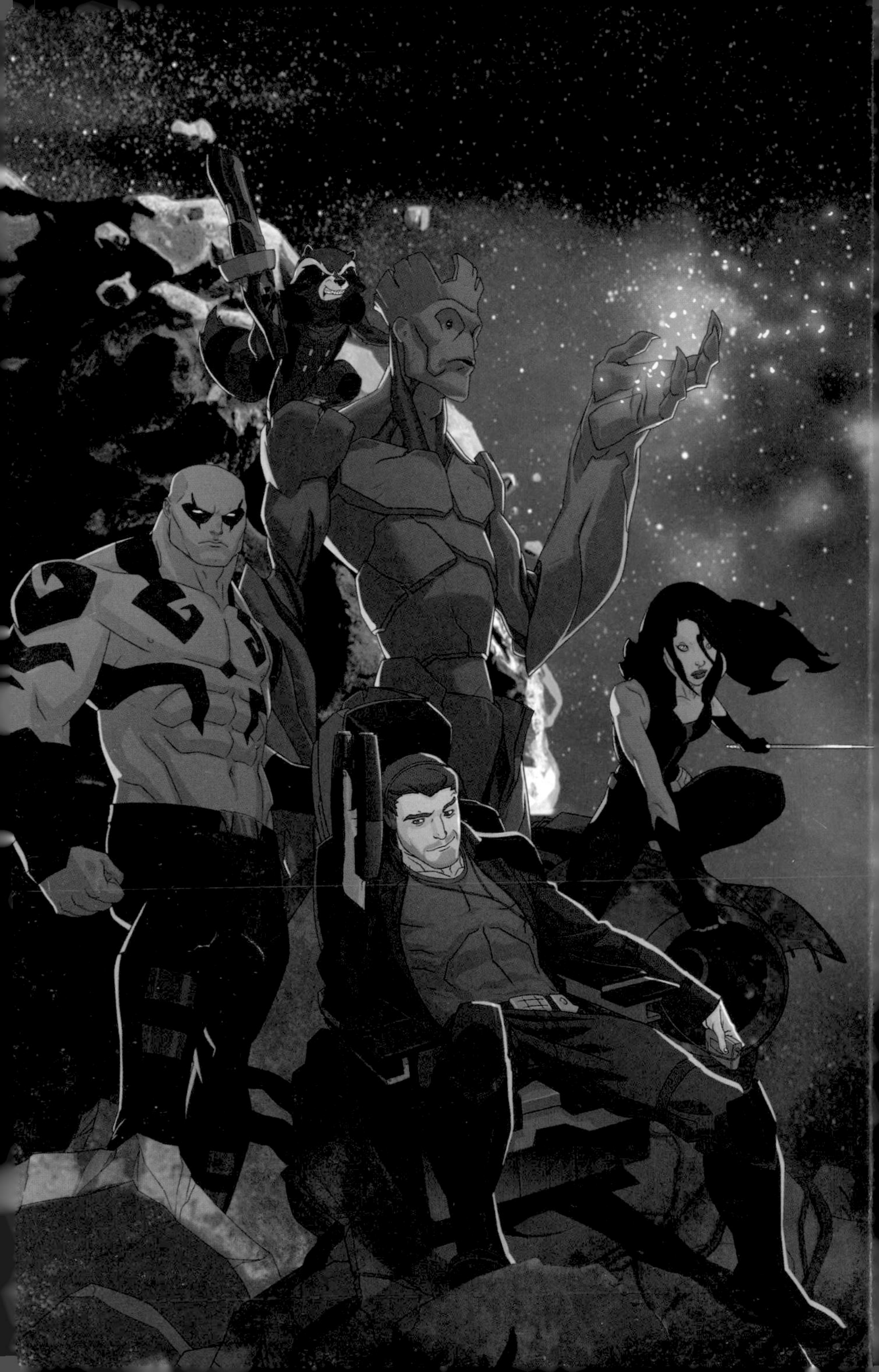

MARVEL
GUARDIANS OF THE GALAXY

BASED ON THE TV SERIES WRITTEN BY
DAVID MCDERMOTT MARSHA F. GRIFFIN
& ANDREW R. ROBINSON

DIRECTED BY
JAMES YANG & JEFF WAMESTER

ANIMATION ART PRODUCED BY
MARVEL ANIMATION STUDIOS

ADAPTED BY
JOE CARAMAGNA

SPECIAL THANKS TO
HANNAH MACDONALD, ANTHONY GAMBINO & PRODUCT FACTORY

EDITOR
MARK BASSO

SENIOR EDITOR
MARK PANICCIA

COLLECTION EDITOR: **ALEX STARBUCK**
ASSOCIATE EDITOR: **SARAH BRUNSTAD**
EDITORS, SPECIAL PROJECTS:
JENNIFER GRÜNWALD & **MARK D. BEAZLEY**
VP, PRODUCTION & SPECIAL PROJECTS: **JEFF YOUNGQUIST**
SVP PRINT, SALES & MARKETING: **DAVID GABRIEL**
HEAD OF MARVEL TELEVISION: **JEPH LOEB**
BOOK DESIGNER: **ADAM DEL RE**

EDITOR IN CHIEF: **AXEL ALONSO**
CHIEF CREATIVE OFFICER: **JOE QUESADA**
PUBLISHER: **DAN BUCKLEY**
EXECUTIVE PRODUCER: **ALAN FINE**

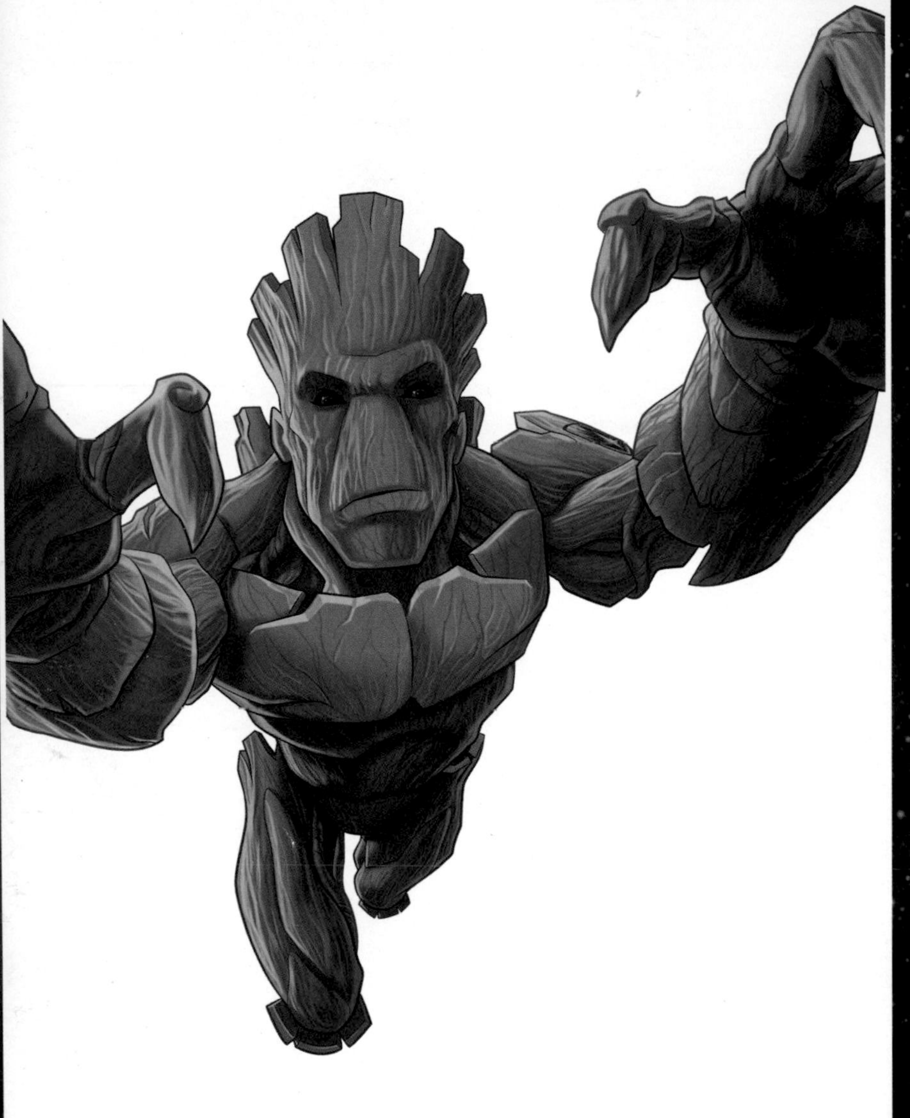

5 BASED ON **"CAN'T FIGHT THIS SEEDLING"**

PREVIOUSLY:
The Guardians came into possession of a mysterious Spartaxan cube that they learned once held an object of immense power called the Cosmic Seed. Half Spartaxan, Star-Lord was able to open the box to discover it contains a partial map to the Seed. The Guardians are now protecting the cube, but need a Pandorian crystal to fully unlock the map. Thanks to the Collector, they know just where to find one...

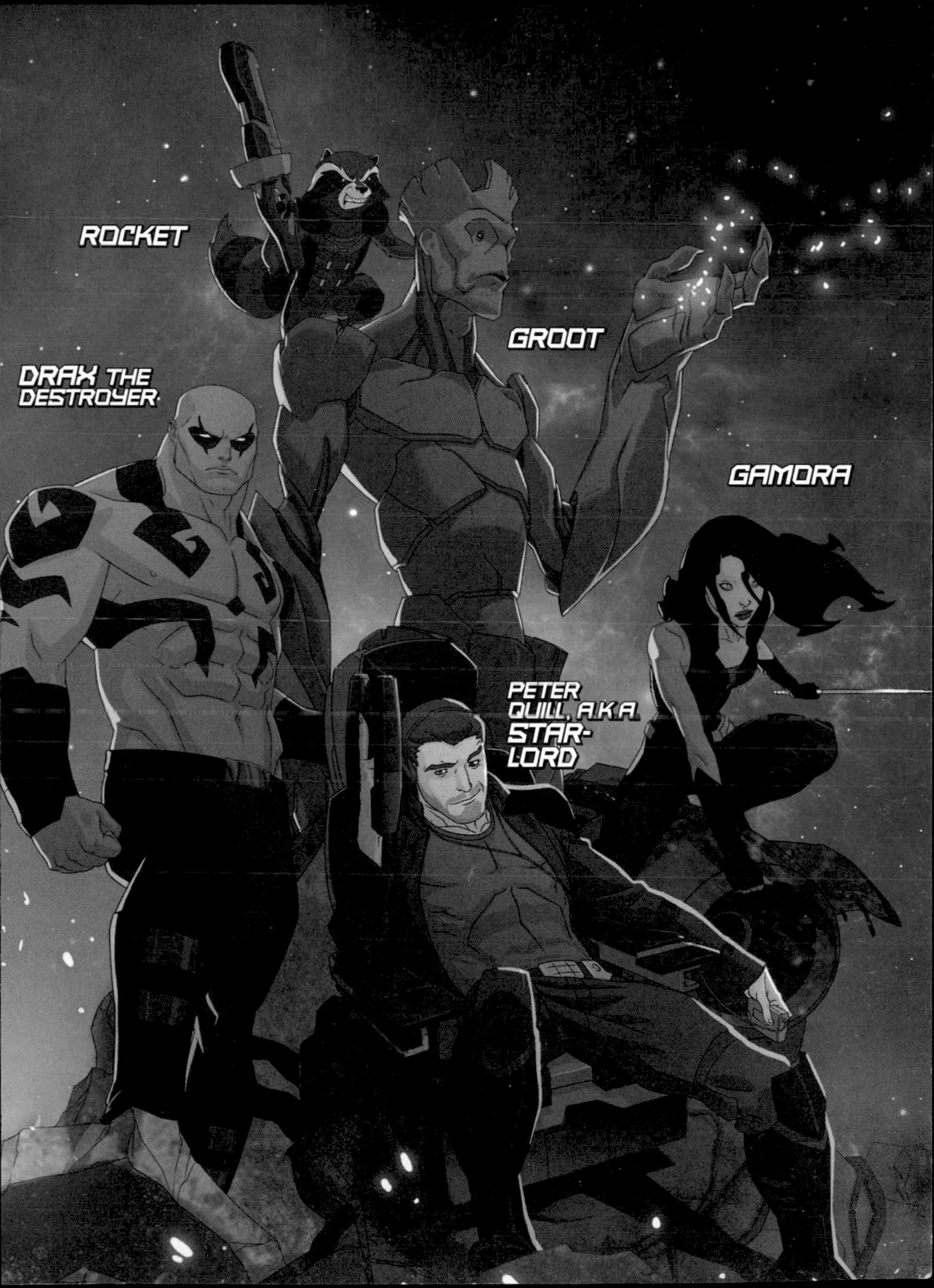
ROCKET
GROOT
DRAX THE DESTROYER
GAMORA
PETER QUILL, A.K.A. STAR-LORD

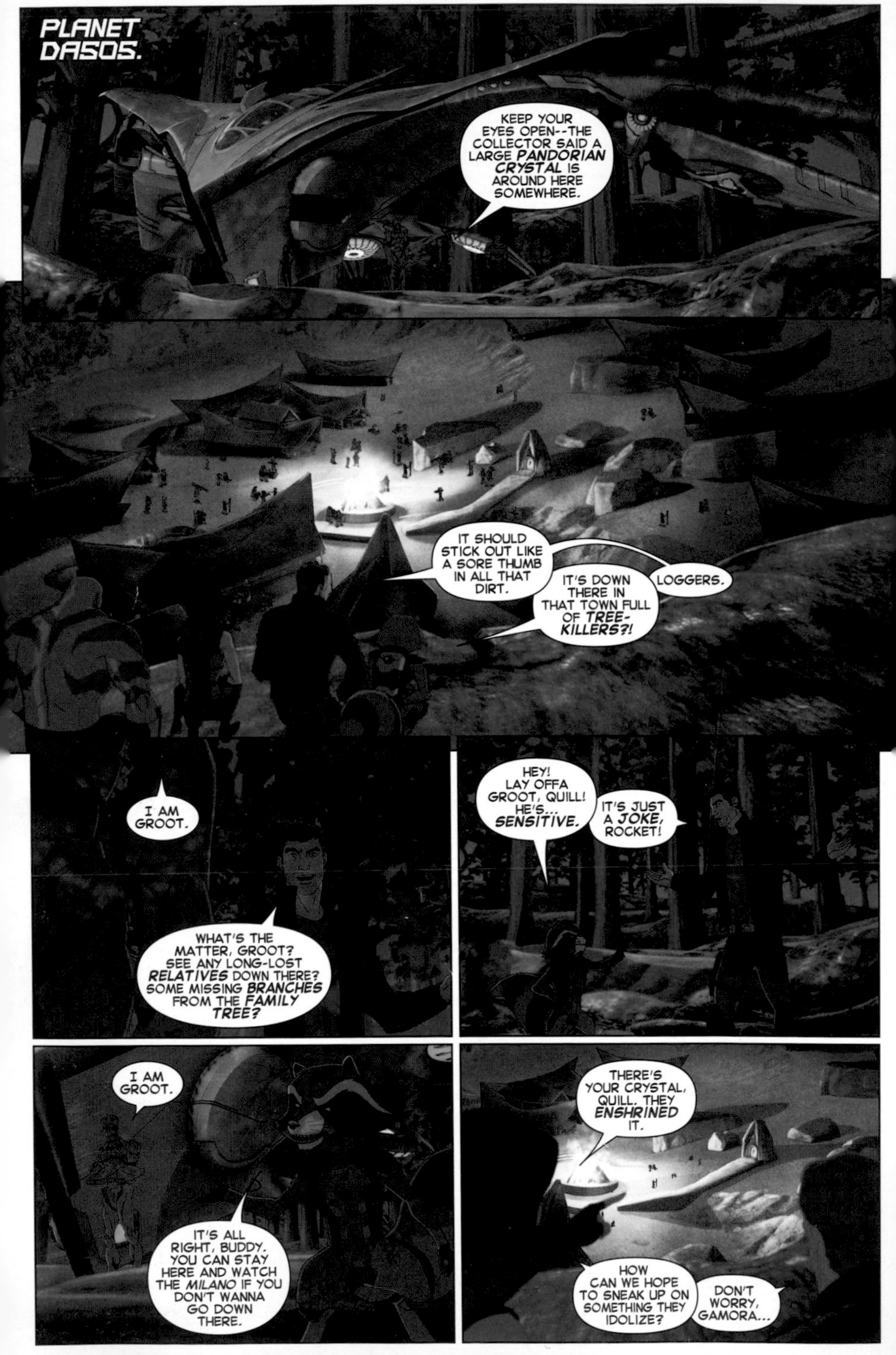
PLANET DASOS.
KEEP YOUR EYES OPEN--THE COLLECTOR SAID A LARGE PANDORIAN CRYSTAL IS AROUND HERE SOMEWHERE.
IT SHOULD STICK OUT LIKE A SORE THUMB IN ALL THAT DIRT.
LOGGERS.
IT'S DOWN THERE IN THAT TOWN FULL OF TREE-KILLERS?!
I AM GROOT.
WHAT'S THE MATTER, GROOT? SEE ANY LONG-LOST RELATIVES DOWN THERE? SOME MISSING BRANCHES FROM THE FAMILY TREE?
HEY! LAY OFFA GROOT, QUILL! HE'S... SENSITIVE.
IT'S JUST A JOKE, ROCKET!
I AM GROOT.
IT'S ALL RIGHT, BUDDY. YOU CAN STAY HERE AND WATCH THE MILANO IF YOU DON'T WANNA GO DOWN THERE.
THERE'S YOUR CRYSTAL, QUILL. THEY ENSHRINED IT.
HOW CAN WE HOPE TO SNEAK UP ON SOMETHING THEY IDOLIZE?
DON'T WORRY, GAMORA...

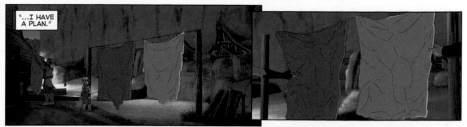

"...I HAVE A PLAN."

MAKE IT **FAST**, QUILL. THIS STOLEN LAUNDRY WON'T KEEP US HIDDEN FOR LONG.

RELAX...

...I'LL SLICE IT OUT BEFORE YOU CAN SAY--

INTRUDER!

WHAT SORT OF **BLADE** IS THAT?

OH, HEY, WE... UH--

WAIT-- **WHAT?!**

WHAT DO YOU **WANT** FOR IT?

YOU MEAN THIS **LITTLE**--

OI!! ERR, IT'S QUITE **VALUABLE**, ACTUALLY.

IT'S PROBABLY WORTH AS MUCH AS YOUR **CRYSTAL**.

THEN IT'S A **TRADE**. THE BLADE FOR THE CRYSTAL.

I CAN'T BELIEVE THAT CHUMP TRADED THE CRYSTAL FOR A **POCKET-KNIFE**!

I CAN'T BELIEVE THAT SIMPLETON TRADED THIS **AMAZING BLADE** FOR THAT WORTHLESS HUNK OF ROCK!

I AM **GROOT!**

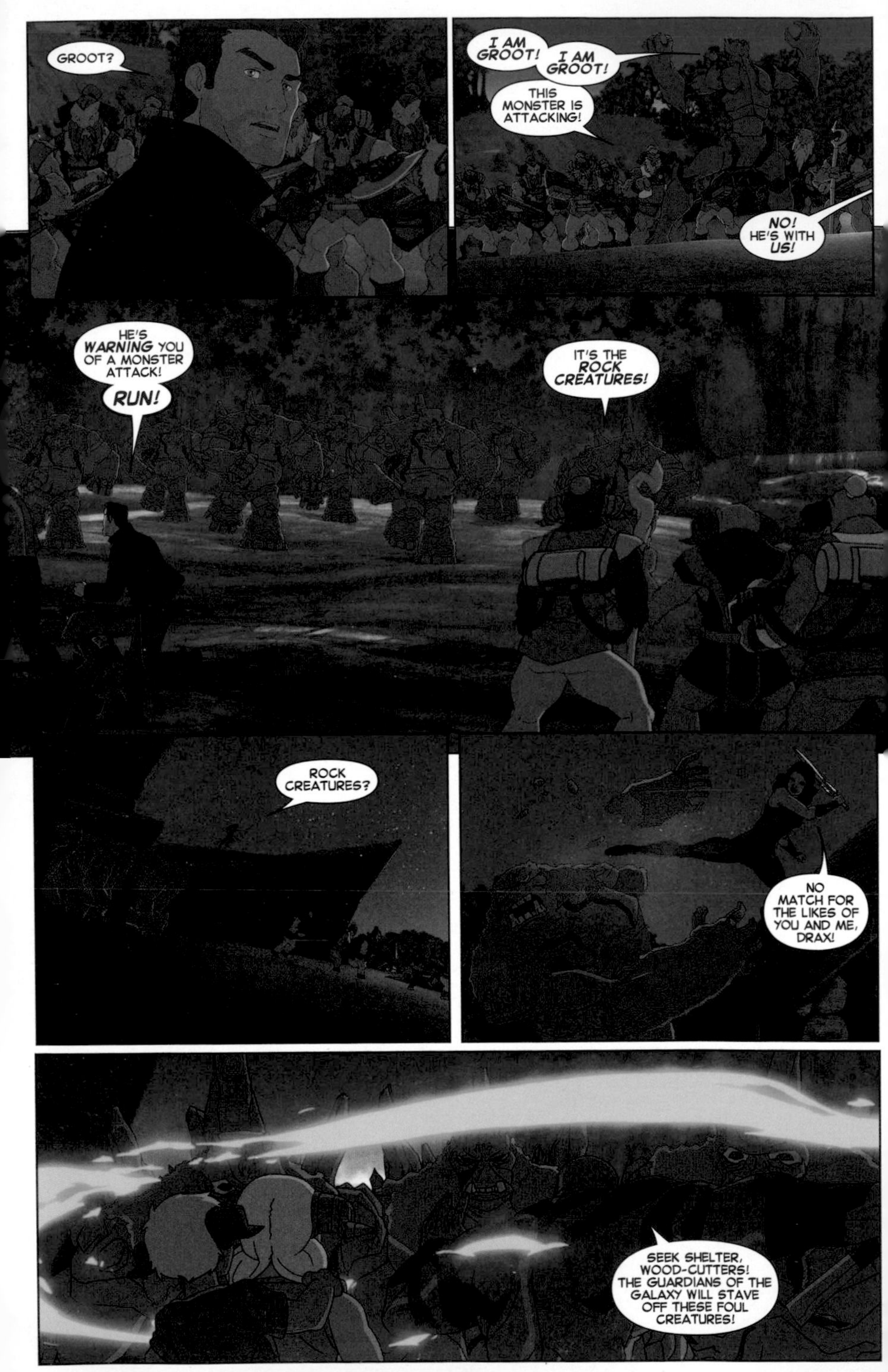
GROOT?
I AM GROOT!
I AM GROOT!
THIS MONSTER IS ATTACKING!
NO! HE'S WITH US!
HE'S WARNING YOU OF A MONSTER ATTACK! RUN!
IT'S THE ROCK CREATURES!
ROCK CREATURES?
NO MATCH FOR THE LIKES OF YOU AND ME, DRAX!
SEEK SHELTER, WOOD-CUTTERS! THE GUARDIANS OF THE GALAXY WILL STAVE OFF THESE FOUL CREATURES!

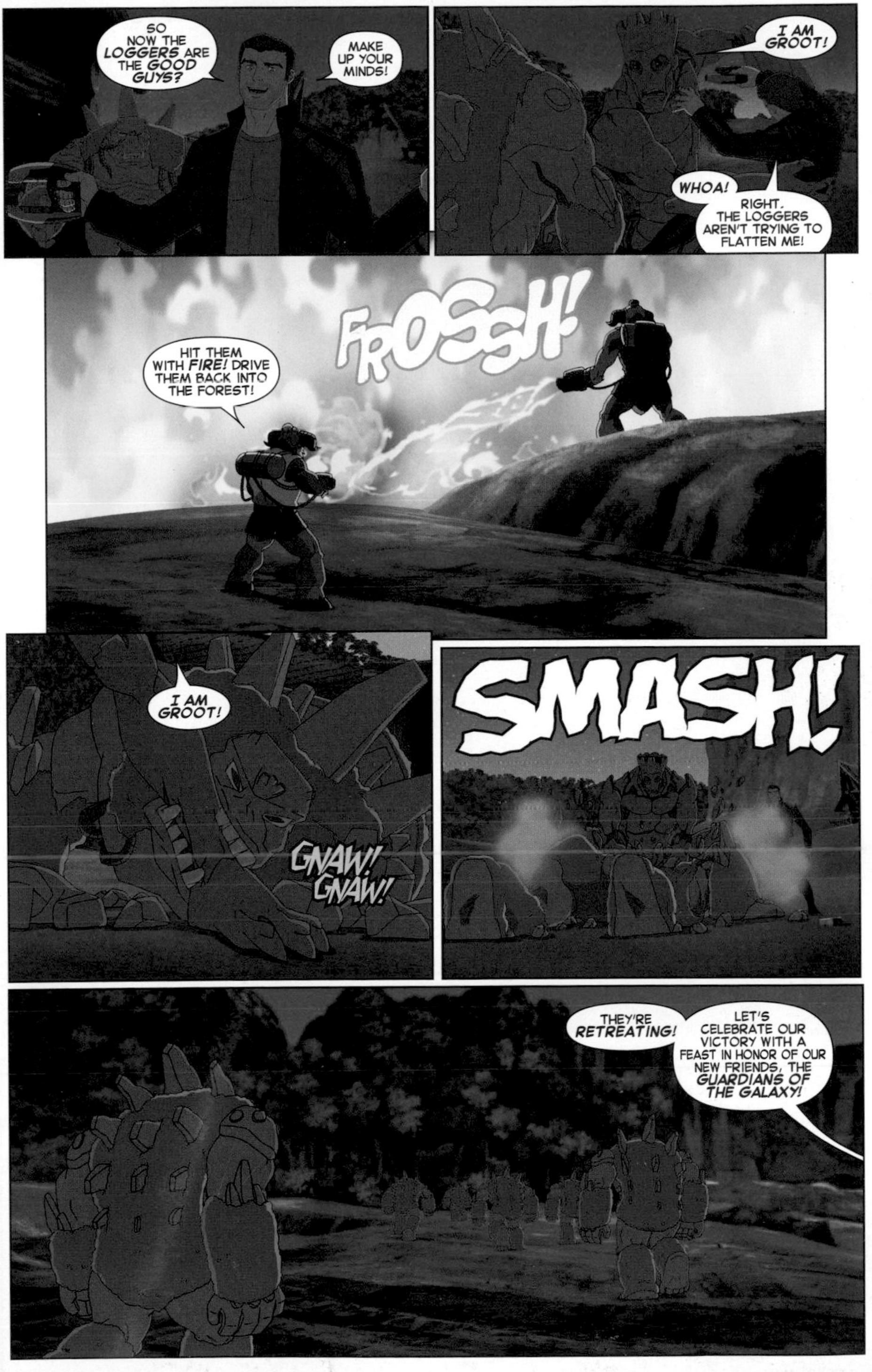
SO NOW THE LOGGERS ARE THE GOOD GUYS?
MAKE UP YOUR MINDS!
I AM GROOT!
WHOA!
RIGHT. THE LOGGERS AREN'T TRYING TO FLATTEN ME!
FROSSH!
HIT THEM WITH FIRE! DRIVE THEM BACK INTO THE FOREST!
I AM GROOT!
GNAW! GNAW!
SMASH!
THEY'RE RETREATING!
LET'S CELEBRATE OUR VICTORY WITH A FEAST IN HONOR OF OUR NEW FRIENDS, THE GUARDIANS OF THE GALAXY!

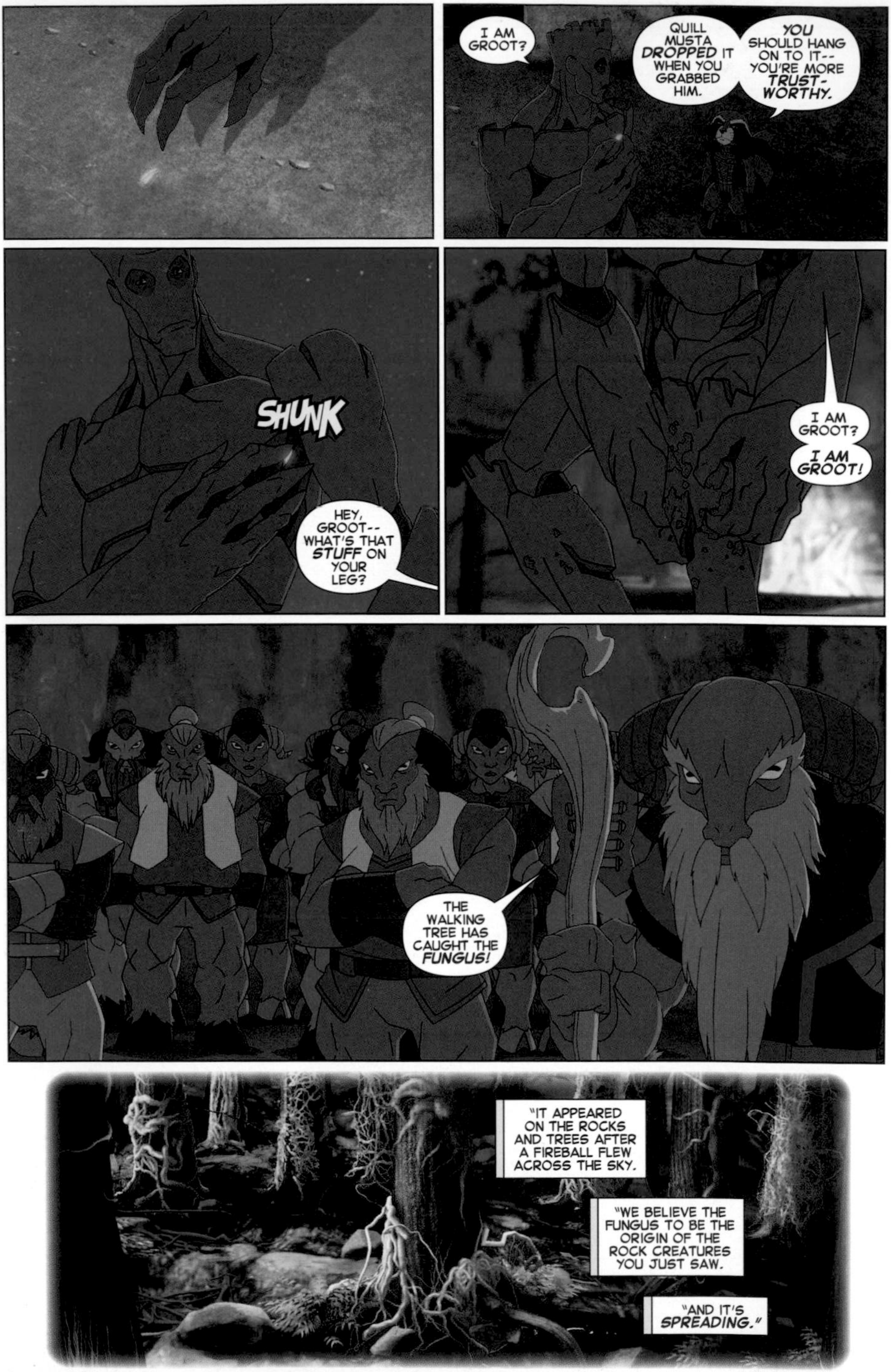
I AM GROOT?
QUILL MUSTA DROPPED IT WHEN YOU GRABBED HIM.
YOU SHOULD HANG ON TO IT-- YOU'RE MORE TRUST-WORTHY.
SHUNK
HEY, GROOT-- WHAT'S THAT STUFF ON YOUR LEG?
I AM GROOT?
I AM GROOT!
THE WALKING TREE HAS CAUGHT THE FUNGUS!
"IT APPEARED ON THE ROCKS AND TREES AFTER A FIREBALL FLEW ACROSS THE SKY.
"WE BELIEVE THE FUNGUS TO BE THE ORIGIN OF THE ROCK CREATURES YOU JUST SAW.
"AND IT'S SPREADING."

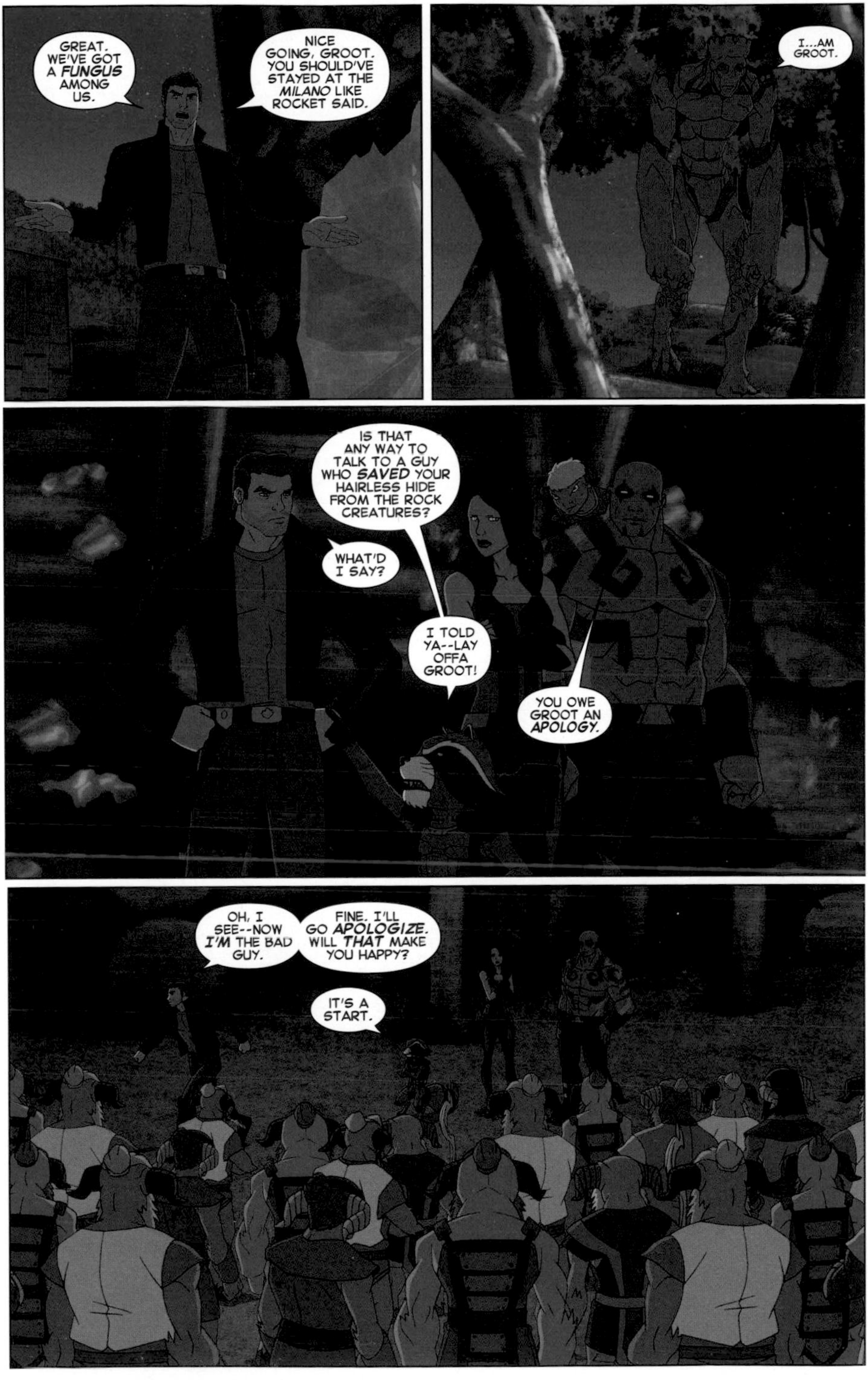
GREAT. WE'VE GOT A *FUNGUS* AMONG US.
NICE GOING, GROOT. YOU SHOULD'VE STAYED AT THE *MILANO* LIKE ROCKET SAID.
I...AM GROOT.
IS THAT ANY WAY TO TALK TO A GUY WHO *SAVED* YOUR HAIRLESS HIDE FROM THE ROCK CREATURES?
WHAT'D I SAY?
I TOLD YA--LAY OFFA GROOT!
YOU OWE GROOT AN *APOLOGY*.
OH, I SEE--NOW *I'M* THE BAD GUY.
FINE. I'LL GO *APOLOGIZE*. WILL *THAT* MAKE YOU HAPPY?
IT'S A START.

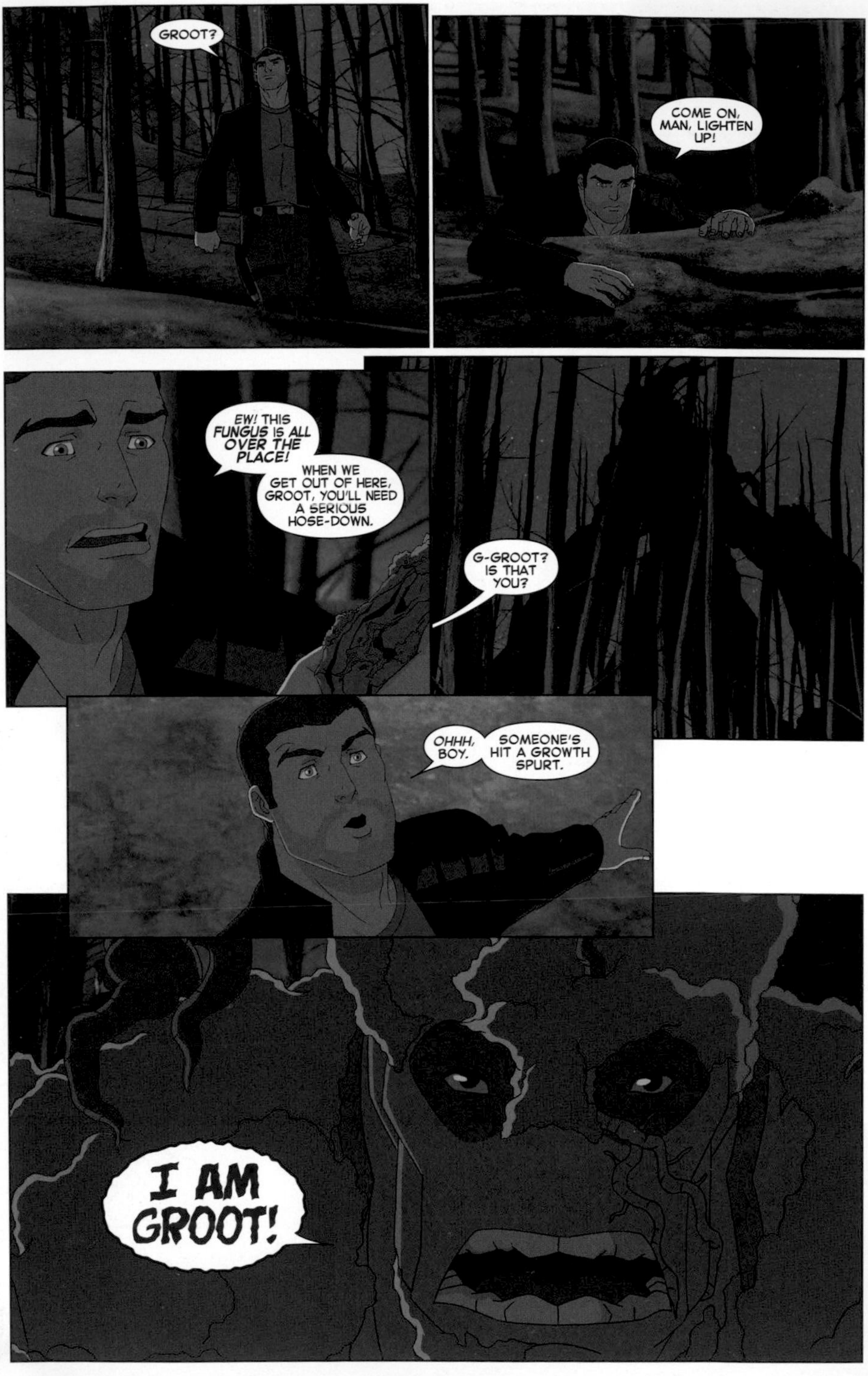
GROOT?
COME ON, MAN, LIGHTEN UP!
EW! THIS FUNGUS IS ALL OVER THE PLACE!
WHEN WE GET OUT OF HERE, GROOT, YOU'LL NEED A SERIOUS HOSE-DOWN.
G-GROOT? IS THAT YOU?
OHHH, BOY.
SOMEONE'S HIT A GROWTH SPURT.
I AM GROOT!

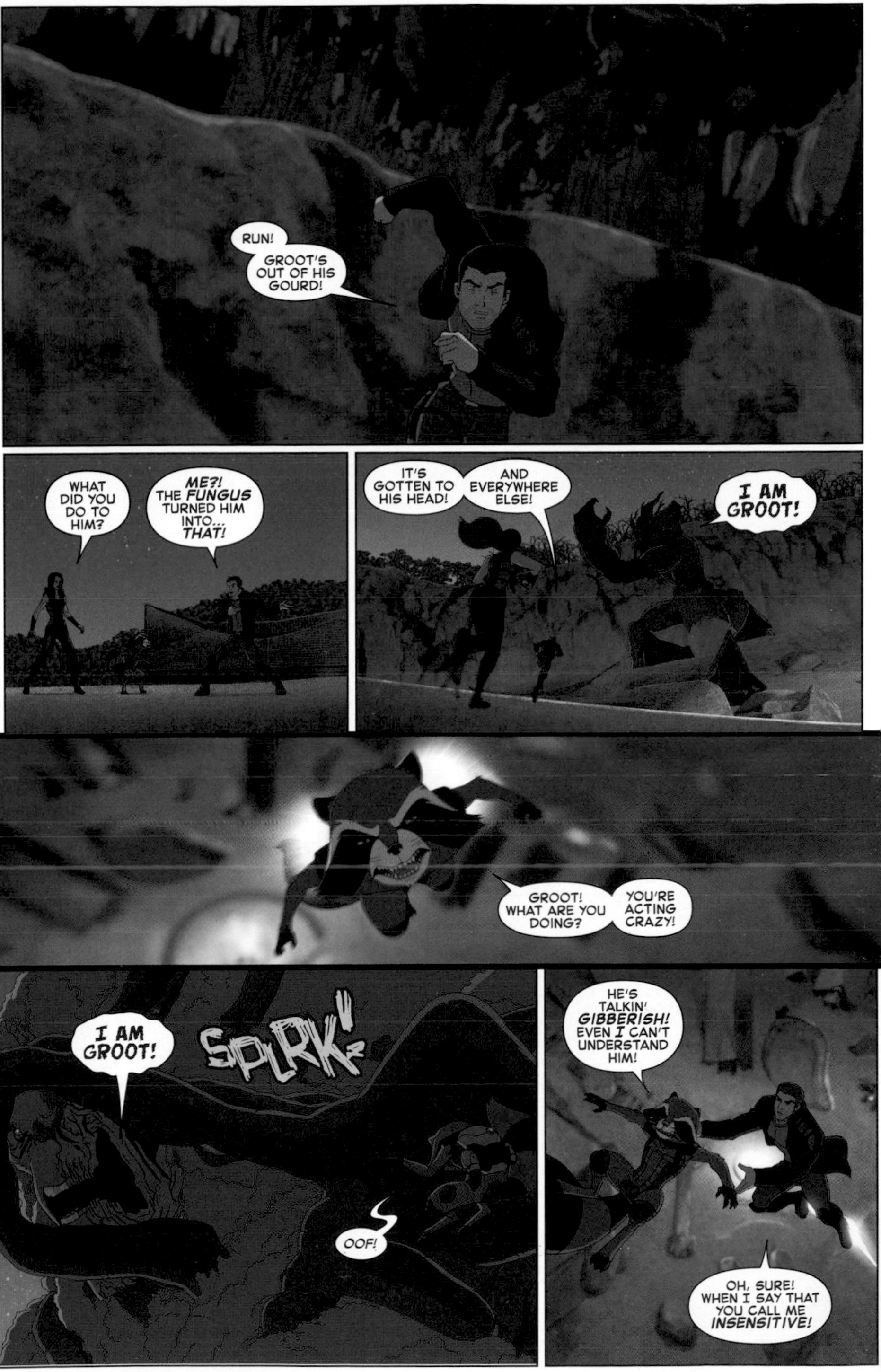
RUN!
GROOT'S OUT OF HIS GOURD!
WHAT DID YOU DO TO HIM?
ME?! THE FUNGUS TURNED HIM INTO... THAT!
IT'S GOTTEN TO HIS HEAD!
AND EVERYWHERE ELSE!
I AM GROOT!
GROOT! WHAT ARE YOU DOING?
YOU'RE ACTING CRAZY!
I AM GROOT!
SPLRK!
OOF!
HE'S TALKIN' GIBBERISH! EVEN I CAN'T UNDERSTAND HIM!
OH, SURE! WHEN I SAY THAT YOU CALL ME INSENSITIVE!

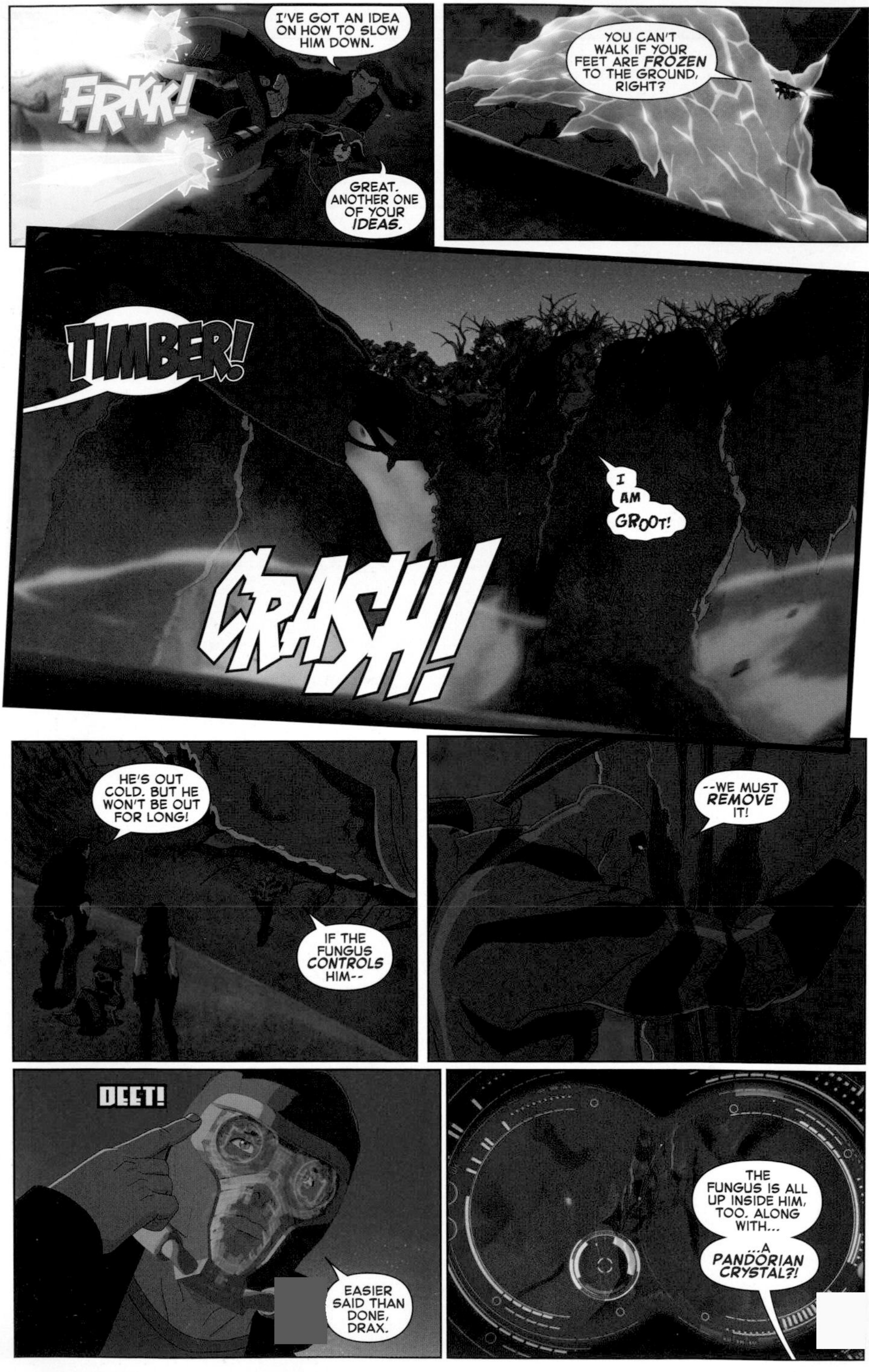
I'VE GOT AN IDEA ON HOW TO SLOW HIM DOWN.
FRKK!
GREAT. ANOTHER ONE OF YOUR IDEAS.
YOU CAN'T WALK IF YOUR FEET ARE FROZEN TO THE GROUND, RIGHT?
TIMBER!
I AM GROOT!
CRASH!
HE'S OUT COLD. BUT HE WON'T BE OUT FOR LONG!
IF THE FUNGUS CONTROLS HIM--
--WE MUST REMOVE IT!
DEET!
EASIER SAID THAN DONE, DRAX.
THE FUNGUS IS ALL UP INSIDE HIM, TOO. ALONG WITH...
...A PANDORIAN CRYSTAL?!

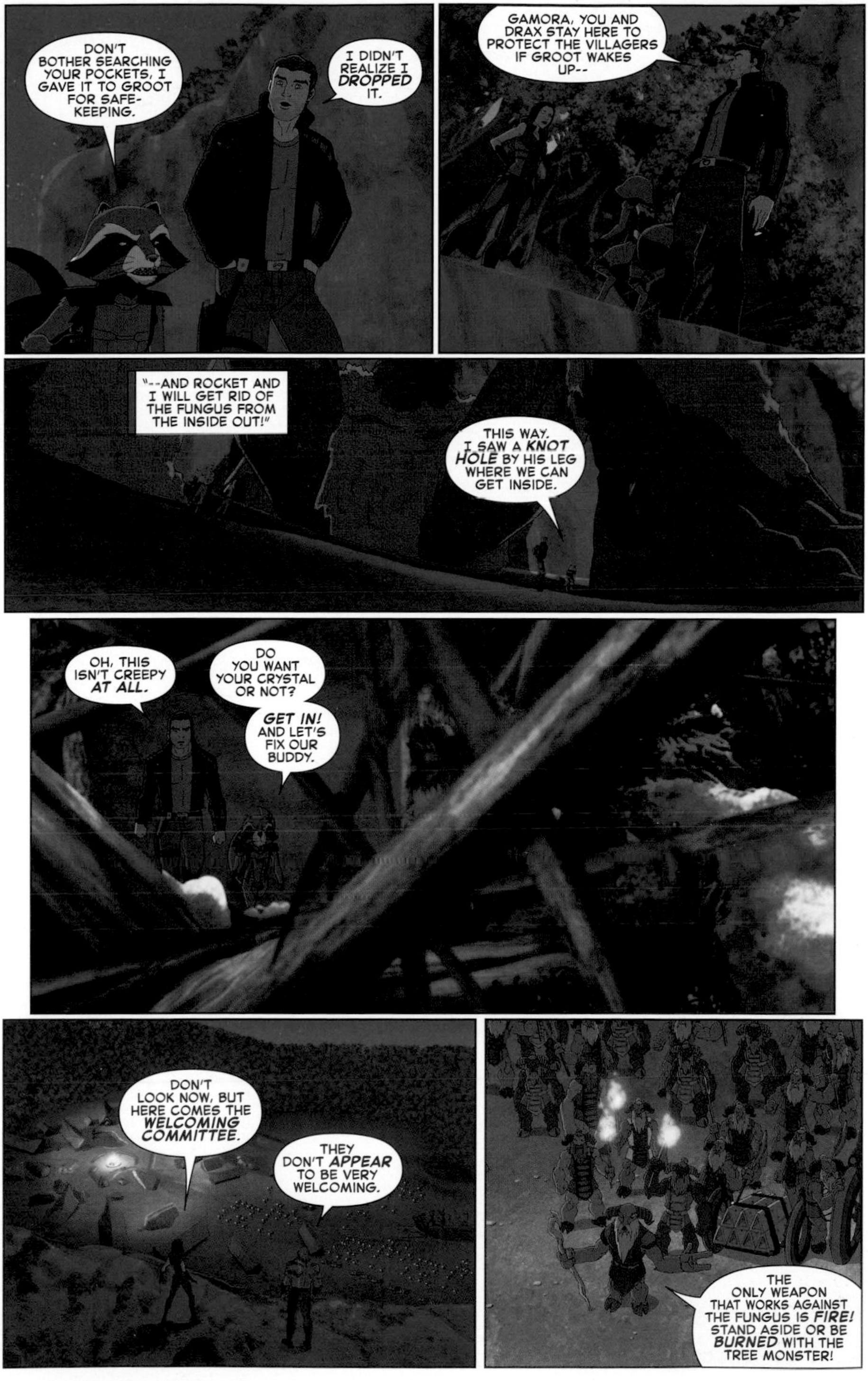
DON'T BOTHER SEARCHING YOUR POCKETS, I GAVE IT TO GROOT FOR SAFE-KEEPING.
I DIDN'T REALIZE I DROPPED IT.
GAMORA, YOU AND DRAX STAY HERE TO PROTECT THE VILLAGERS IF GROOT WAKES UP--
"--AND ROCKET AND I WILL GET RID OF THE FUNGUS FROM THE INSIDE OUT!"
THIS WAY. I SAW A KNOT HOLE BY HIS LEG WHERE WE CAN GET INSIDE.
OH, THIS ISN'T CREEPY AT ALL.
DO YOU WANT YOUR CRYSTAL OR NOT?
GET IN! AND LET'S FIX OUR BUDDY.
DON'T LOOK NOW, BUT HERE COMES THE WELCOMING COMMITTEE.
THEY DON'T APPEAR TO BE VERY WELCOMING.
THE ONLY WEAPON THAT WORKS AGAINST THE FUNGUS IS FIRE! STAND ASIDE OR BE BURNED WITH THE TREE MONSTER!

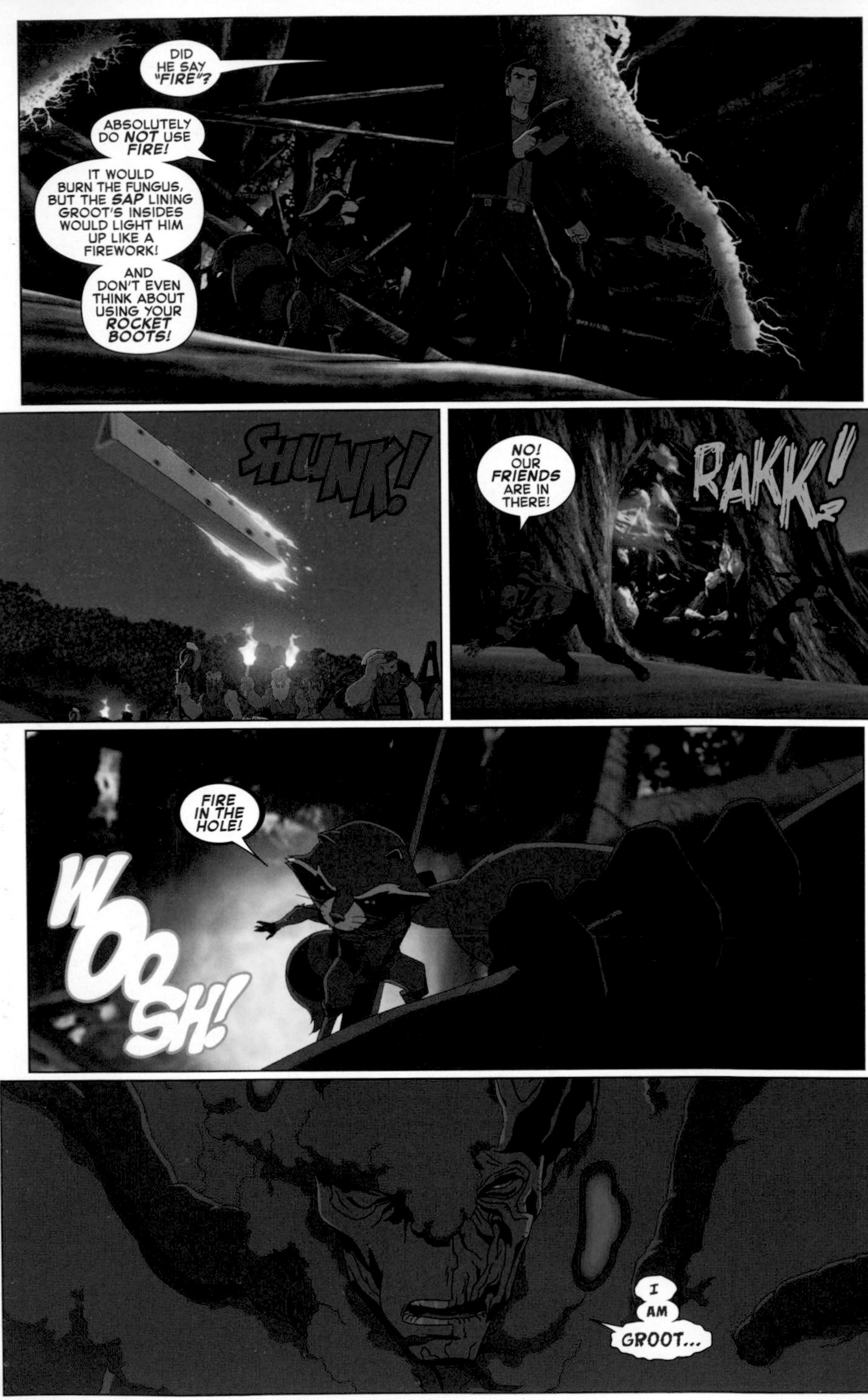
DID HE SAY "FIRE"?
ABSOLUTELY DO NOT USE FIRE!
IT WOULD BURN THE FUNGUS, BUT THE SAP LINING GROOT'S INSIDES WOULD LIGHT HIM UP LIKE A FIREWORK!
AND DON'T EVEN THINK ABOUT USING YOUR ROCKET BOOTS!
SHUNK!
NO! OUR FRIENDS ARE IN THERE!
RAKK!
FIRE IN THE HOLE!
WOOOSH!
I AM GROOT...

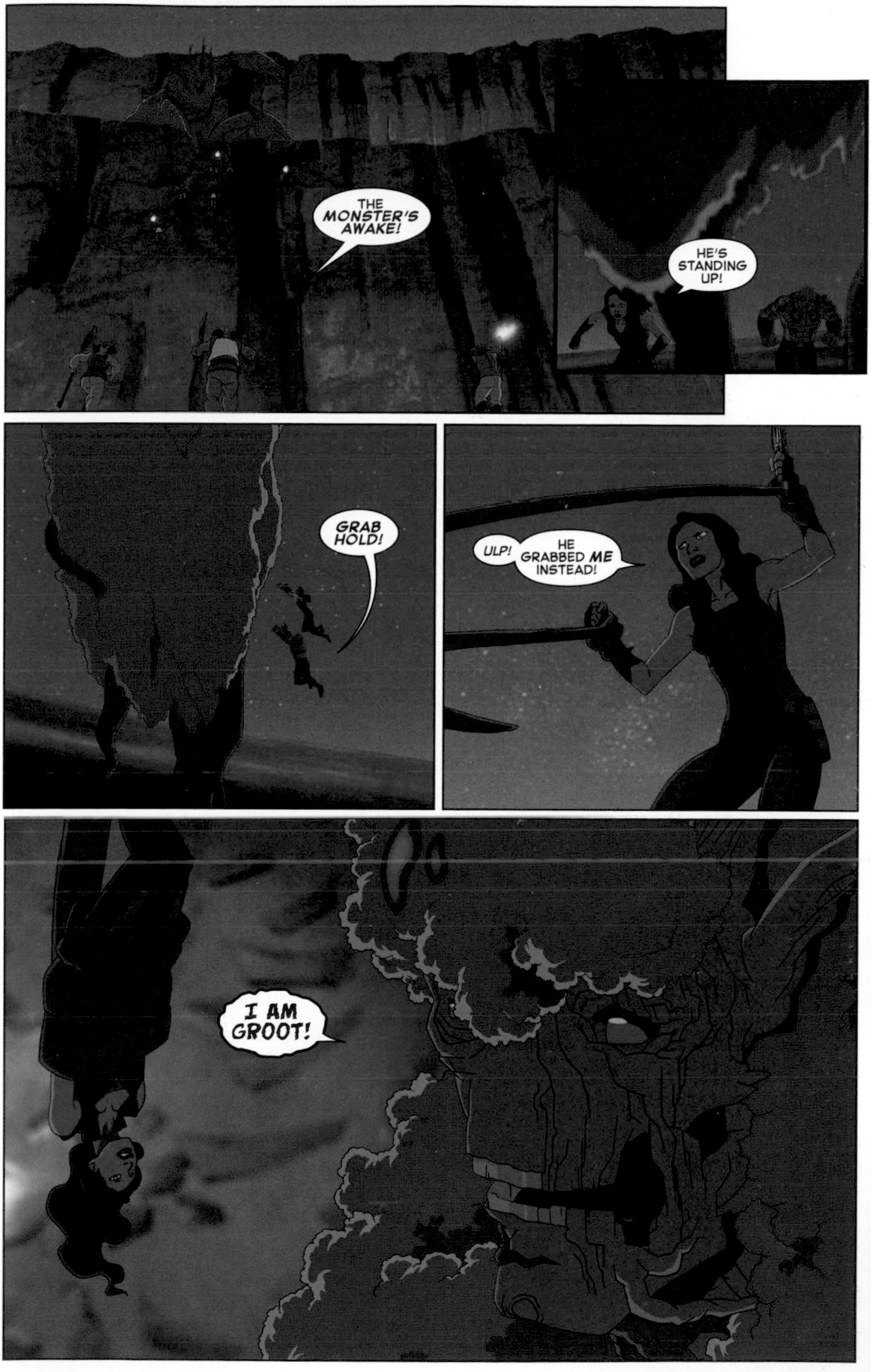
THE MONSTER'S AWAKE!
HE'S STANDING UP!
GRAB HOLD!
ULP!
HE GRABBED ME INSTEAD!
I AM GROOT!

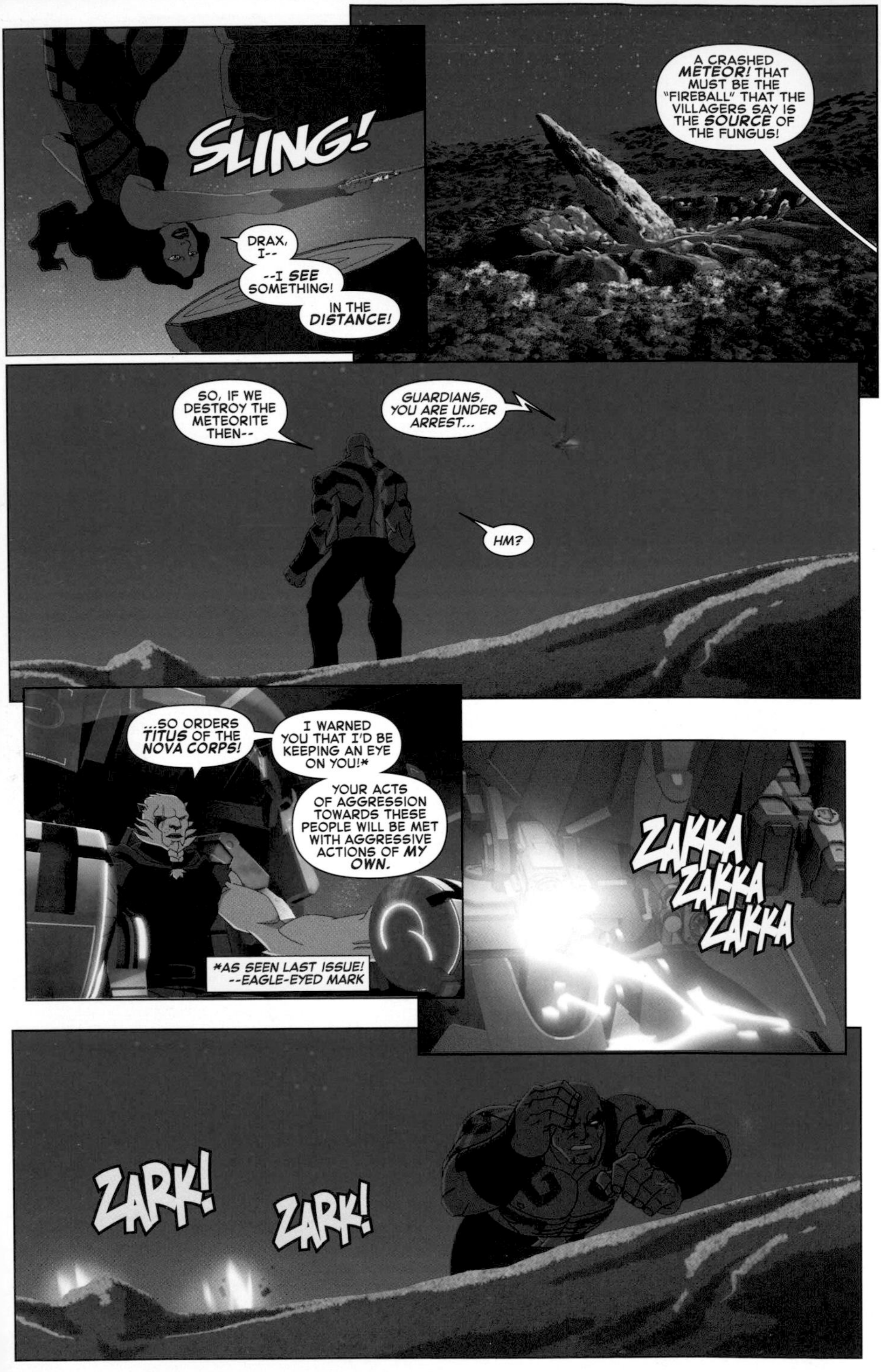
SLING!
DRAX, I--
--I SEE SOMETHING!
IN THE DISTANCE!
A CRASHED METEOR! THAT MUST BE THE "FIREBALL" THAT THE VILLAGERS SAY IS THE SOURCE OF THE FUNGUS!
SO, IF WE DESTROY THE METEORITE THEN--
GUARDIANS, YOU ARE UNDER ARREST...
HM?
...SO ORDERS TITUS OF THE NOVA CORPS!
I WARNED YOU THAT I'D BE KEEPING AN EYE ON YOU!*
YOUR ACTS OF AGGRESSION TOWARDS THESE PEOPLE WILL BE MET WITH AGGRESSIVE ACTIONS OF MY OWN.
*AS SEEN LAST ISSUE! --EAGLE-EYED MARK
ZAKKA ZAKKA ZAKKA
ZARK!
ZARK!

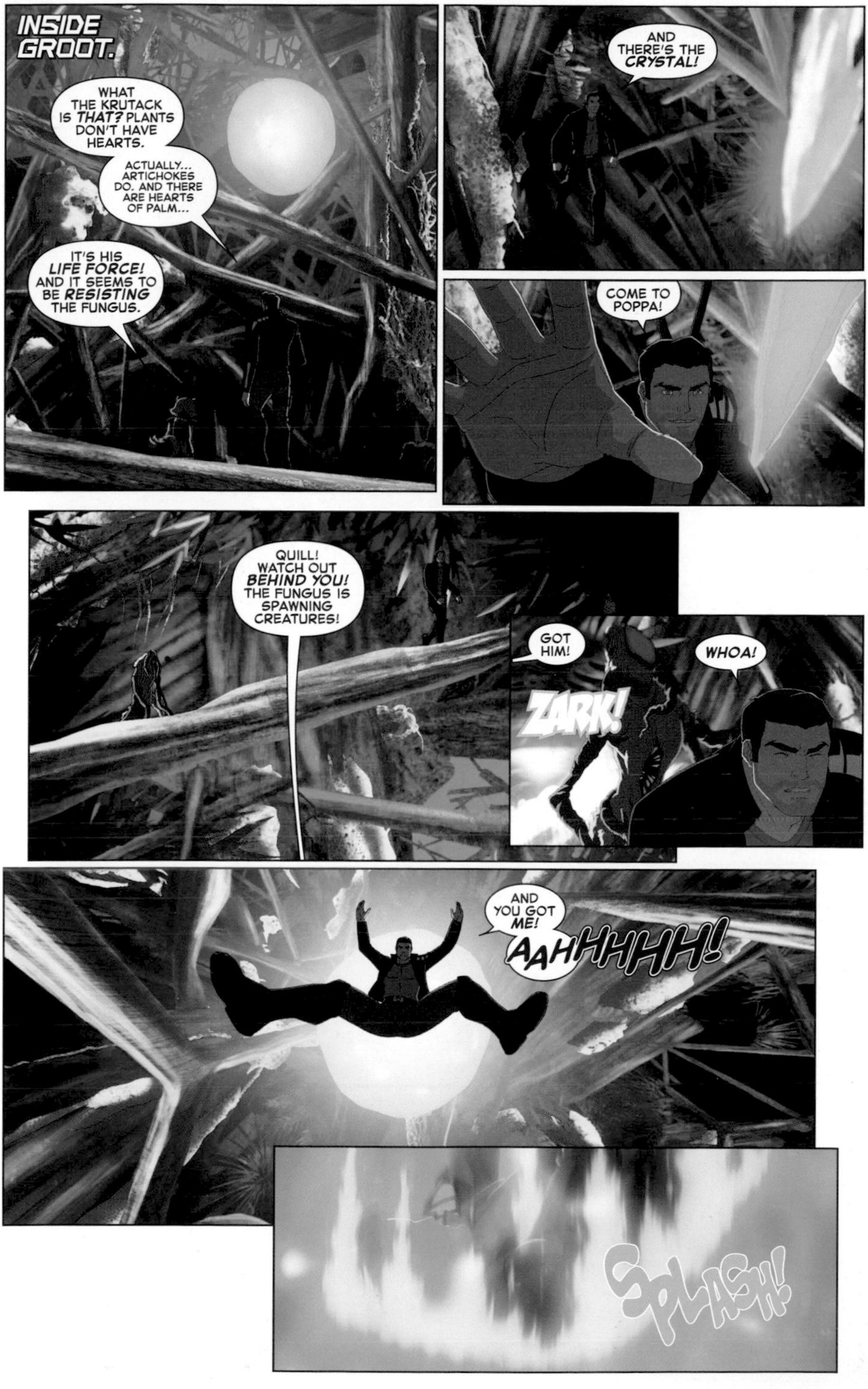
INSIDE GROOT.
WHAT THE KRUTACK IS THAT? PLANTS DON'T HAVE HEARTS.
ACTUALLY... ARTICHOKES DO. AND THERE ARE HEARTS OF PALM...
IT'S HIS LIFE FORCE! AND IT SEEMS TO BE RESISTING THE FUNGUS.
AND THERE'S THE CRYSTAL!
COME TO POPPA!
QUILL! WATCH OUT BEHIND YOU! THE FUNGUS IS SPAWNING CREATURES!
GOT HIM!
ZARK!
WHOA!
AND YOU GOT ME!
AAHHHHH!
SPLASH!

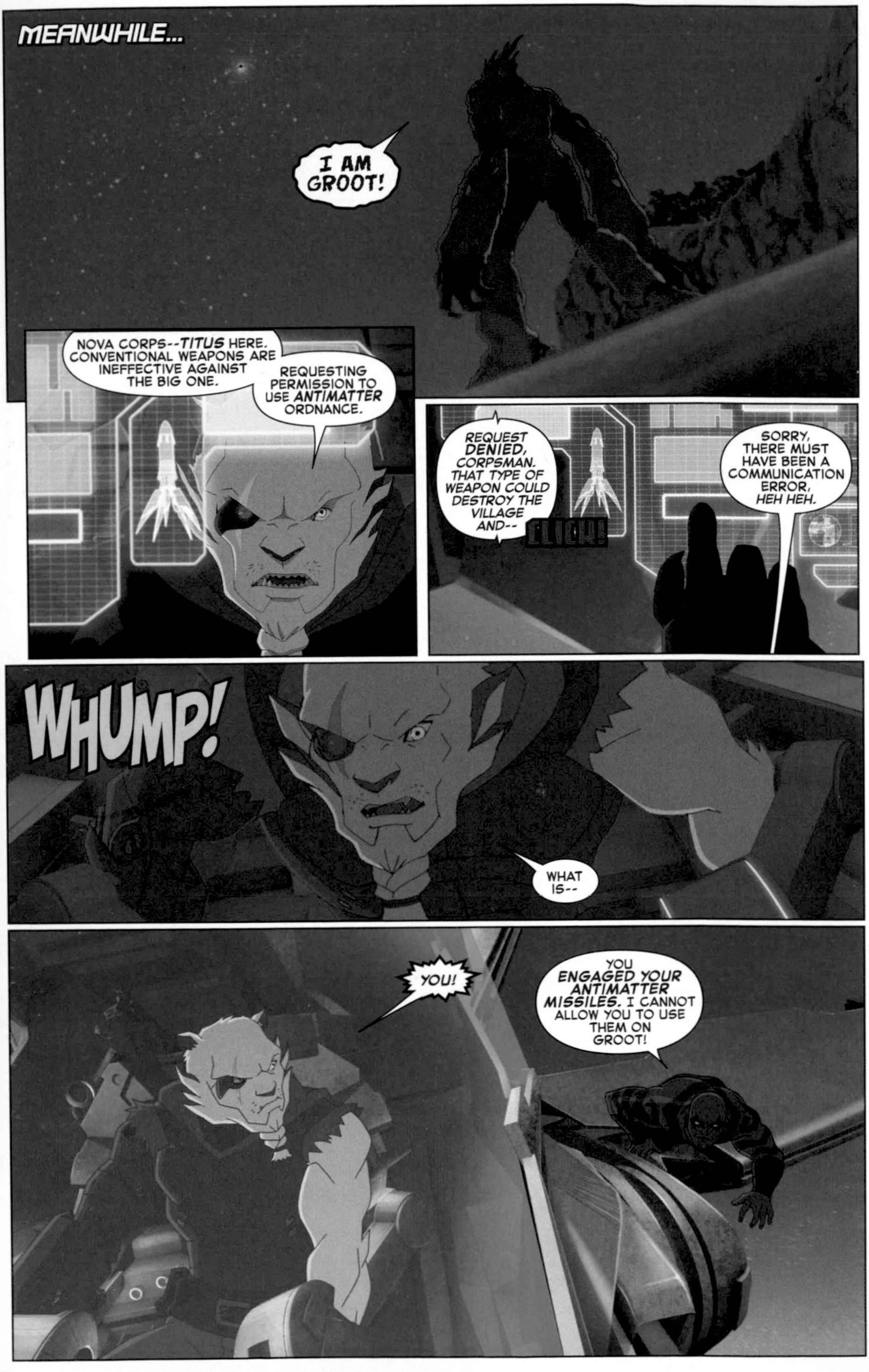
MEANWHILE...
I AM GROOT!
NOVA CORPS--TITUS HERE. CONVENTIONAL WEAPONS ARE INEFFECTIVE AGAINST THE BIG ONE.
REQUESTING PERMISSION TO USE ANTIMATTER ORDNANCE.
REQUEST DENIED, CORPSMAN. THAT TYPE OF WEAPON COULD DESTROY THE VILLAGE AND--
CLICK!
SORRY, THERE MUST HAVE BEEN A COMMUNICATION ERROR, HEH HEH.
WHUMP!
WHAT IS--
YOU!
YOU ENGAGED YOUR ANTIMATTER MISSILES. I CANNOT ALLOW YOU TO USE THEM ON GROOT!

THIS IS OUT OF YOUR HANDS NOW, DESTROYER!

FROOSH!

NO, IT IS *NOT!*

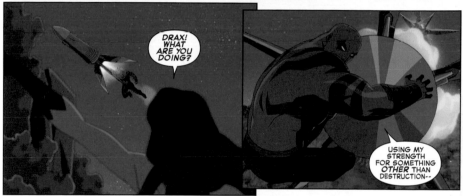

DRAX! WHAT ARE YOU DOING?

USING MY STRENGTH FOR SOMETHING *OTHER* THAN DESTRUCTION--

WHUD!

--LIKE *DEFENSE!*

YAAH!

BWOM!

DRAX, YOU DID IT! YOU REDIRECTED THE MISSILE RIGHT INTO THE *METEORITE!*

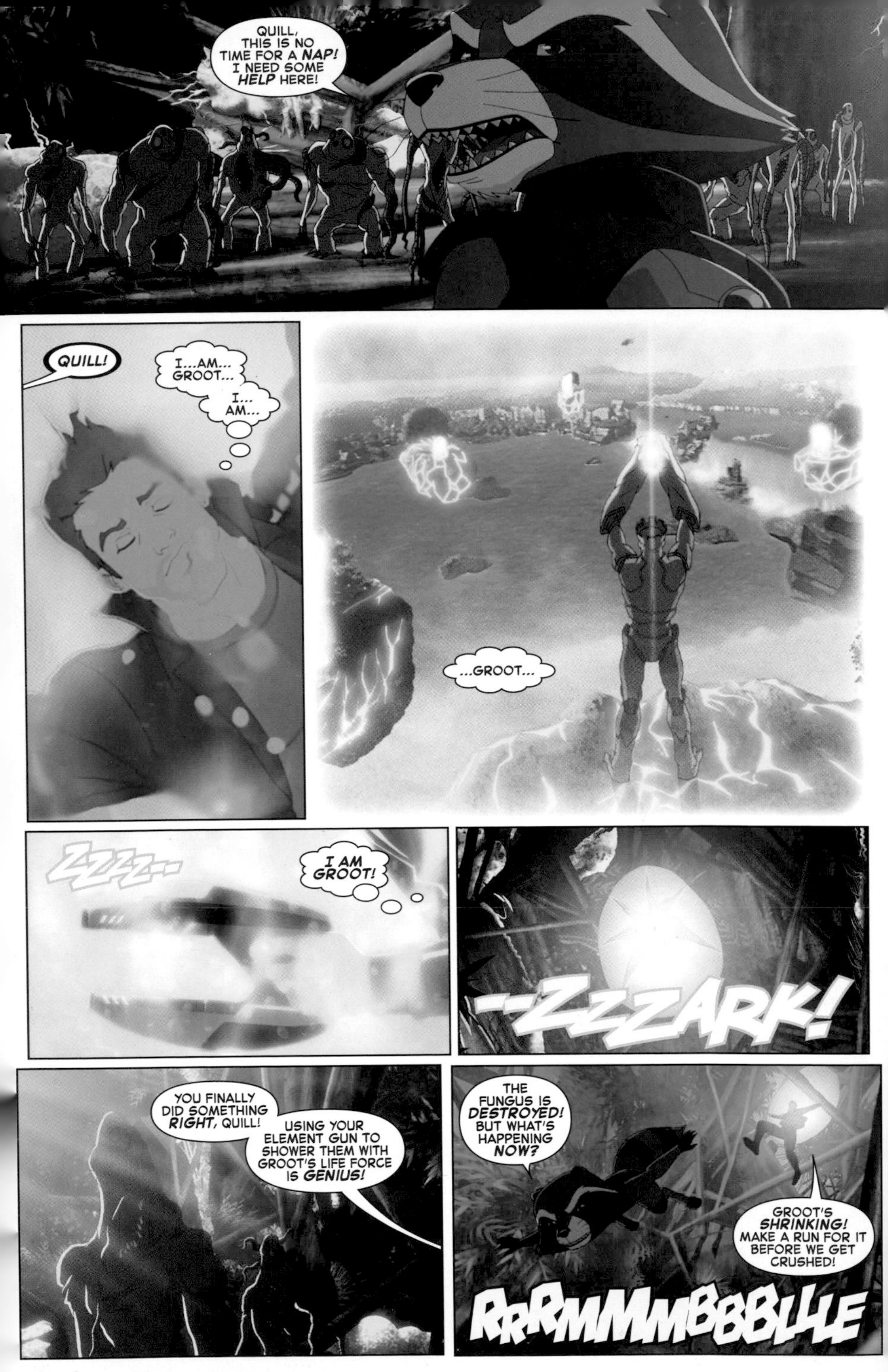
QUILL, THIS IS NO TIME FOR A NAP! I NEED SOME HELP HERE!
QUILL!
I...AM... GROOT...
I... AM...
...GROOT...
ZZZZ--
I AM GROOT!
--ZZZZARK!
YOU FINALLY DID SOMETHING RIGHT, QUILL!
USING YOUR ELEMENT GUN TO SHOWER THEM WITH GROOT'S LIFE FORCE IS GENIUS!
THE FUNGUS IS DESTROYED! BUT WHAT'S HAPPENING NOW?
GROOT'S SHRINKING! MAKE A RUN FOR IT BEFORE WE GET CRUSHED!
RRRMMMMBBBLLLE

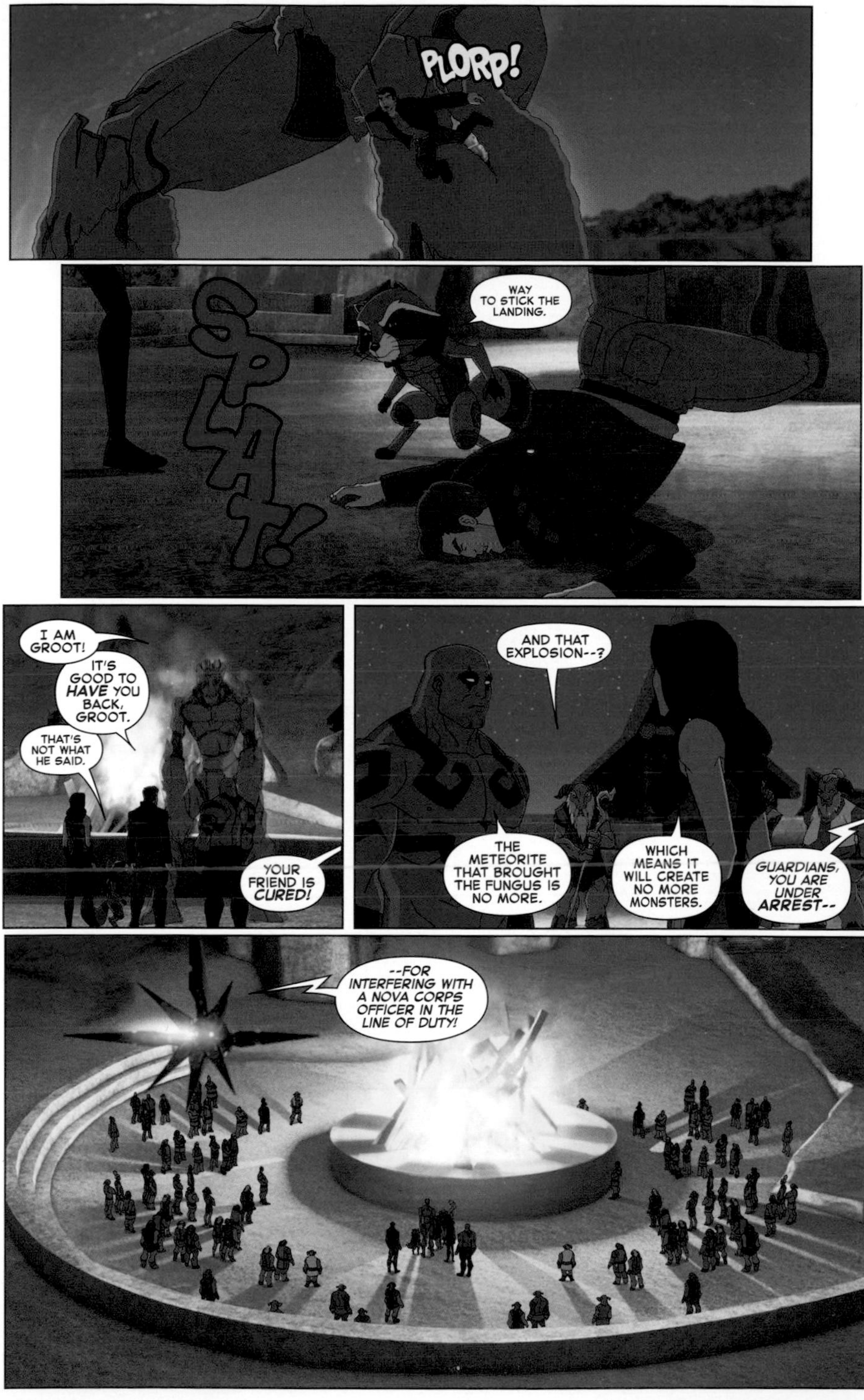
PLORP!
WAY TO STICK THE LANDING.
SPLAT!
I AM GROOT!
IT'S GOOD TO HAVE YOU BACK, GROOT.
THAT'S NOT WHAT HE SAID.
YOUR FRIEND IS CURED!
AND THAT EXPLOSION--?
THE METEORITE THAT BROUGHT THE FUNGUS IS NO MORE.
WHICH MEANS IT WILL CREATE NO MORE MONSTERS.
GUARDIANS, YOU ARE UNDER ARREST--
--FOR INTERFERING WITH A NOVA CORPS OFFICER IN THE LINE OF DUTY!

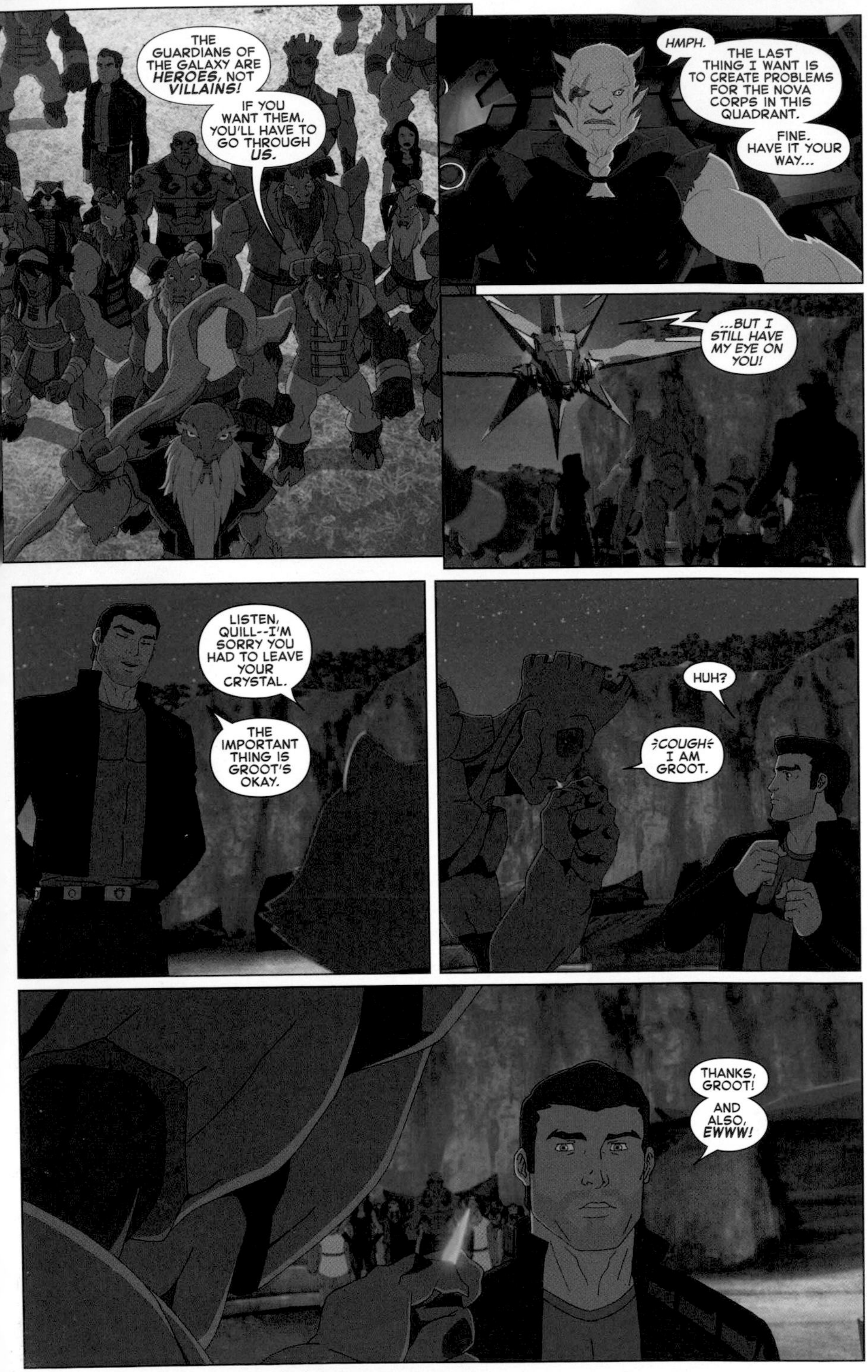
THE GUARDIANS OF THE GALAXY ARE *HEROES*, NOT *VILLAINS!*
IF YOU WANT THEM, YOU'LL HAVE TO GO THROUGH *US.*
HMPH.
THE LAST THING I WANT IS TO CREATE PROBLEMS FOR THE NOVA CORPS IN THIS QUADRANT.
FINE. HAVE IT YOUR WAY...
...BUT I STILL HAVE MY EYE ON YOU!
LISTEN, QUILL--I'M SORRY YOU HAD TO LEAVE YOUR CRYSTAL.
THE IMPORTANT THING IS GROOT'S OKAY.
HUH?
COUGH I AM GROOT.
THANKS, GROOT!
AND ALSO, *EWWW!*

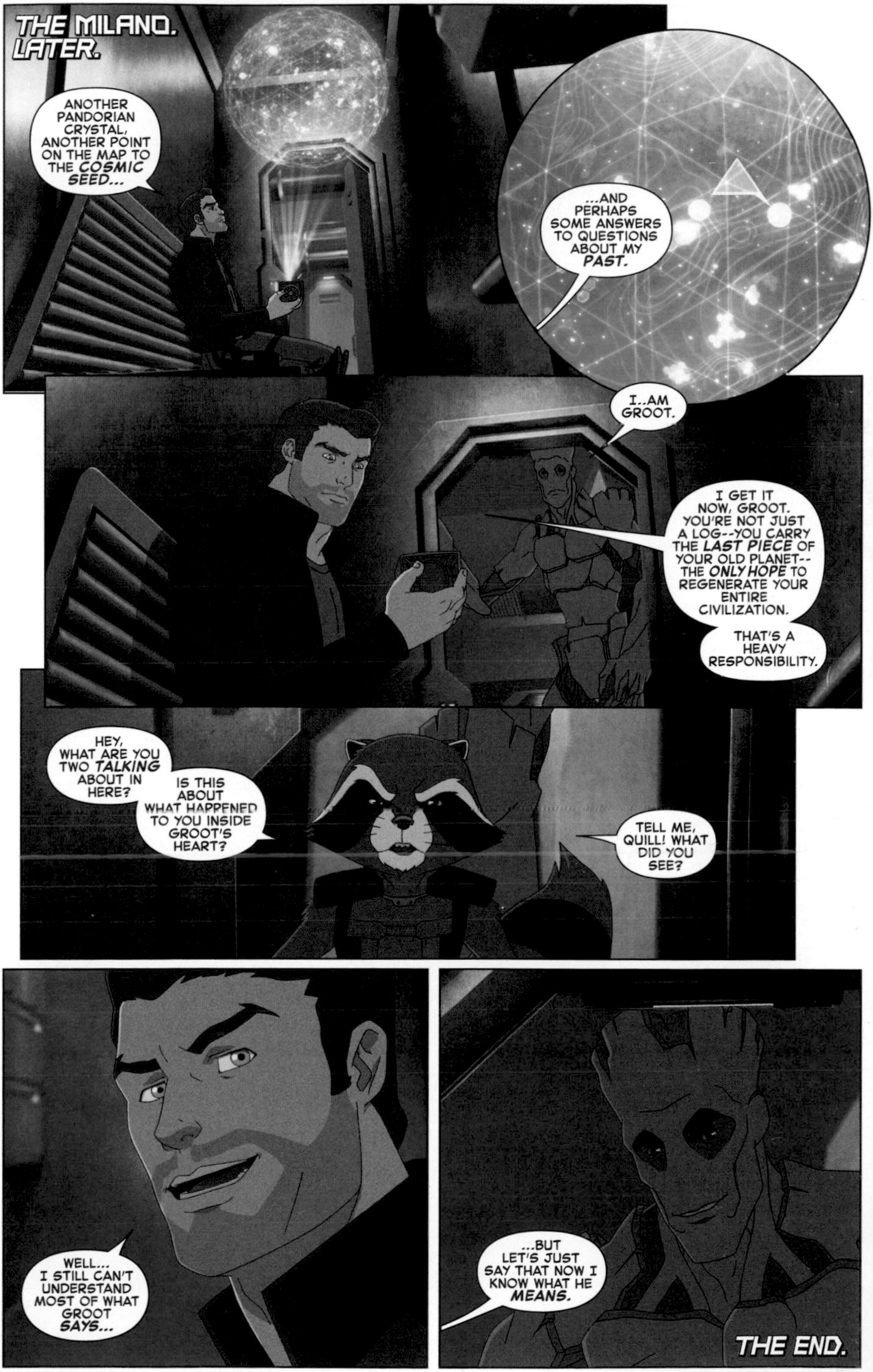
THE MILANO. LATER.
ANOTHER PANDORIAN CRYSTAL, ANOTHER POINT ON THE MAP TO THE COSMIC SEED...
...AND PERHAPS SOME ANSWERS TO QUESTIONS ABOUT MY PAST.
I..AM GROOT.
I GET IT NOW, GROOT. YOU'RE NOT JUST A LOG--YOU CARRY THE LAST PIECE OF YOUR OLD PLANET--THE ONLY HOPE TO REGENERATE YOUR ENTIRE CIVILIZATION.
THAT'S A HEAVY RESPONSIBILITY.
HEY, WHAT ARE YOU TWO TALKING ABOUT IN HERE?
IS THIS ABOUT WHAT HAPPENED TO YOU INSIDE GROOT'S HEART?
TELL ME, QUILL! WHAT DID YOU SEE?
WELL... I STILL CAN'T UNDERSTAND MOST OF WHAT GROOT SAYS...
...BUT LET'S JUST SAY THAT NOW I KNOW WHAT HE MEANS.
THE END.

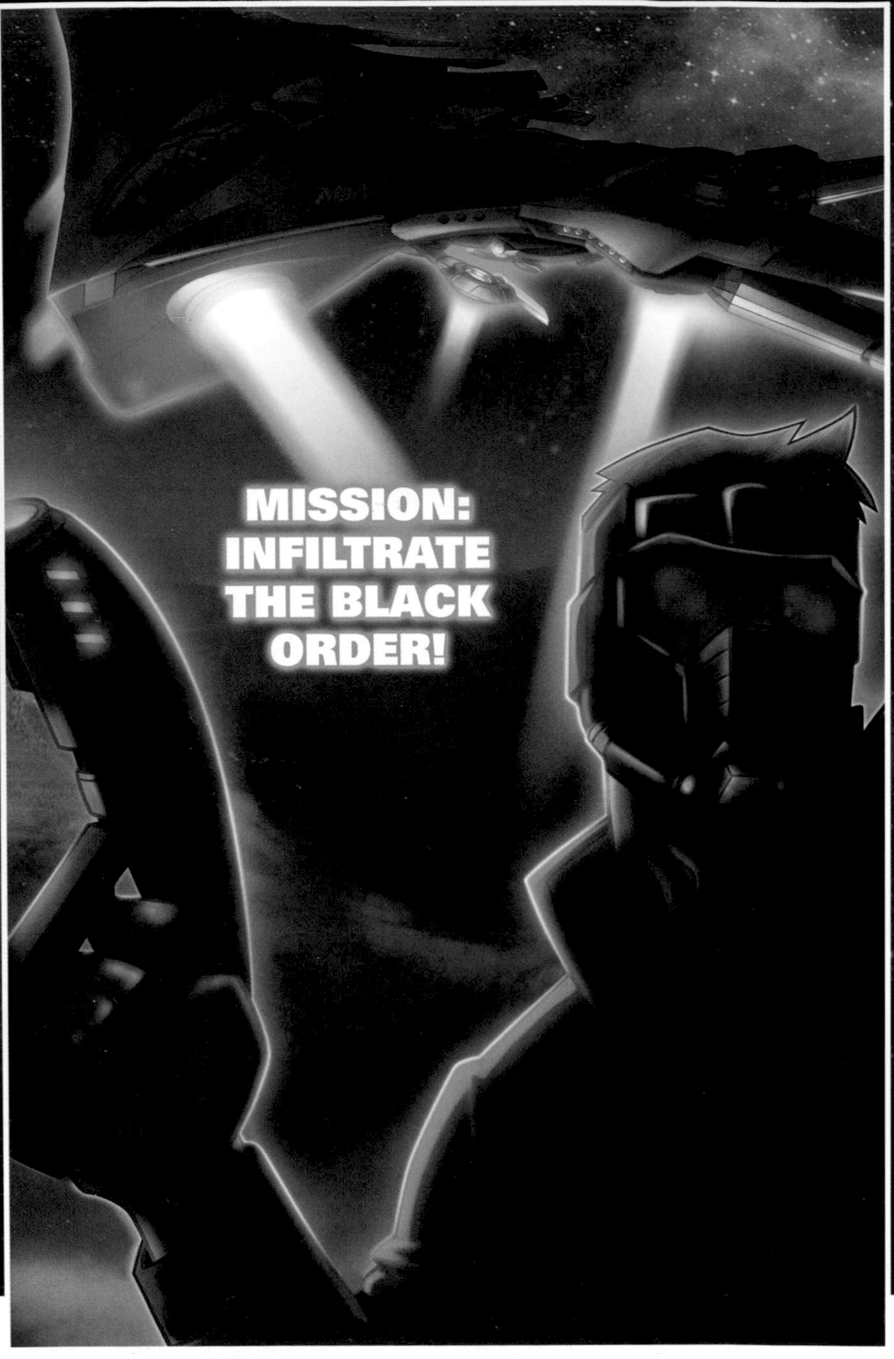
MISSION: INFILTRATE THE BLACK ORDER!

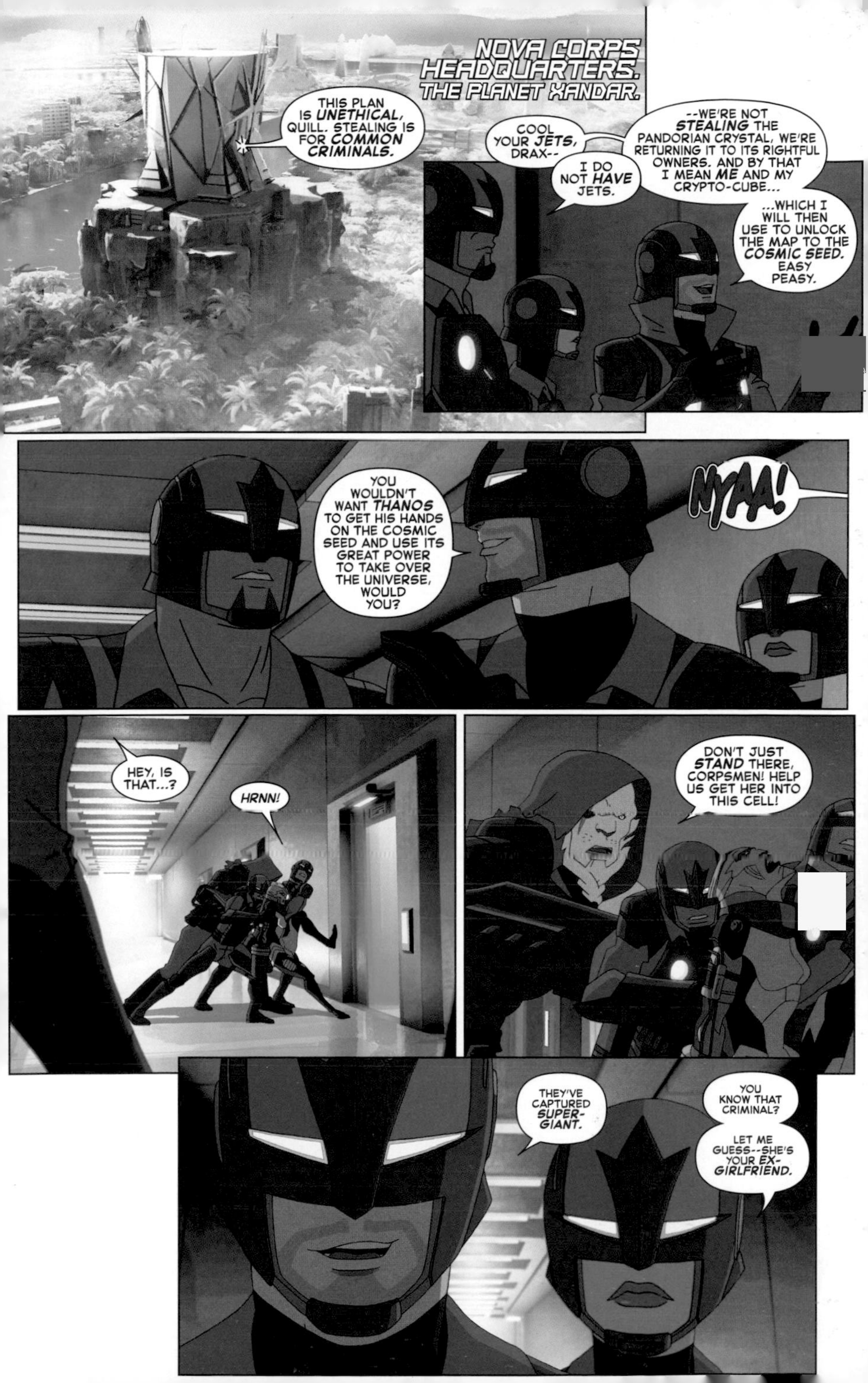

NOVA CORPS HEADQUARTERS. THE PLANET XANDAR.
THIS PLAN IS UNETHICAL, QUILL. STEALING IS FOR COMMON CRIMINALS.
COOL YOUR JETS, DRAX--
I DO NOT HAVE JETS.
--WE'RE NOT STEALING THE PANDORIAN CRYSTAL, WE'RE RETURNING IT TO ITS RIGHTFUL OWNERS. AND BY THAT I MEAN ME AND MY CRYPTO-CUBE...
...WHICH I WILL THEN USE TO UNLOCK THE MAP TO THE COSMIC SEED. EASY PEASY.
YOU WOULDN'T WANT THANOS TO GET HIS HANDS ON THE COSMIC SEED AND USE ITS GREAT POWER TO TAKE OVER THE UNIVERSE, WOULD YOU?
NYAA!
HEY, IS THAT...?
HRNN!
DON'T JUST STAND THERE, CORPSMEN! HELP US GET HER INTO THIS CELL!
THEY'VE CAPTURED SUPER-GIANT.
YOU KNOW THAT CRIMINAL?
LET ME GUESS--SHE'S YOUR EX-GIRLFRIEND.

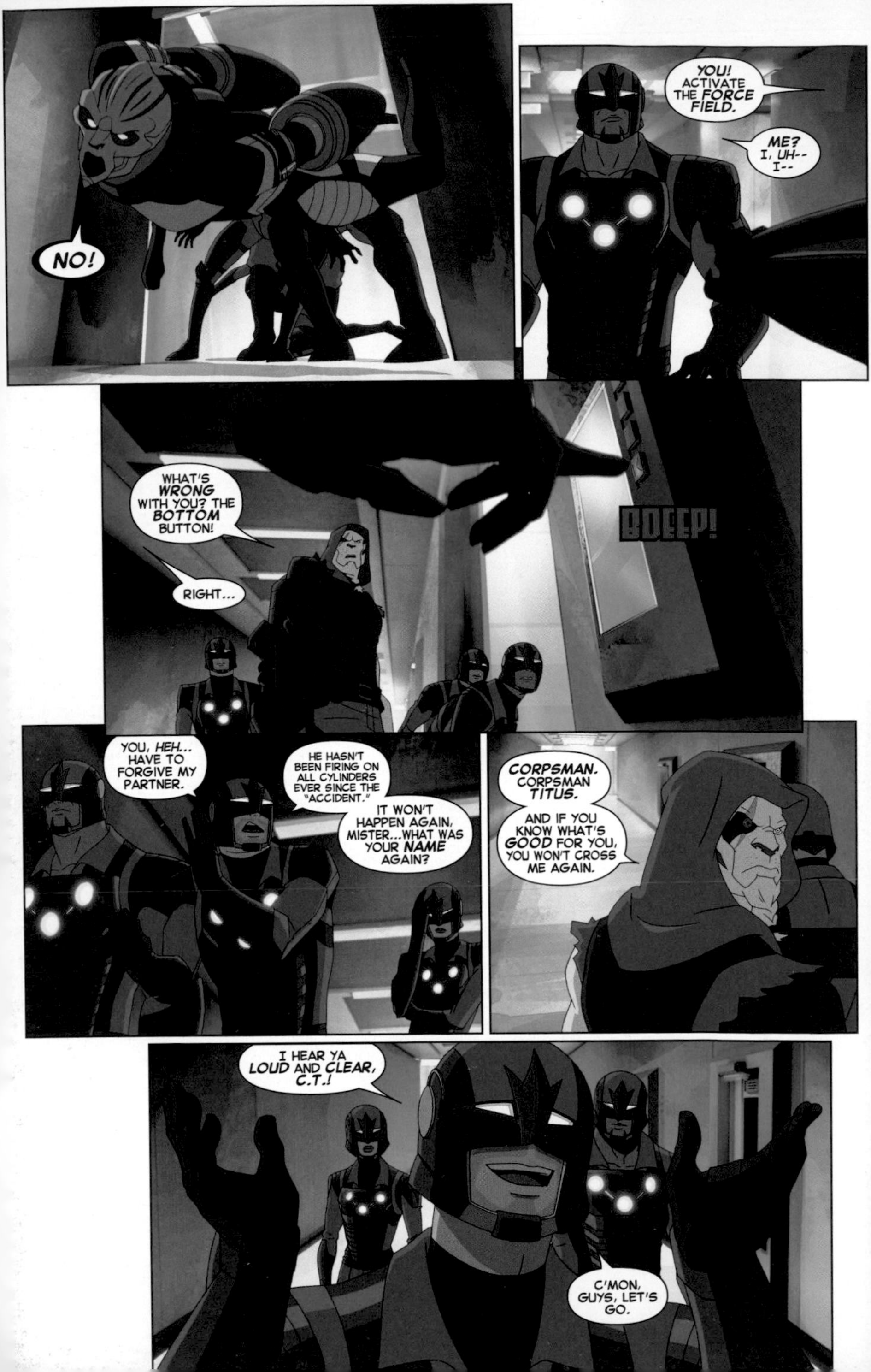
NO!
YOU! ACTIVATE THE FORCE FIELD.
ME? I, UH-- I--
WHAT'S WRONG WITH YOU? THE BOTTOM BUTTON!
RIGHT...
BDEEP!
YOU, HEH... HAVE TO FORGIVE MY PARTNER.
HE HASN'T BEEN FIRING ON ALL CYLINDERS EVER SINCE THE "ACCIDENT."
IT WON'T HAPPEN AGAIN, MISTER...WHAT WAS YOUR NAME AGAIN?
CORPSMAN. CORPSMAN TITUS.
AND IF YOU KNOW WHAT'S GOOD FOR YOU, YOU WON'T CROSS ME AGAIN.
I HEAR YA LOUD AND CLEAR, C.T.!
C'MON, GUYS, LET'S GO.

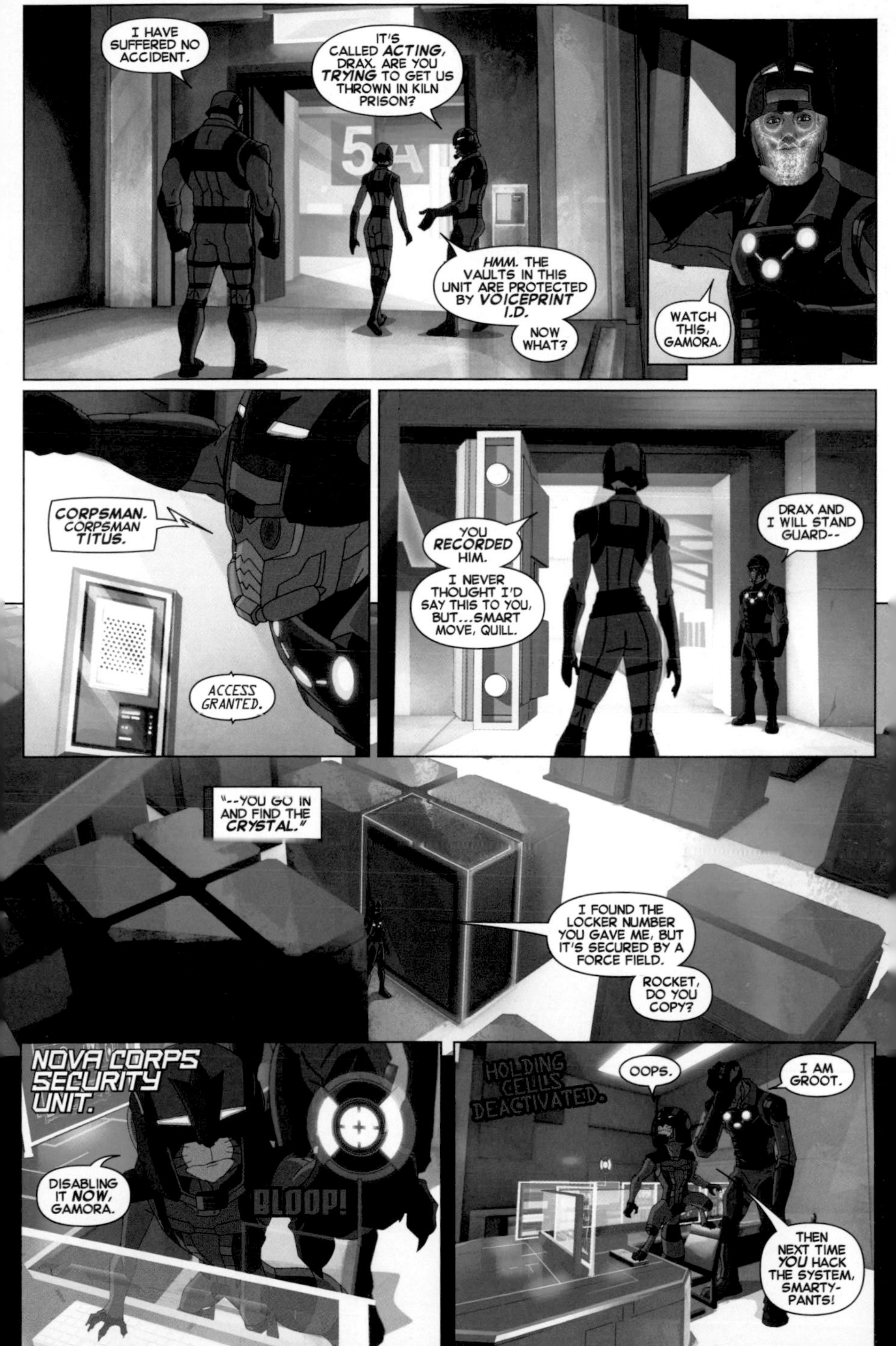
I HAVE SUFFERED NO ACCIDENT.
IT'S CALLED ACTING, DRAX. ARE YOU TRYING TO GET US THROWN IN KILN PRISON?
HMM. THE VAULTS IN THIS UNIT ARE PROTECTED BY VOICEPRINT I.D.
NOW WHAT?
WATCH THIS, GAMORA.
CORPSMAN. CORPSMAN TITUS.
ACCESS GRANTED.
YOU RECORDED HIM.
I NEVER THOUGHT I'D SAY THIS TO YOU, BUT...SMART MOVE, QUILL.
DRAX AND I WILL STAND GUARD--
"--YOU GO IN AND FIND THE CRYSTAL."
I FOUND THE LOCKER NUMBER YOU GAVE ME, BUT IT'S SECURED BY A FORCE FIELD.
ROCKET, DO YOU COPY?
NOVA CORPS SECURITY UNIT.
DISABLING IT NOW, GAMORA.
BLOOP!
HOLDING CELLS DEACTIVATED.
OOPS.
I AM GROOT.
THEN NEXT TIME YOU HACK THE SYSTEM, SMARTY-PANTS!

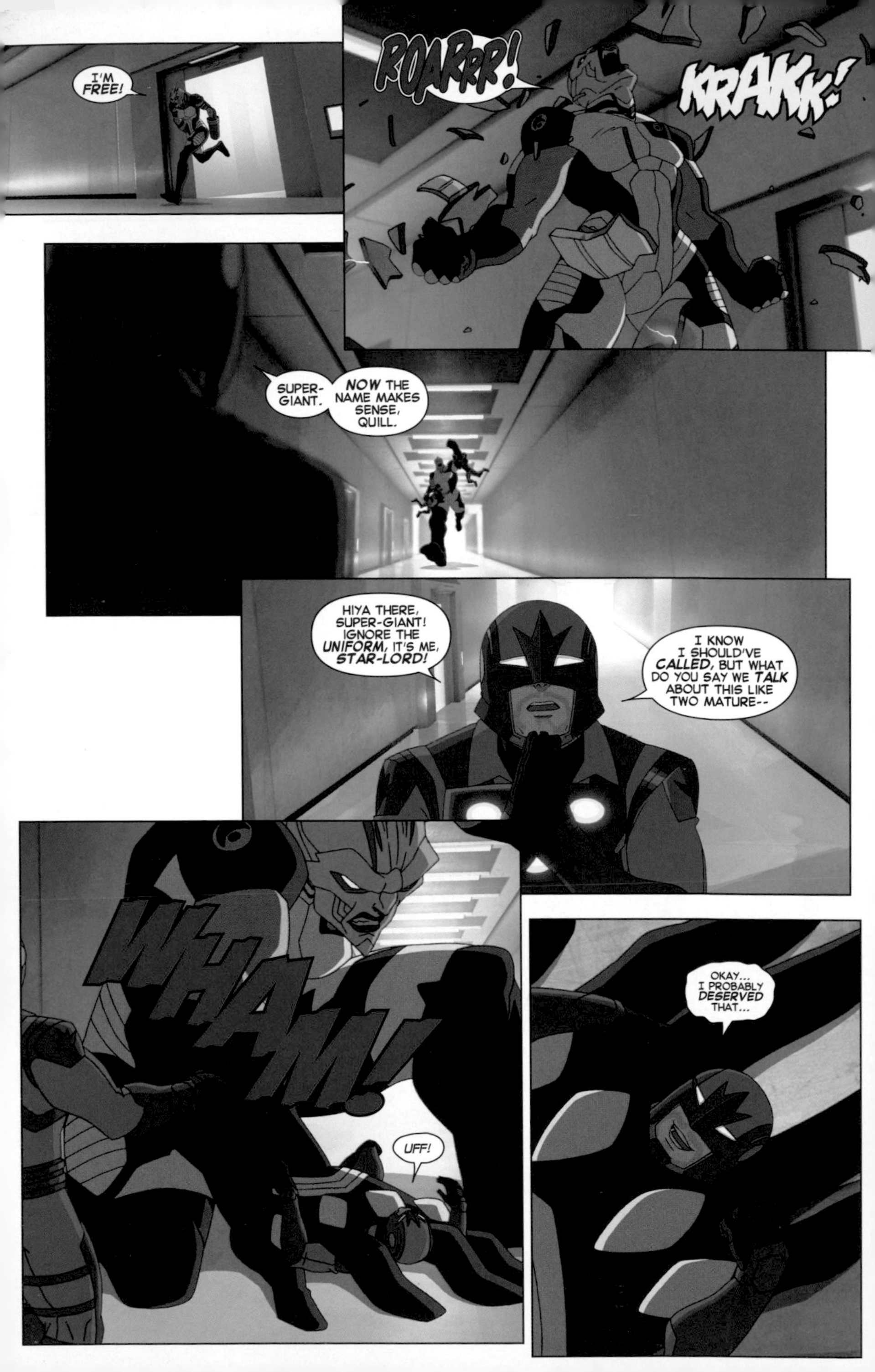
I'M FREE!
ROARRR!
KRAKK!
SUPER-GIANT.
NOW THE NAME MAKES SENSE, QUILL.
HIYA THERE, SUPER-GIANT! IGNORE THE UNIFORM, IT'S ME, STAR-LORD!
I KNOW I SHOULD'VE CALLED, BUT WHAT DO YOU SAY WE TALK ABOUT THIS LIKE TWO MATURE--
WHAM!
UFF!
OKAY... I PROBABLY DESERVED THAT...

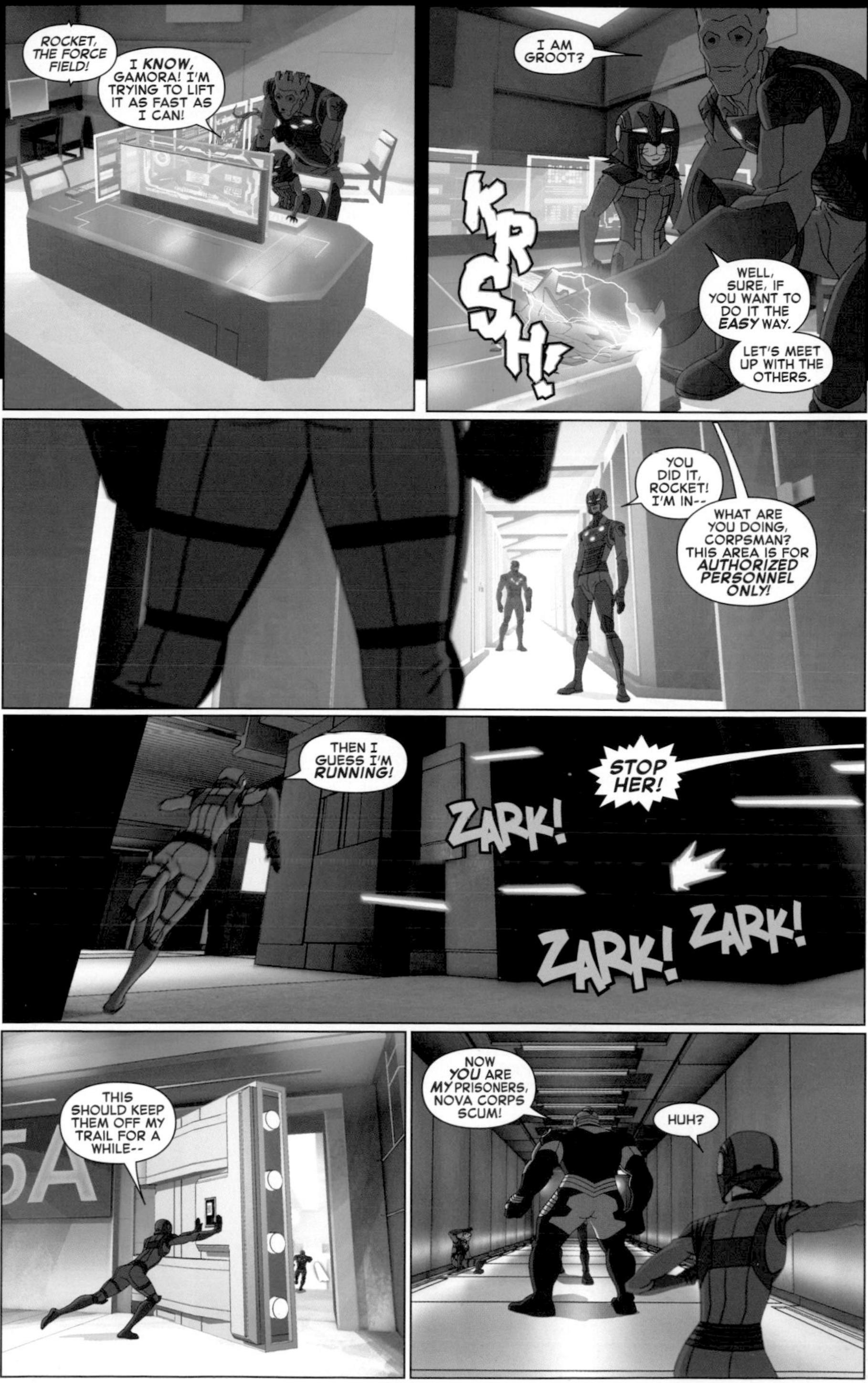
ROCKET, THE FORCE FIELD!
I KNOW, GAMORA! I'M TRYING TO LIFT IT AS FAST AS I CAN!
I AM GROOT?
KRSH!
WELL, SURE, IF YOU WANT TO DO IT THE EASY WAY.
LET'S MEET UP WITH THE OTHERS.
YOU DID IT, ROCKET! I'M IN--
WHAT ARE YOU DOING, CORPSMAN? THIS AREA IS FOR AUTHORIZED PERSONNEL ONLY!
THEN I GUESS I'M RUNNING!
STOP HER!
ZARK!
ZARK! ZARK!
THIS SHOULD KEEP THEM OFF MY TRAIL FOR A WHILE--
5A
NOW YOU ARE MY PRISONERS, NOVA CORPS SCUM!
HUH?

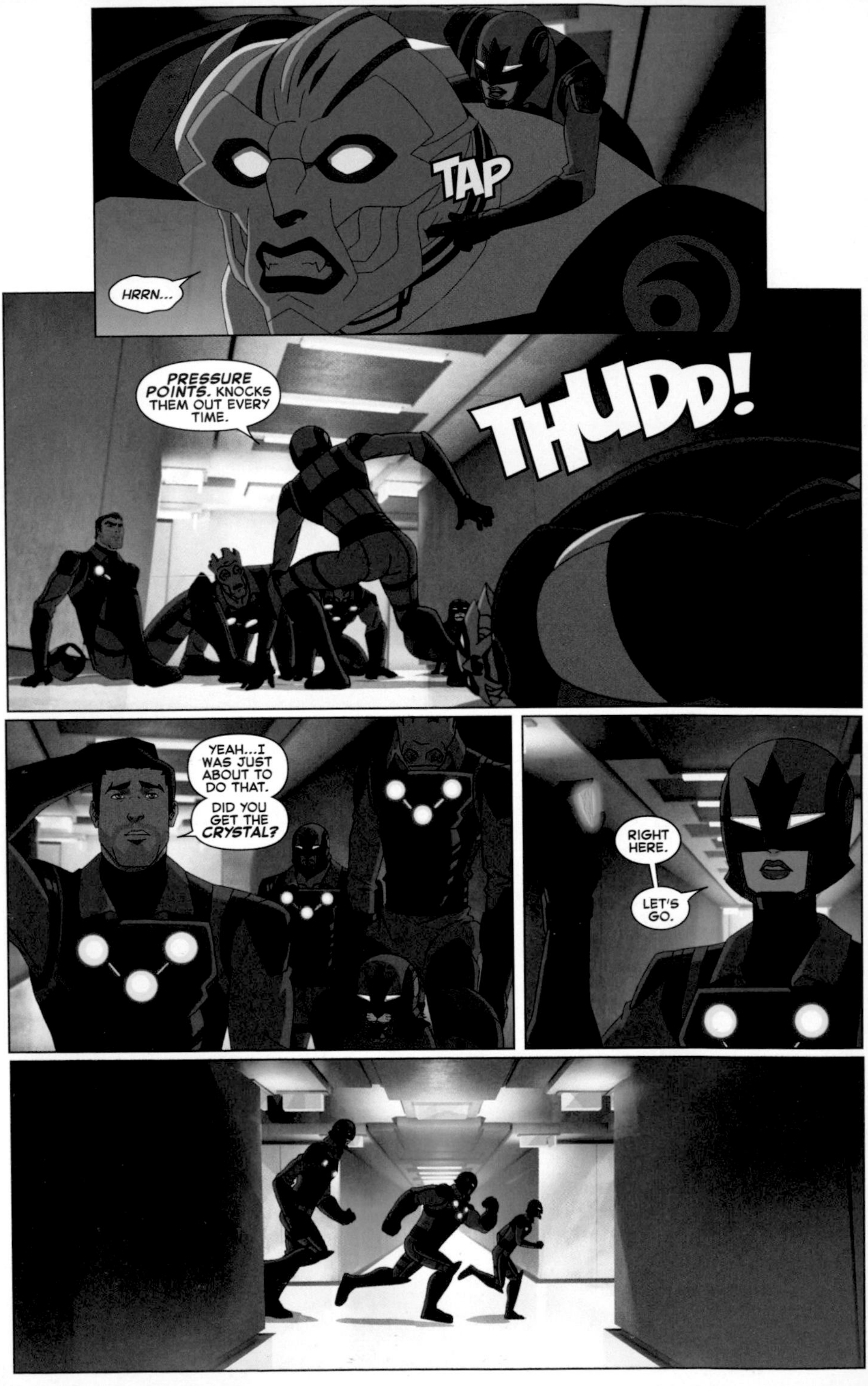
TAP
HRRN...
PRESSURE POINTS. KNOCKS THEM OUT EVERY TIME.
THUDD!
YEAH...I WAS JUST ABOUT TO DO THAT.
DID YOU GET THE CRYSTAL?
RIGHT HERE.
LET'S GO.

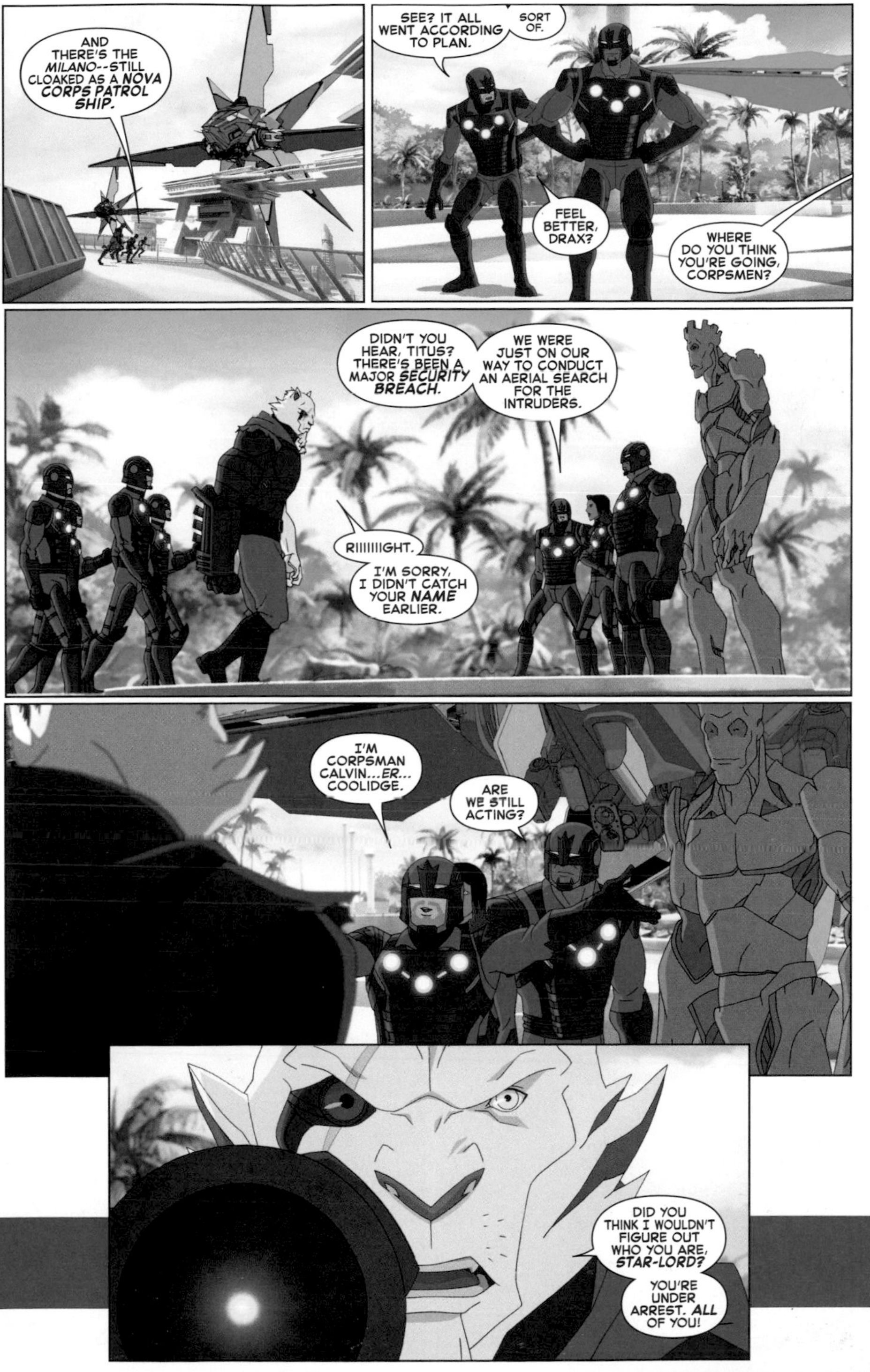
AND THERE'S THE MILANO--STILL CLOAKED AS A NOVA CORPS PATROL SHIP.
SEE? IT ALL WENT ACCORDING TO PLAN.
SORT OF.
FEEL BETTER, DRAX?
WHERE DO YOU THINK YOU'RE GOING, CORPSMEN?
DIDN'T YOU HEAR, TITUS? THERE'S BEEN A MAJOR SECURITY BREACH.
WE WERE JUST ON OUR WAY TO CONDUCT AN AERIAL SEARCH FOR THE INTRUDERS.
RIIIIIIGHT.
I'M SORRY, I DIDN'T CATCH YOUR NAME EARLIER.
I'M CORPSMAN CALVIN...ER... COOLIDGE.
ARE WE STILL ACTING?
DID YOU THINK I WOULDN'T FIGURE OUT WHO YOU ARE, STAR-LORD?
YOU'RE UNDER ARREST. ALL OF YOU!

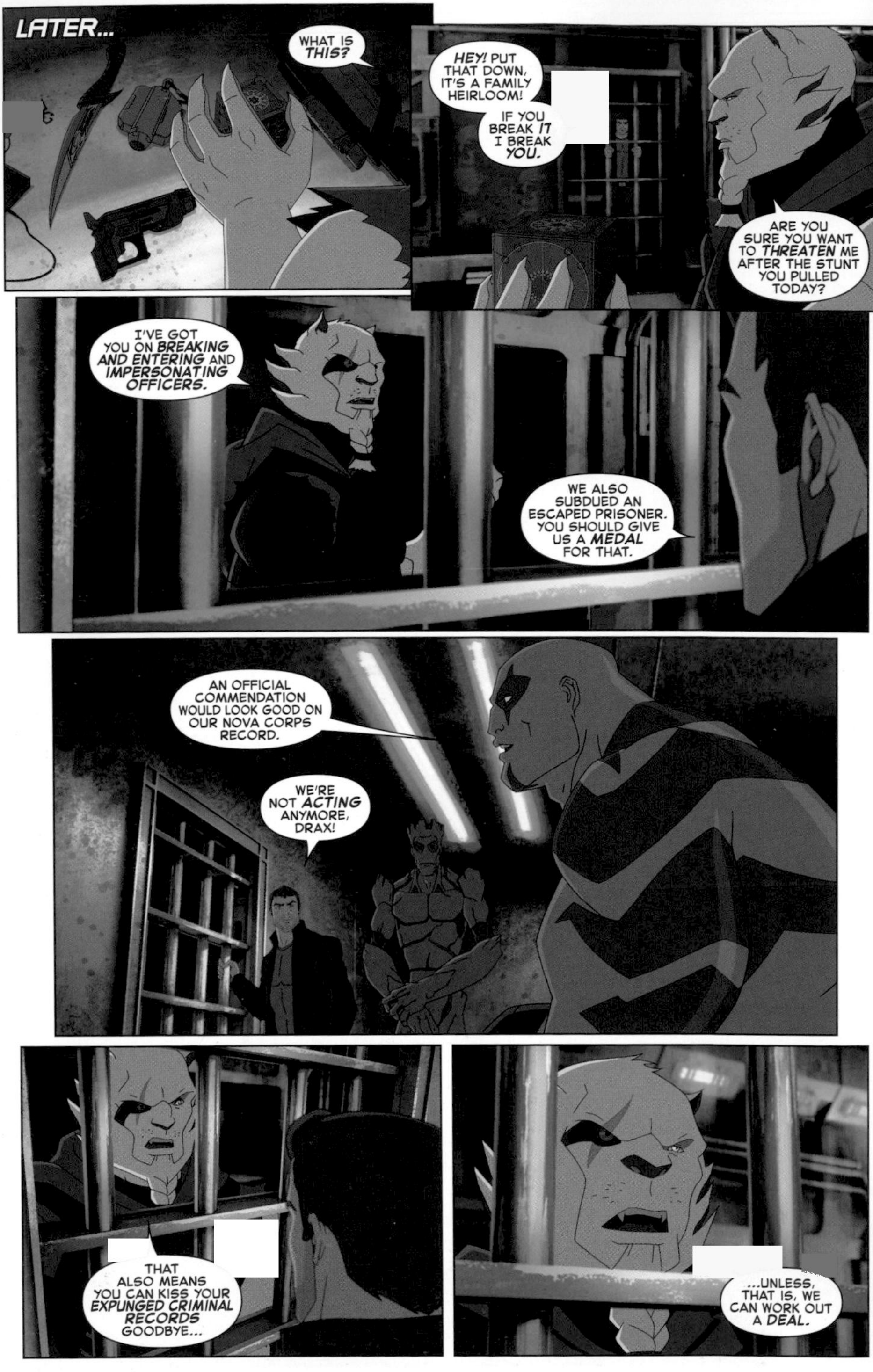
LATER...
WHAT IS THIS?
HEY! PUT THAT DOWN, IT'S A FAMILY HEIRLOOM!
IF YOU BREAK IT I BREAK YOU.
ARE YOU SURE YOU WANT TO THREATEN ME AFTER THE STUNT YOU PULLED TODAY?
I'VE GOT YOU ON BREAKING AND ENTERING AND IMPERSONATING OFFICERS.
WE ALSO SUBDUED AN ESCAPED PRISONER. YOU SHOULD GIVE US A MEDAL FOR THAT.
AN OFFICIAL COMMENDATION WOULD LOOK GOOD ON OUR NOVA CORPS RECORD.
WE'RE NOT ACTING ANYMORE, DRAX!
THAT ALSO MEANS YOU CAN KISS YOUR EXPUNGED CRIMINAL RECORDS GOODBYE...
...UNLESS, THAT IS, WE CAN WORK OUT A DEAL.

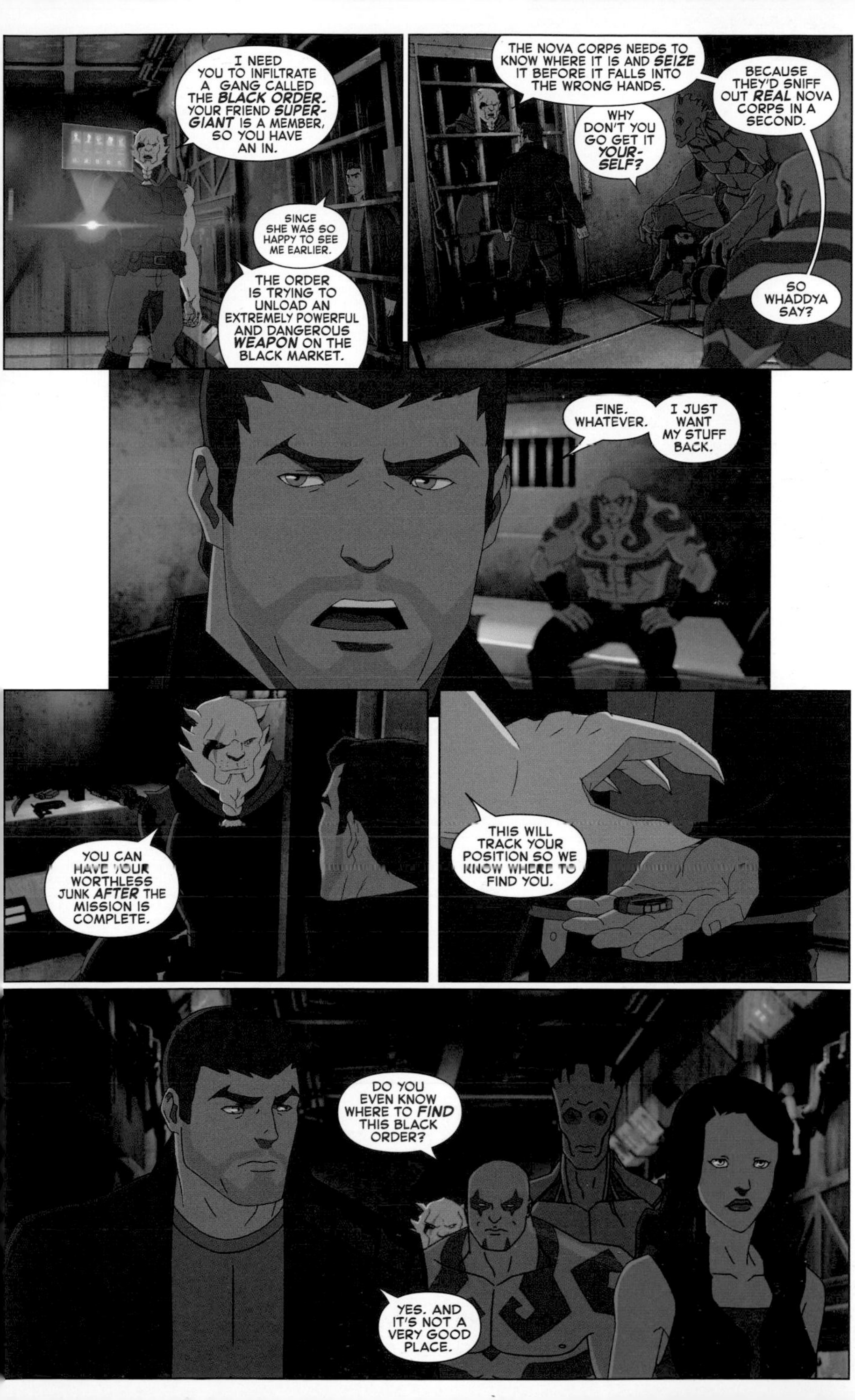
I NEED YOU TO INFILTRATE A GANG CALLED THE BLACK ORDER. YOUR FRIEND SUPER-GIANT IS A MEMBER, SO YOU HAVE AN IN.
SINCE SHE WAS SO HAPPY TO SEE ME EARLIER.
THE ORDER IS TRYING TO UNLOAD AN EXTREMELY POWERFUL AND DANGEROUS WEAPON ON THE BLACK MARKET.
THE NOVA CORPS NEEDS TO KNOW WHERE IT IS AND SEIZE IT BEFORE IT FALLS INTO THE WRONG HANDS.
WHY DON'T YOU GO GET IT YOUR-SELF?
BECAUSE THEY'D SNIFF OUT REAL NOVA CORPS IN A SECOND.
SO WHADDYA SAY?
FINE. WHATEVER.
I JUST WANT MY STUFF BACK.
YOU CAN HAVE YOUR WORTHLESS JUNK AFTER THE MISSION IS COMPLETE.
THIS WILL TRACK YOUR POSITION SO WE KNOW WHERE TO FIND YOU.
DO YOU EVEN KNOW WHERE TO FIND THIS BLACK ORDER?
YES. AND IT'S NOT A VERY GOOD PLACE.

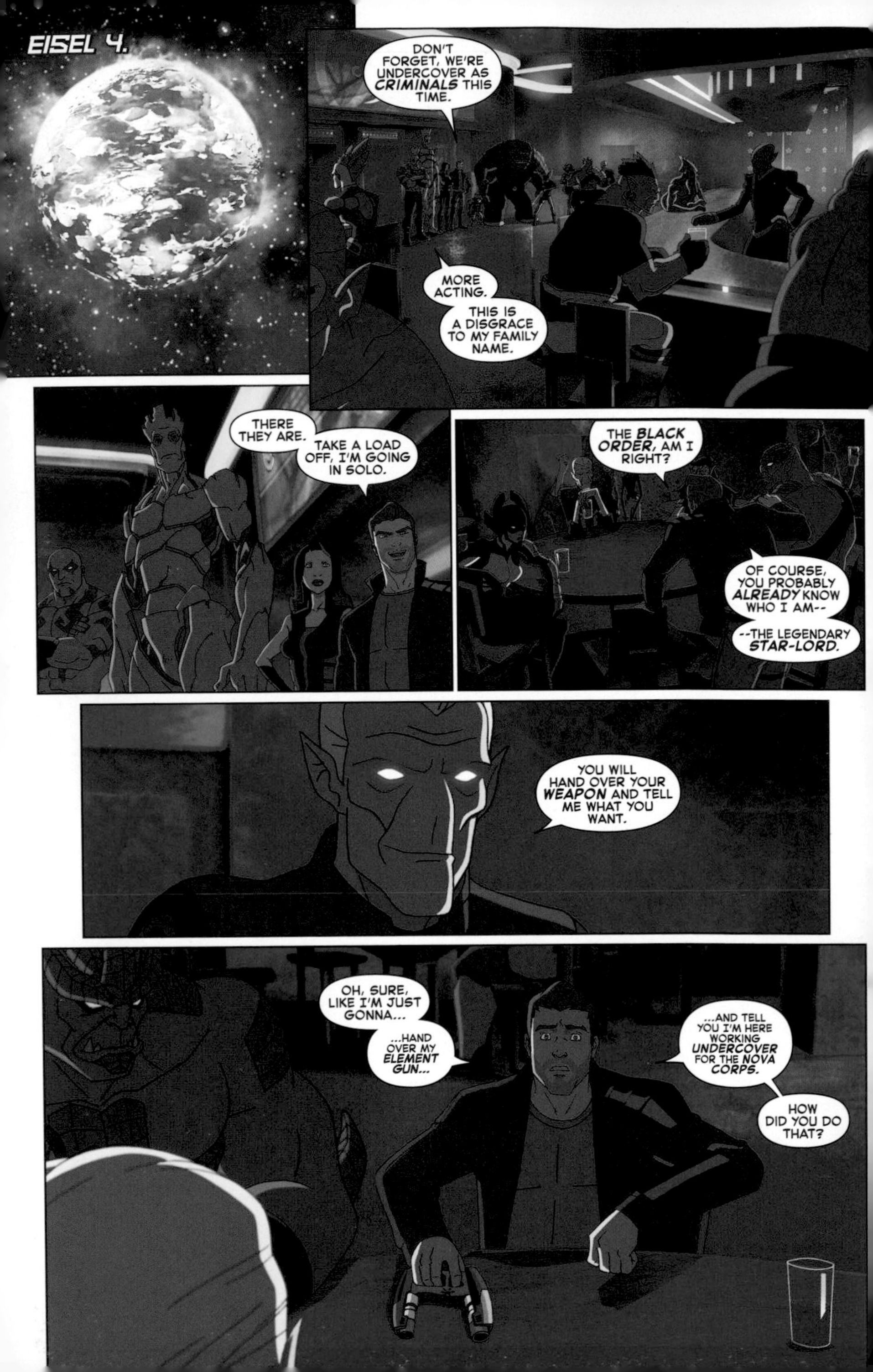
EISEL 4.
DON'T FORGET, WE'RE UNDERCOVER AS CRIMINALS THIS TIME.
MORE ACTING.
THIS IS A DISGRACE TO MY FAMILY NAME.
THERE THEY ARE.
TAKE A LOAD OFF, I'M GOING IN SOLO.
THE BLACK ORDER, AM I RIGHT?
OF COURSE, YOU PROBABLY ALREADY KNOW WHO I AM--
--THE LEGENDARY STAR-LORD.
YOU WILL HAND OVER YOUR WEAPON AND TELL ME WHAT YOU WANT.
OH, SURE, LIKE I'M JUST GONNA...
...HAND OVER MY ELEMENT GUN...
...AND TELL YOU I'M HERE WORKING UNDERCOVER FOR THE NOVA CORPS.
HOW DID YOU DO THAT?

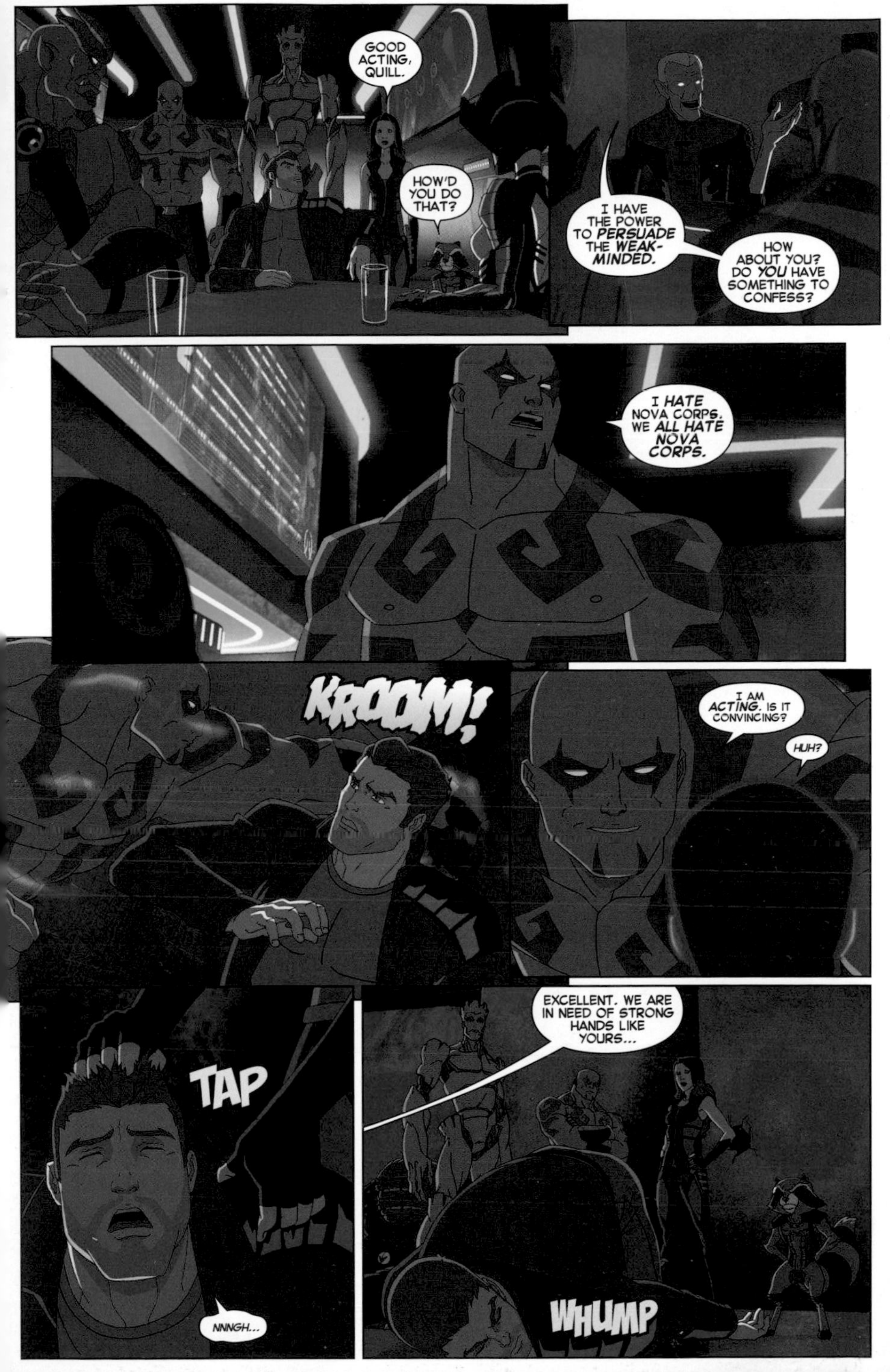
GOOD ACTING, QUILL.
HOW'D YOU DO THAT?
I HAVE THE POWER TO PERSUADE THE WEAK-MINDED.
HOW ABOUT YOU? DO YOU HAVE SOMETHING TO CONFESS?
I HATE NOVA CORPS. WE ALL HATE NOVA CORPS.
KROOM!
I AM ACTING. IS IT CONVINCING?
HUH?
TAP
NNNGH...
EXCELLENT. WE ARE IN NEED OF STRONG HANDS LIKE YOURS...
WHUMP

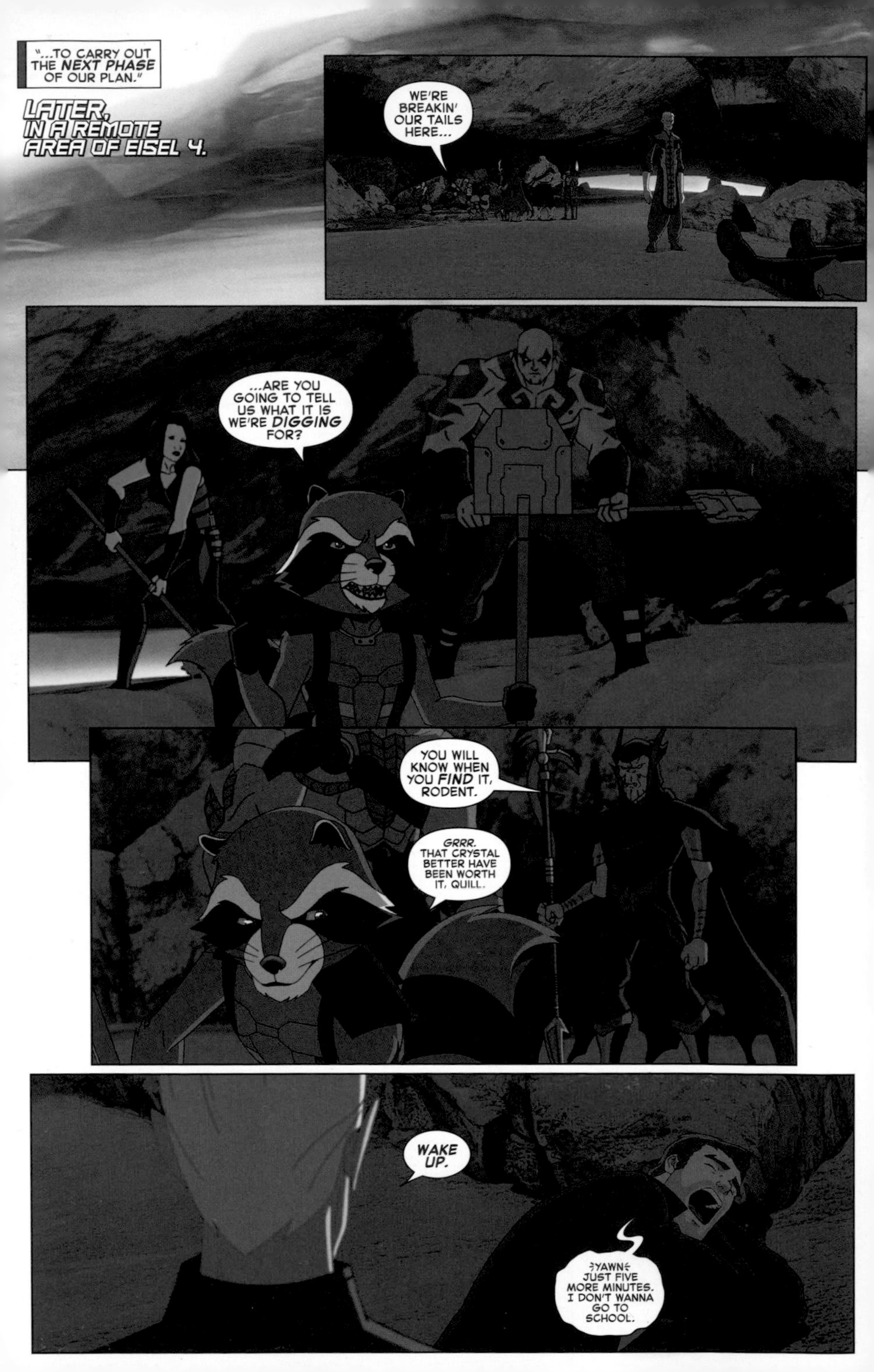
"...TO CARRY OUT THE NEXT PHASE OF OUR PLAN."
LATER, IN A REMOTE AREA OF EISEL 4.
WE'RE BREAKIN' OUR TAILS HERE...
...ARE YOU GOING TO TELL US WHAT IT IS WE'RE DIGGING FOR?
YOU WILL KNOW WHEN YOU FIND IT, RODENT.
GRRR. THAT CRYSTAL BETTER HAVE BEEN WORTH IT, QUILL.
WAKE UP.
YAWN JUST FIVE MORE MINUTES. I DON'T WANNA GO TO SCHOOL.

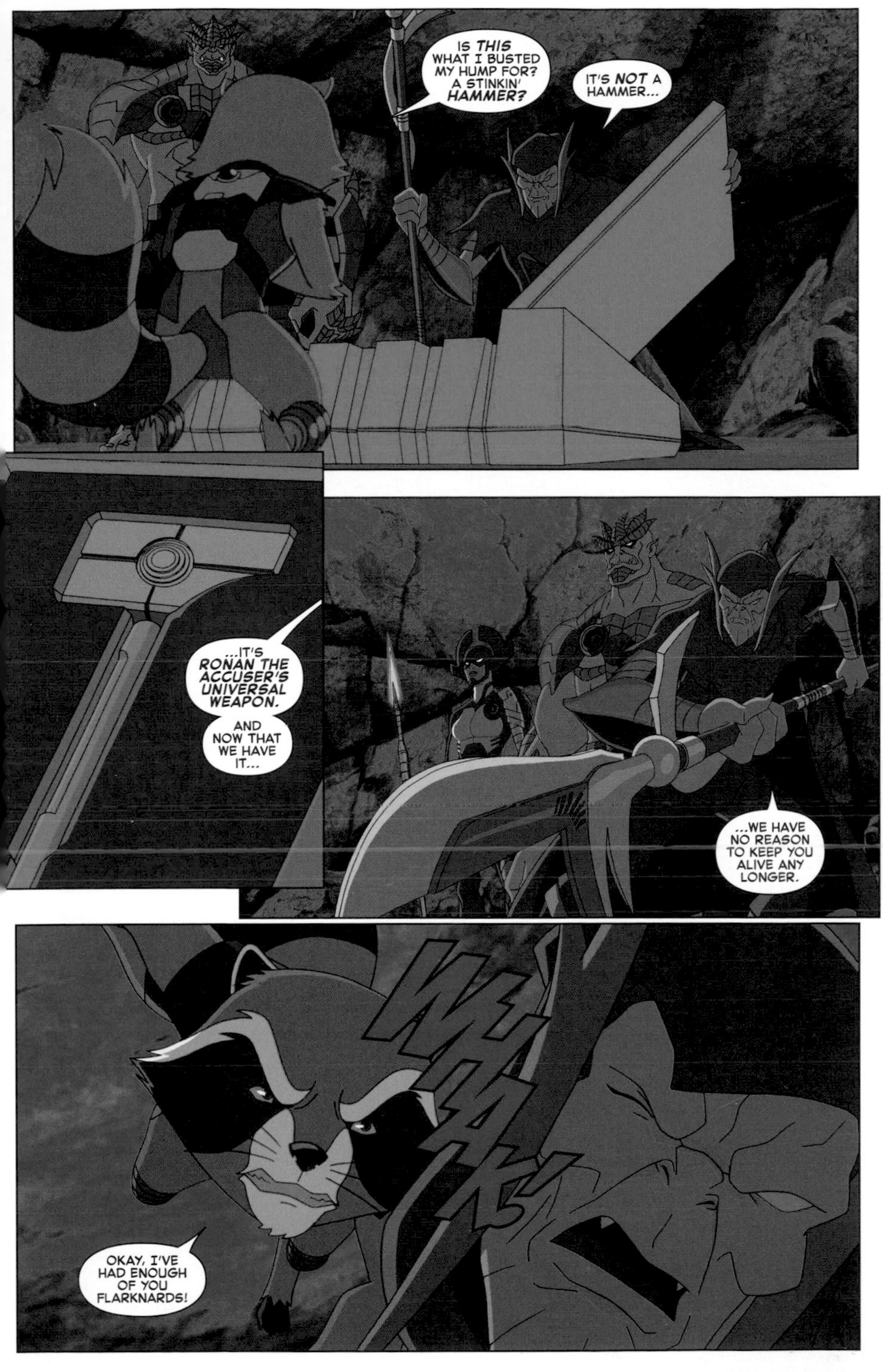
IS *THIS* WHAT I BUSTED MY HUMP FOR? A STINKIN' *HAMMER?*
IT'S *NOT* A HAMMER...
...IT'S *RONAN THE ACCUSER'S UNIVERSAL WEAPON.*
AND NOW THAT WE HAVE IT...
...WE HAVE NO REASON TO KEEP YOU ALIVE ANY LONGER.
WHAK!
OKAY, I'VE HAD ENOUGH OF YOU FLARKNARDS!

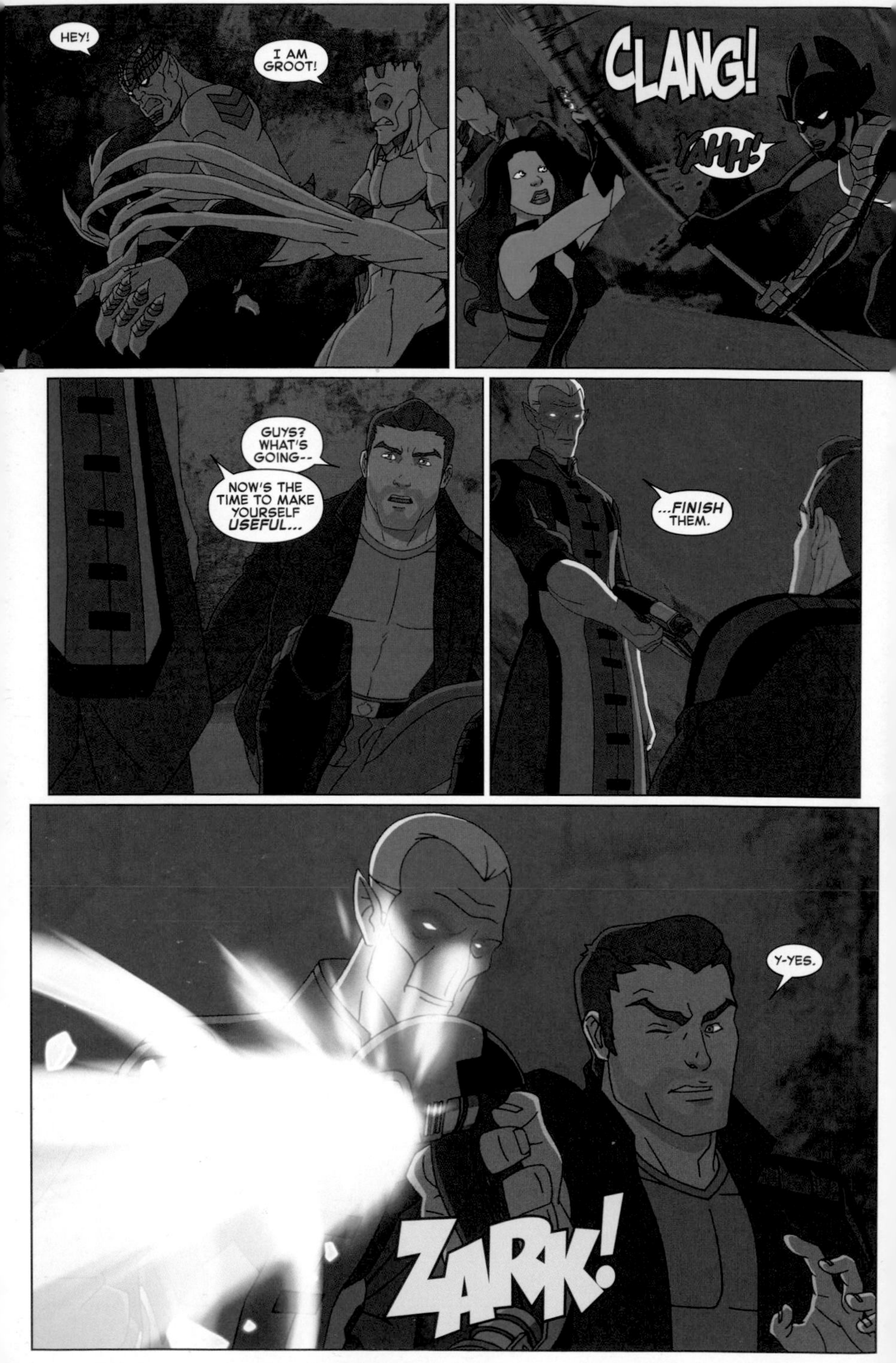
HEY!
I AM GROOT!
CLANG!
YAHH!
GUYS? WHAT'S GOING--
NOW'S THE TIME TO MAKE YOURSELF USEFUL...
...FINISH THEM.
Y-YES.
ZARK!

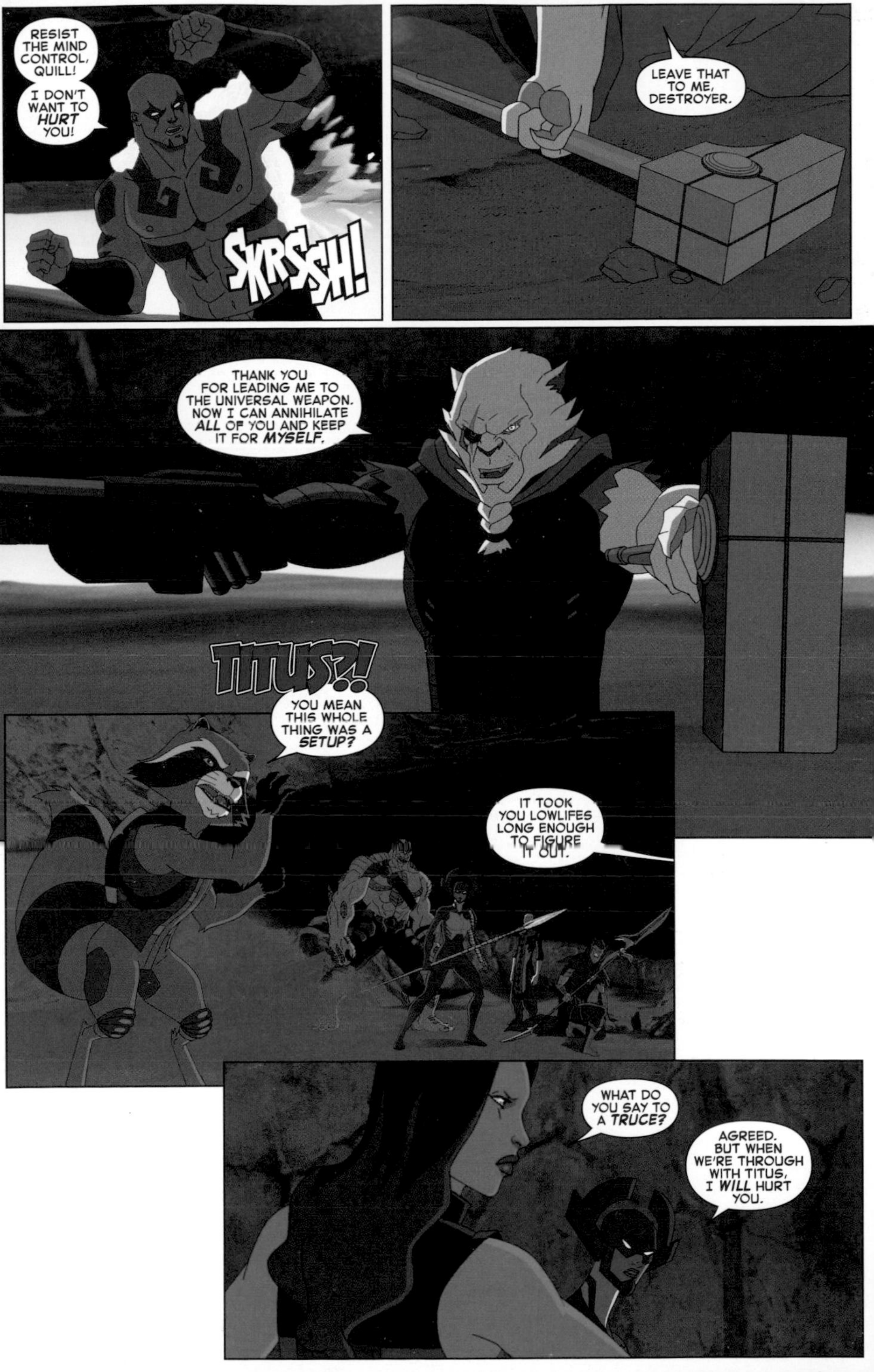
RESIST THE MIND CONTROL, QUILL!
I DON'T WANT TO HURT YOU!
SKRSSH!
LEAVE THAT TO ME, DESTROYER.
THANK YOU FOR LEADING ME TO THE UNIVERSAL WEAPON. NOW I CAN ANNIHILATE ALL OF YOU AND KEEP IT FOR MYSELF.
TITUS?!
YOU MEAN THIS WHOLE THING WAS A SETUP?
IT TOOK YOU LOWLIFES LONG ENOUGH TO FIGURE IT OUT.
WHAT DO YOU SAY TO A TRUCE?
AGREED. BUT WHEN WE'RE THROUGH WITH TITUS, I WILL HURT YOU.

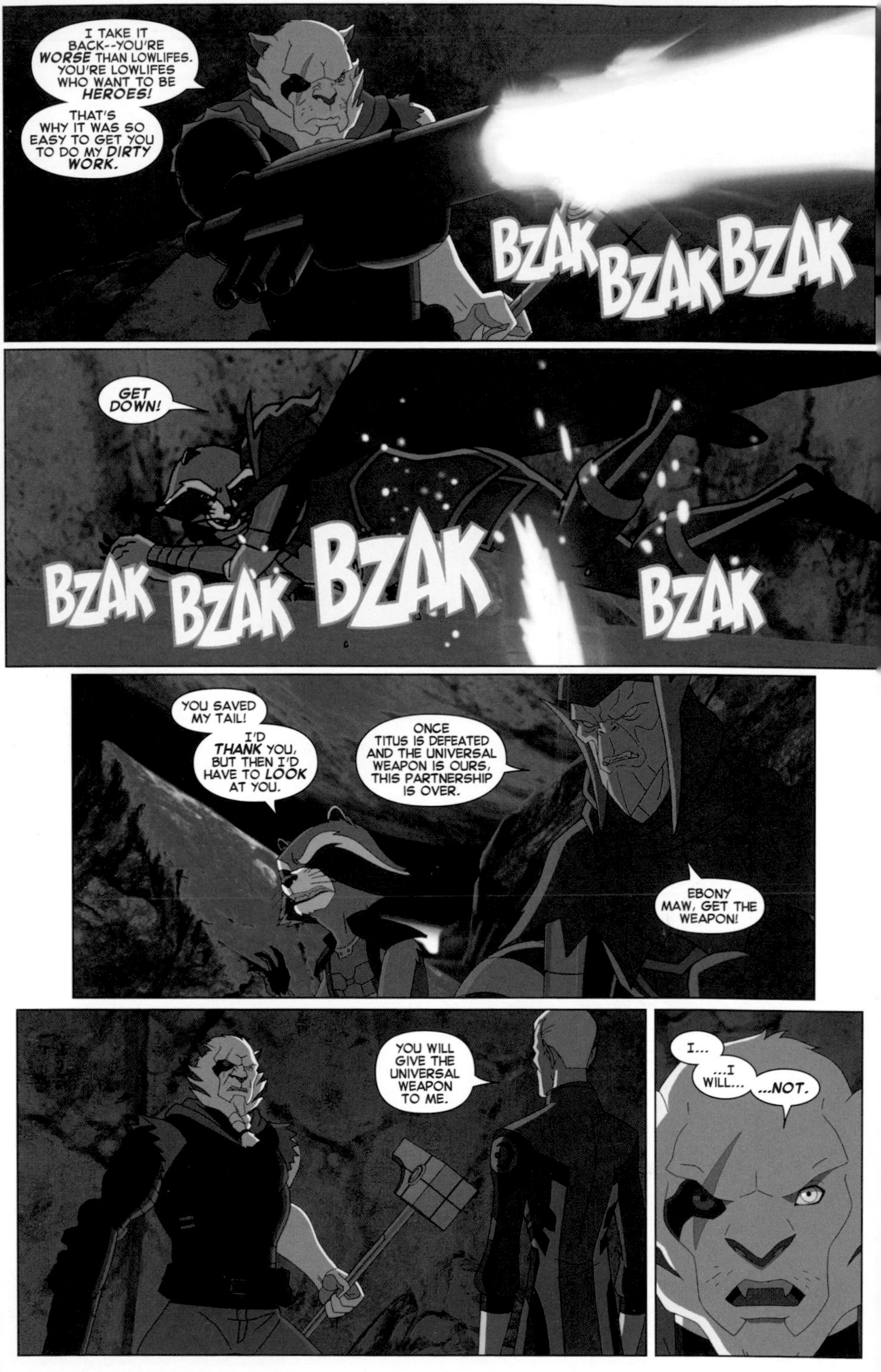

I TAKE IT BACK--YOU'RE *WORSE* THAN LOWLIFES. YOU'RE LOWLIFES WHO WANT TO BE *HEROES!*
THAT'S WHY IT WAS SO EASY TO GET YOU TO DO MY *DIRTY WORK.*
BZAK BZAK BZAK
GET DOWN!
BZAK BZAK BZAK BZAK
YOU SAVED MY TAIL!
I'D *THANK* YOU, BUT THEN I'D HAVE TO *LOOK* AT YOU.
ONCE TITUS IS DEFEATED AND THE UNIVERSAL WEAPON IS OURS, THIS PARTNERSHIP IS OVER.
EBONY MAW, GET THE WEAPON!
YOU WILL GIVE THE UNIVERSAL WEAPON TO ME.
I...
...I WILL...
...NOT.

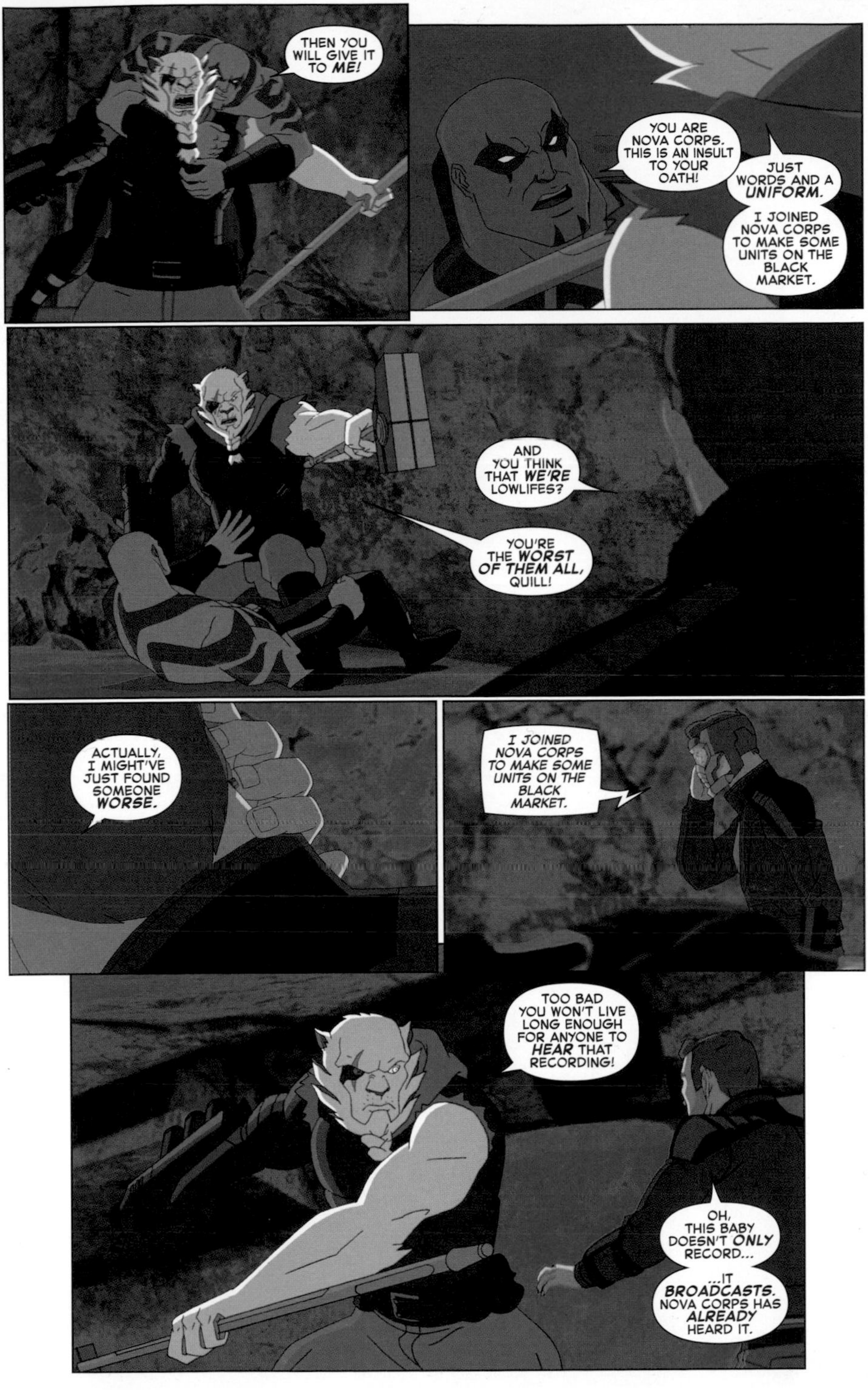
THEN YOU WILL GIVE IT TO *ME!*
YOU ARE NOVA CORPS. THIS IS AN INSULT TO YOUR OATH!
JUST WORDS AND A *UNIFORM.*
I JOINED NOVA CORPS TO MAKE SOME UNITS ON THE BLACK MARKET.
AND YOU THINK THAT *WE'RE* LOWLIFES?
YOU'RE THE *WORST OF THEM ALL,* QUILL!
ACTUALLY, I MIGHT'VE JUST FOUND SOMEONE *WORSE.*
I JOINED NOVA CORPS TO MAKE SOME UNITS ON THE BLACK MARKET.
TOO BAD YOU WON'T LIVE LONG ENOUGH FOR ANYONE TO *HEAR* THAT RECORDING!
OH, THIS BABY DOESN'T *ONLY* RECORD...
...IT *BROADCASTS.* NOVA CORPS HAS *ALREADY* HEARD IT.

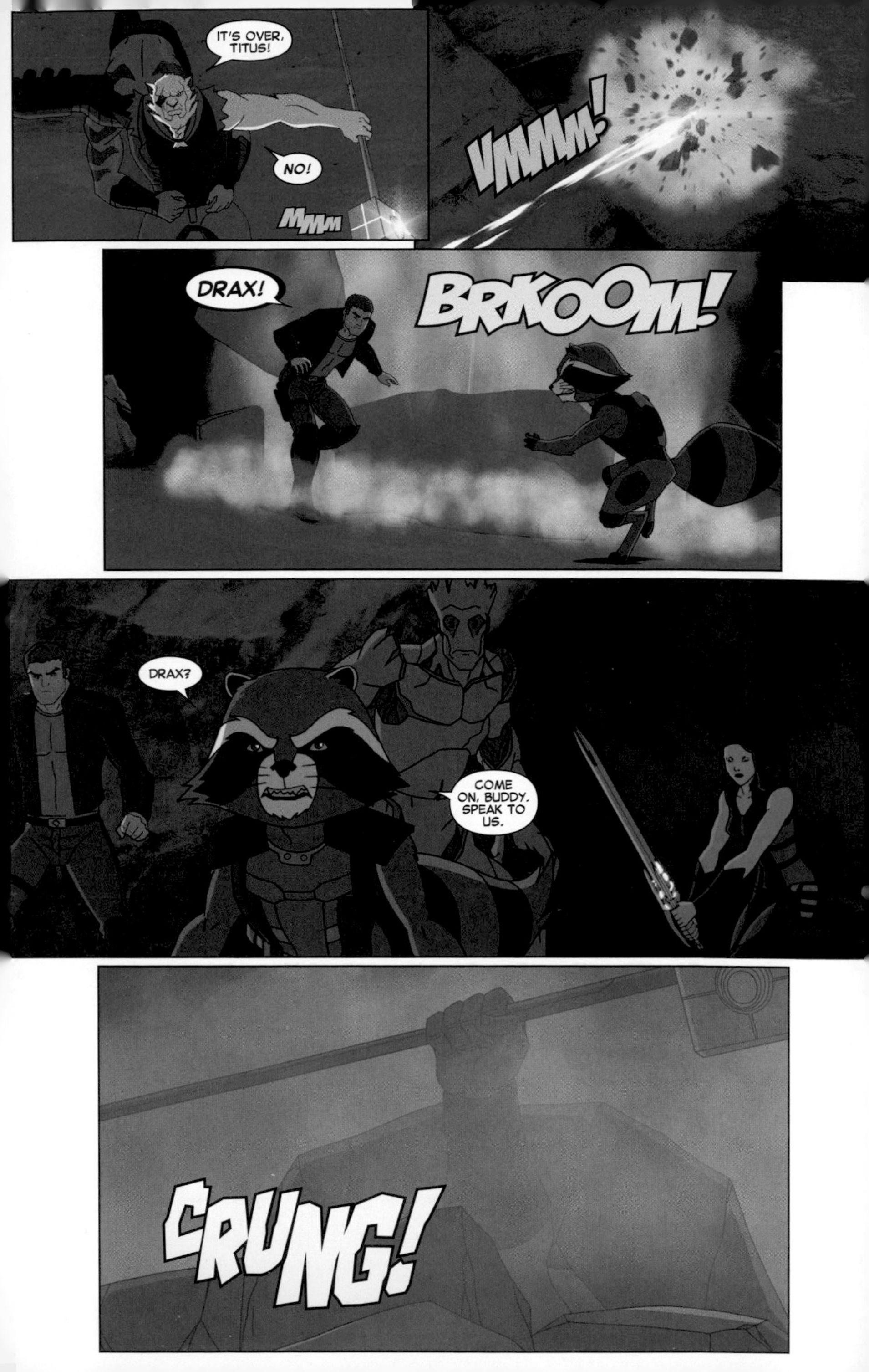
IT'S OVER, TITUS!
NO!
MMM
VMMMM!
DRAX!
BRKOOM!
DRAX?
COME ON, BUDDY. SPEAK TO US.
CRUNG!

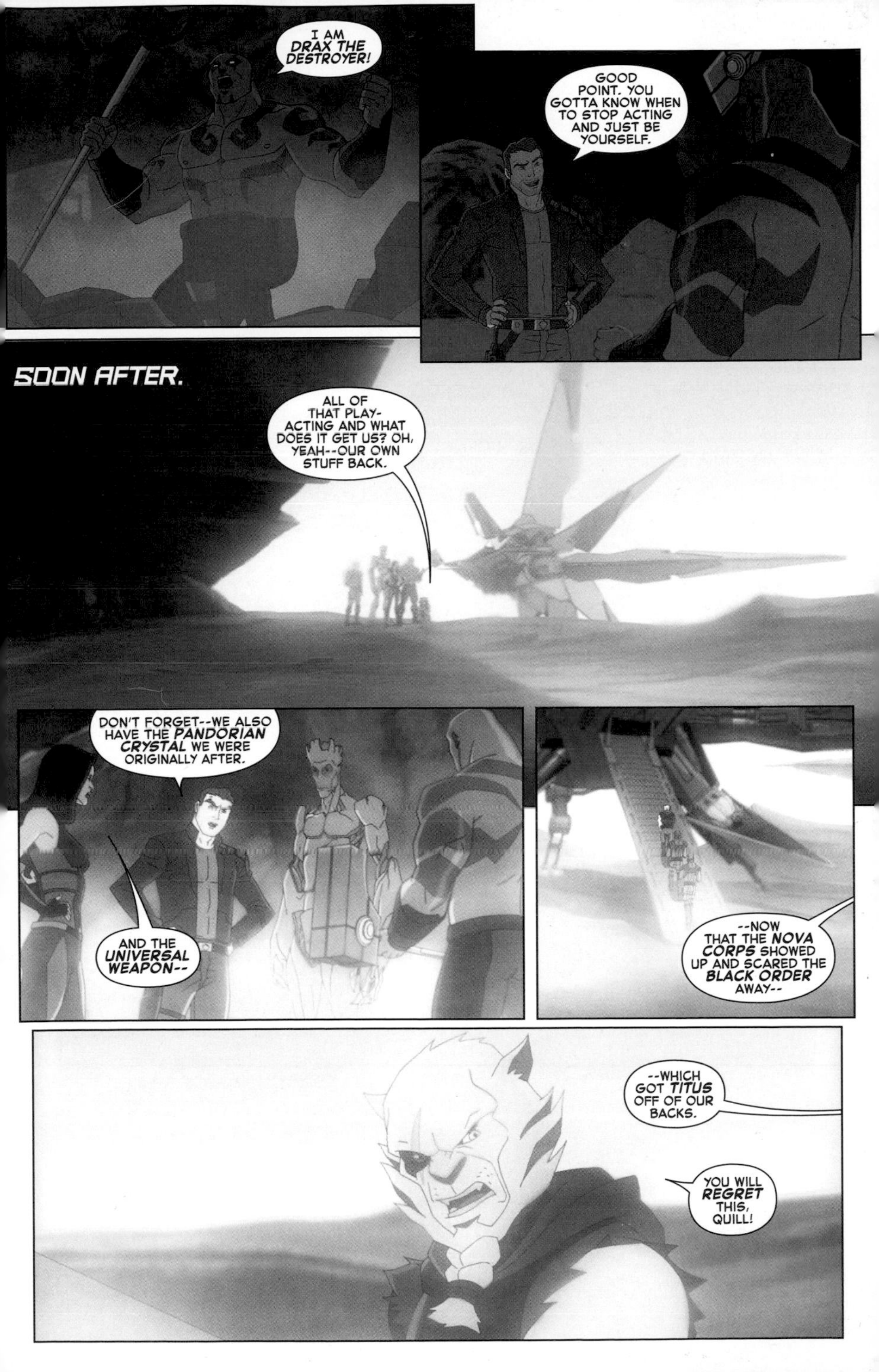
I AM DRAX THE DESTROYER!
GOOD POINT. YOU GOTTA KNOW WHEN TO STOP ACTING AND JUST BE YOURSELF.
SOON AFTER.
ALL OF THAT PLAY-ACTING AND WHAT DOES IT GET US? OH, YEAH--OUR OWN STUFF BACK.
DON'T FORGET--WE ALSO HAVE THE PANDORIAN CRYSTAL WE WERE ORIGINALLY AFTER.
AND THE UNIVERSAL WEAPON--
--NOW THAT THE NOVA CORPS SHOWED UP AND SCARED THE BLACK ORDER AWAY--
--WHICH GOT TITUS OFF OF OUR BACKS.
YOU WILL REGRET THIS, QUILL!

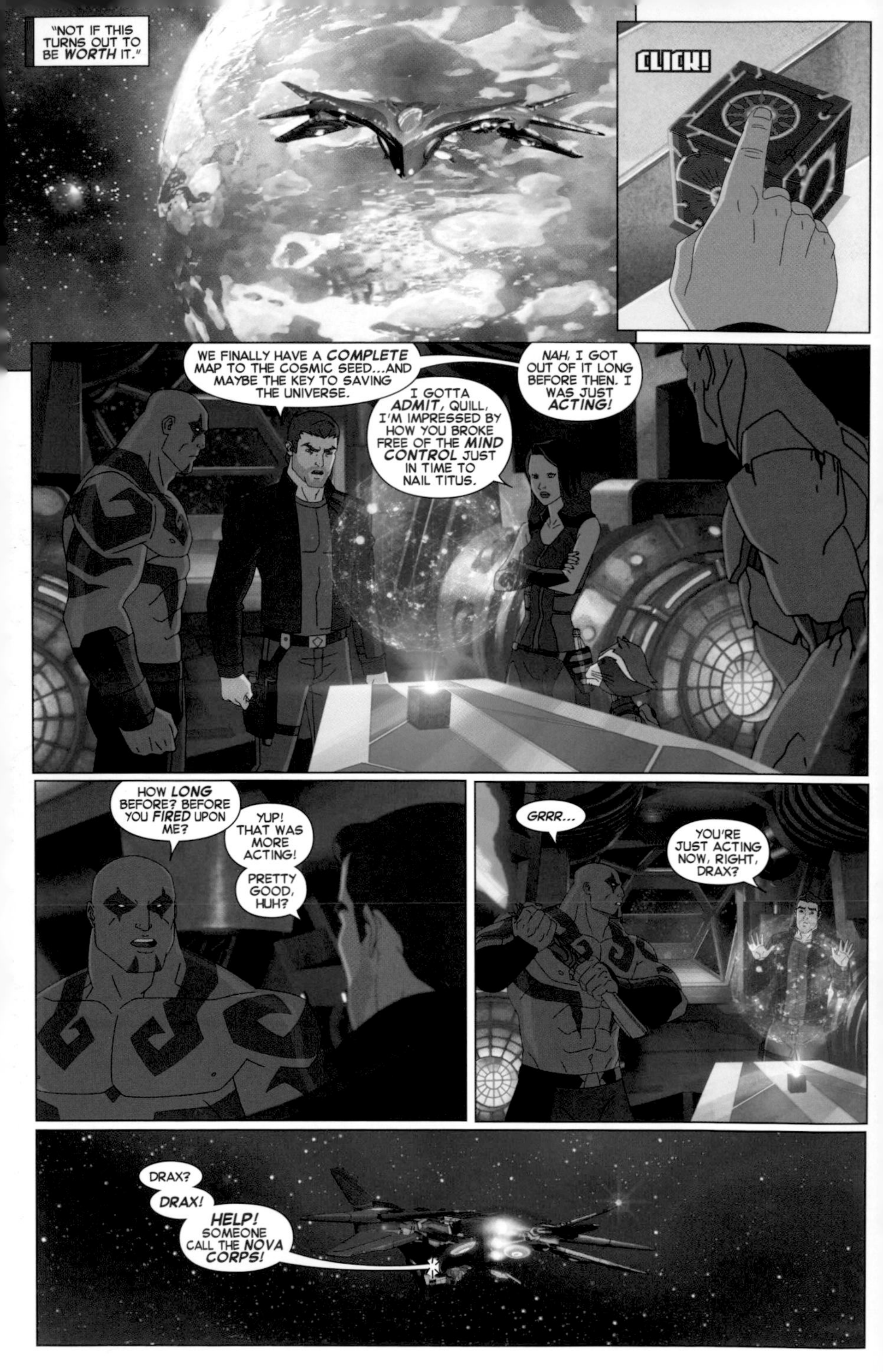
"NOT IF THIS TURNS OUT TO BE WORTH IT."
CLICK!
WE FINALLY HAVE A COMPLETE MAP TO THE COSMIC SEED...AND MAYBE THE KEY TO SAVING THE UNIVERSE.
I GOTTA ADMIT, QUILL, I'M IMPRESSED BY HOW YOU BROKE FREE OF THE MIND CONTROL JUST IN TIME TO NAIL TITUS.
NAH, I GOT OUT OF IT LONG BEFORE THEN. I WAS JUST ACTING!
HOW LONG BEFORE? BEFORE YOU FIRED UPON ME?
YUP! THAT WAS MORE ACTING!
PRETTY GOOD, HUH?
GRRR...
YOU'RE JUST ACTING NOW, RIGHT, DRAX?
DRAX?
DRAX!
HELP! SOMEONE CALL THE NOVA CORPS!

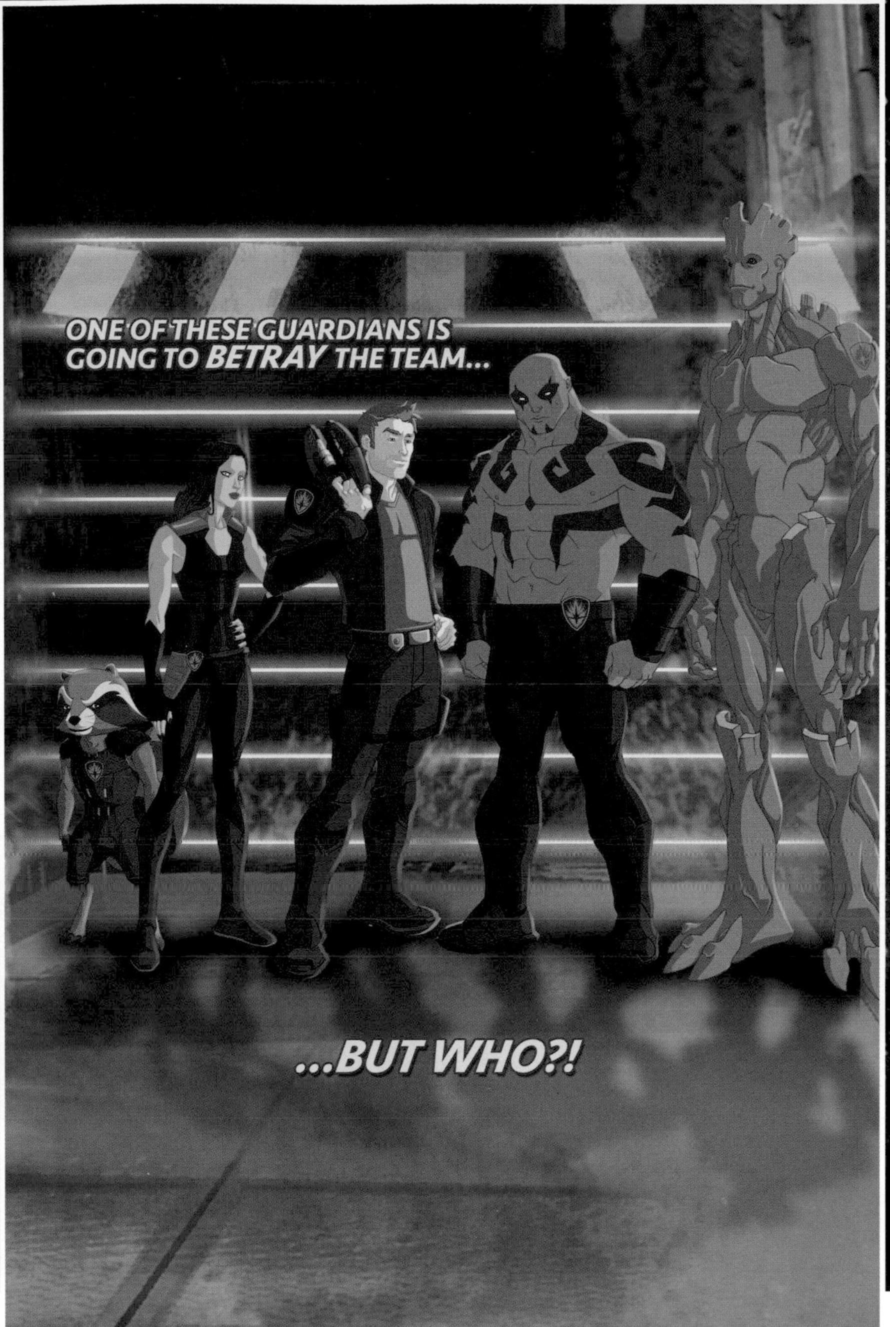
ONE OF THESE GUARDIANS IS
GOING TO BETRAY THE TEAM...
...BUT WHO?!

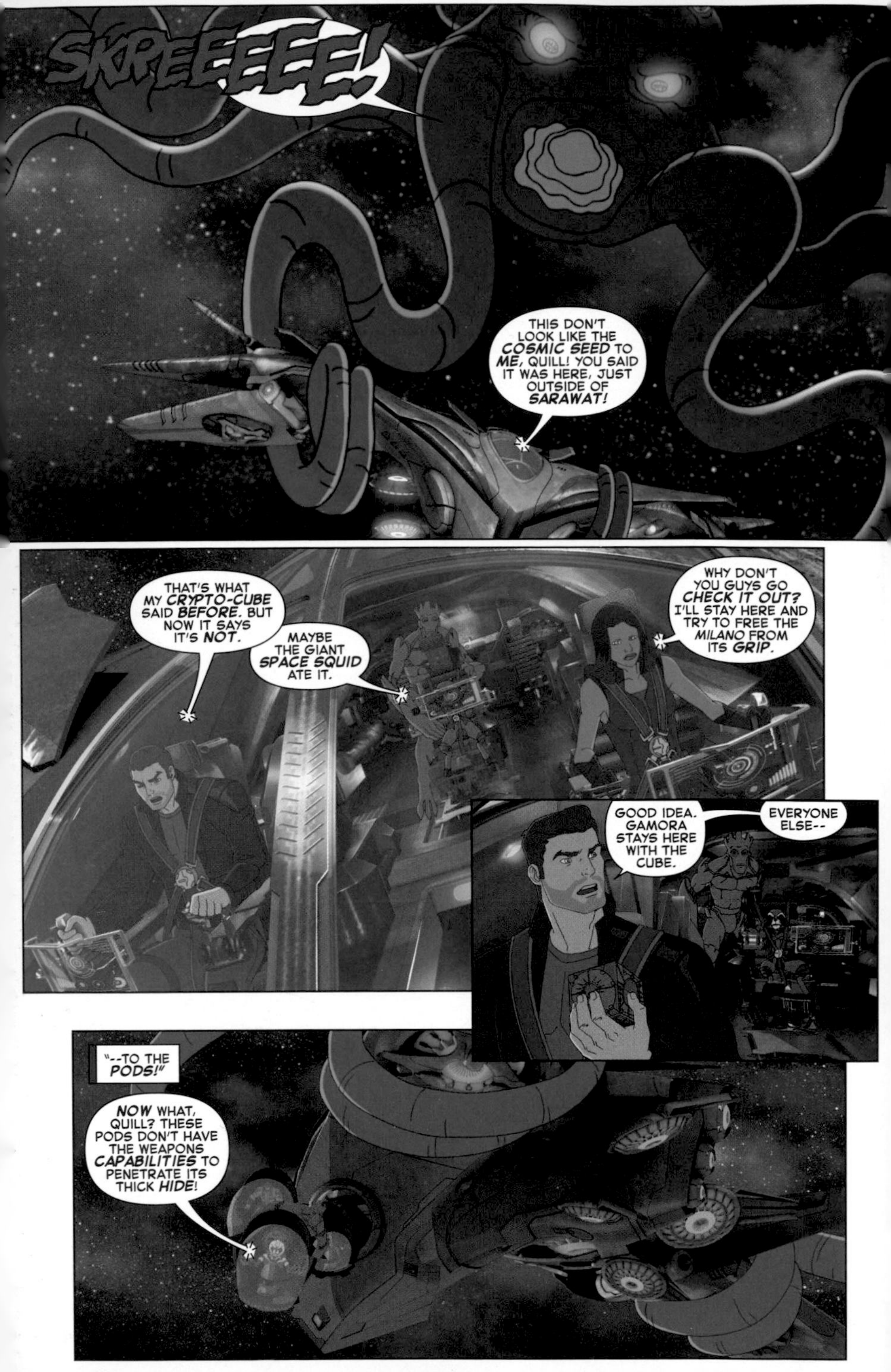
SKREEEEEE!
THIS DON'T LOOK LIKE THE COSMIC SEED TO ME, QUILL! YOU SAID IT WAS HERE, JUST OUTSIDE OF SARAWAT!
THAT'S WHAT MY CRYPTO-CUBE SAID BEFORE. BUT NOW IT SAYS IT'S NOT.
MAYBE THE GIANT SPACE SQUID ATE IT.
WHY DON'T YOU GUYS GO CHECK IT OUT? I'LL STAY HERE AND TRY TO FREE THE MILANO FROM ITS GRIP.
GOOD IDEA. GAMORA STAYS HERE WITH THE CUBE.
EVERYONE ELSE--
"--TO THE PODS!"
NOW WHAT, QUILL? THESE PODS DON'T HAVE THE WEAPONS CAPABILITIES TO PENETRATE ITS THICK HIDE!

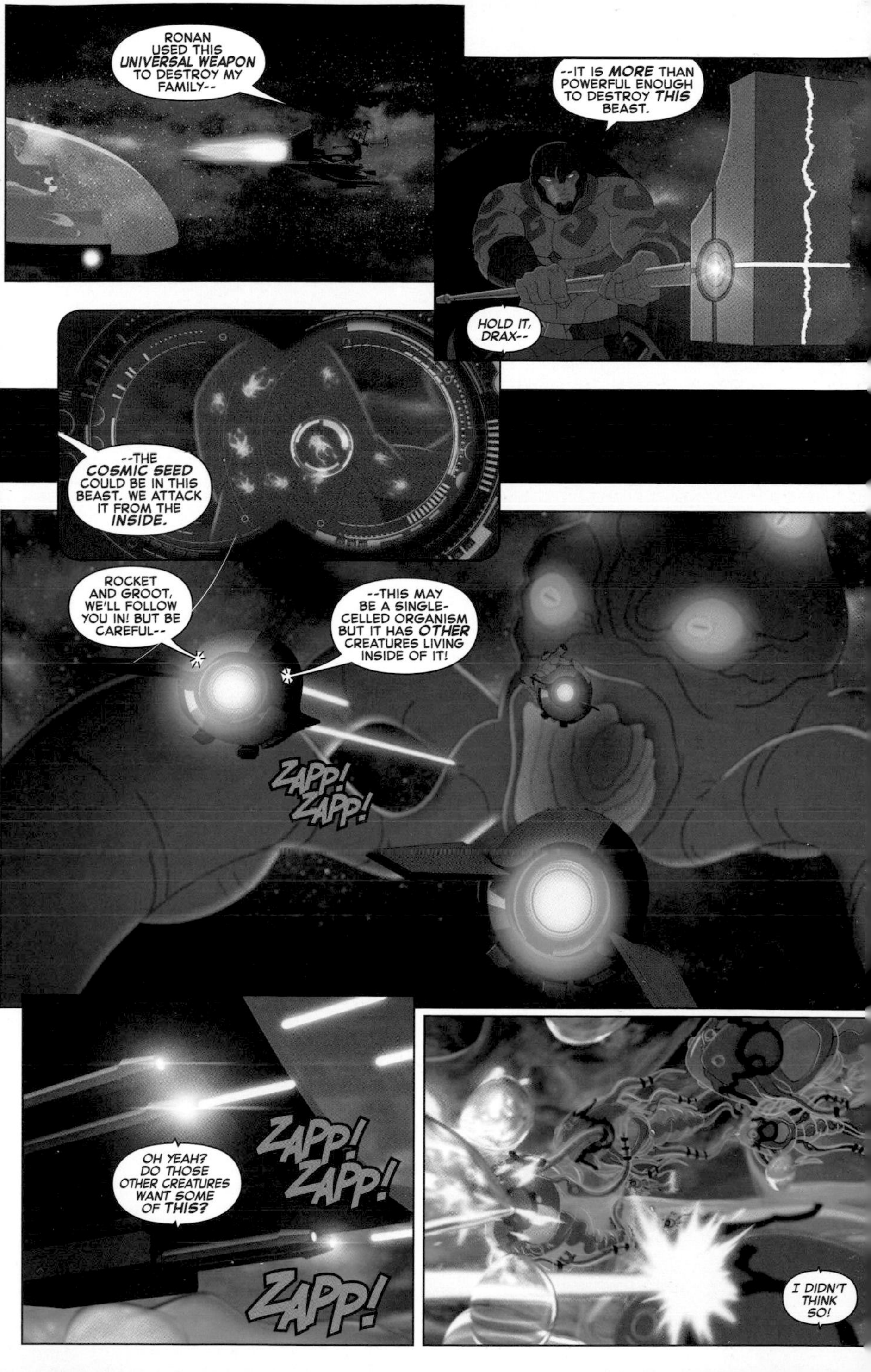
RONAN USED THIS UNIVERSAL WEAPON TO DESTROY MY FAMILY--
--IT IS MORE THAN POWERFUL ENOUGH TO DESTROY THIS BEAST.
HOLD IT, DRAX--
--THE COSMIC SEED COULD BE IN THIS BEAST. WE ATTACK IT FROM THE INSIDE.
ROCKET AND GROOT, WE'LL FOLLOW YOU IN! BUT BE CAREFUL--
--THIS MAY BE A SINGLE-CELLED ORGANISM BUT IT HAS OTHER CREATURES LIVING INSIDE OF IT!
ZAPP! ZAPP!
ZAPP! ZAPP!
OH YEAH? DO THOSE OTHER CREATURES WANT SOME OF THIS?
ZAPP!
I DIDN'T THINK SO!

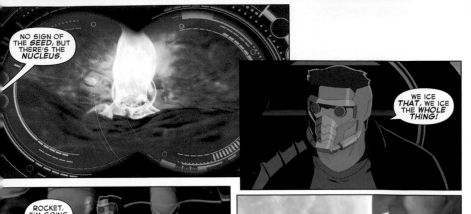

NO SIGN OF THE *SEED*, BUT THERE'S THE *NUCLEUS*.

WE ICE *THAT*, WE ICE THE *WHOLE* THING!

ROCKET, I'M GOING AFTER IT!

QUILL, WAIT--

ZARK!

PRMMB~~

--SHOULDN'T THE *REST* OF US GET OUT FIRST--?

FLOORB!

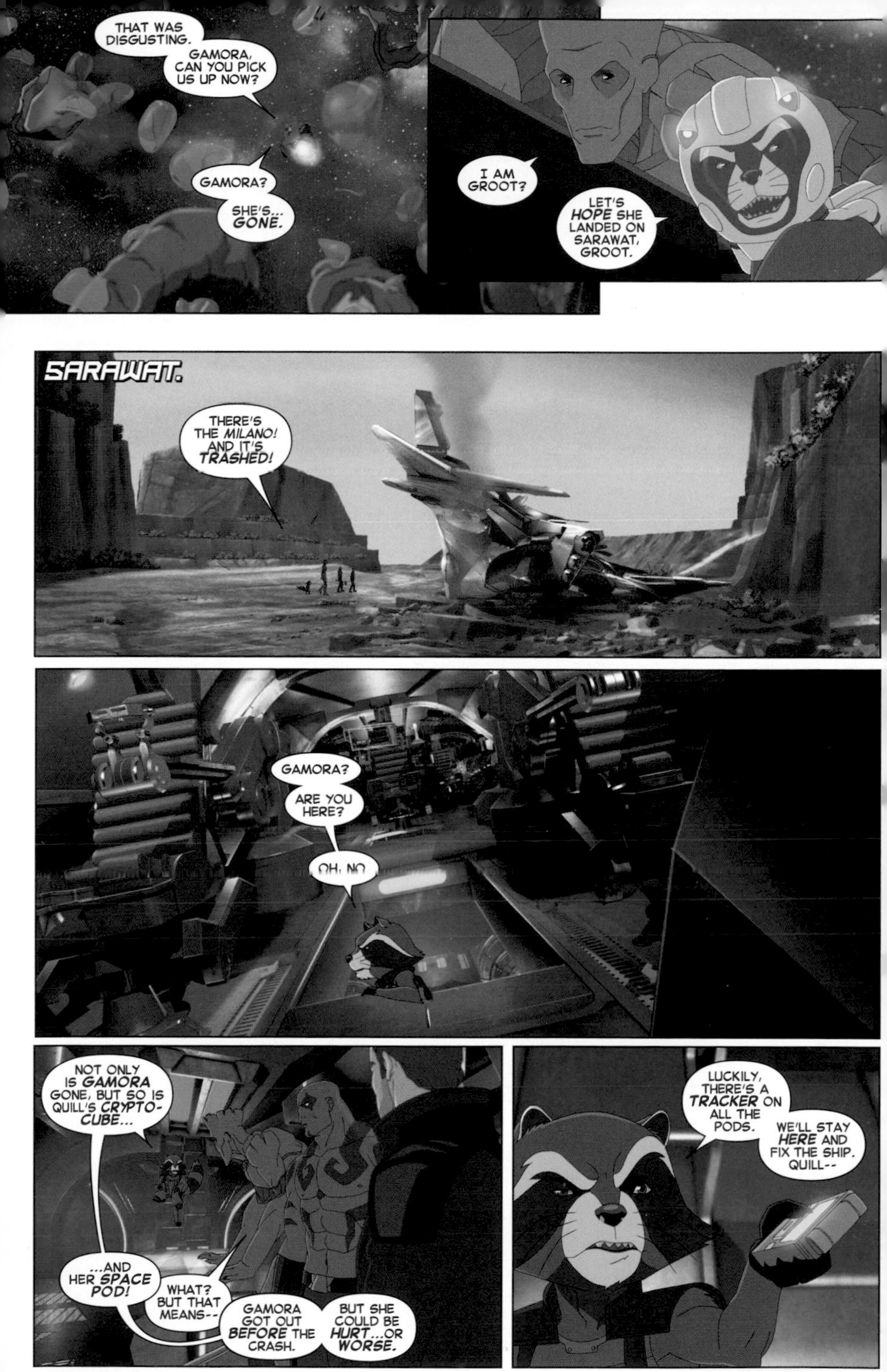
THAT WAS DISGUSTING.
GAMORA, CAN YOU PICK US UP NOW?
GAMORA?
SHE'S... GONE.
I AM GROOT?
LET'S HOPE SHE LANDED ON SARAWAT, GROOT.
SARAWAT.
THERE'S THE MILANO! AND IT'S TRASHED!
GAMORA?
ARE YOU HERE?
OH, NO
NOT ONLY IS GAMORA GONE, BUT SO IS QUILL'S CRYPTO-CUBE...
...AND HER SPACE POD!
WHAT? BUT THAT MEANS--
GAMORA GOT OUT BEFORE THE CRASH.
BUT SHE COULD BE HURT...OR WORSE.
LUCKILY, THERE'S A TRACKER ON ALL THE PODS.
WE'LL STAY HERE AND FIX THE SHIP. QUILL--

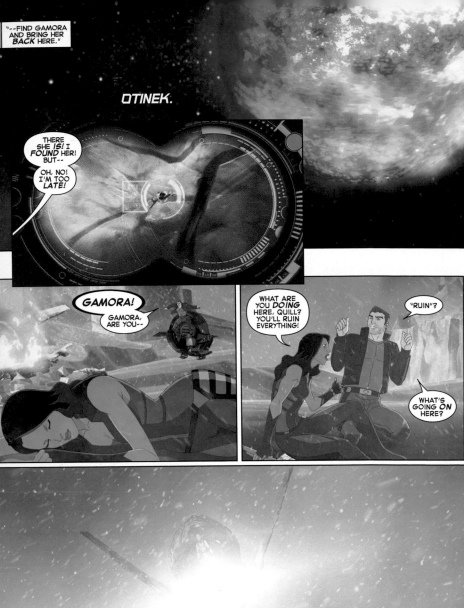

"--FIND GAMORA AND BRING HER *BACK* HERE."

OTINEK.

THERE SHE *IS!* I *FOUND* HER! BUT--

OH, NO! I'M TOO *LATE!*

GAMORA!

GAMORA, ARE YOU--

WHAT ARE YOU *DOING* HERE, QUILL? YOU'LL RUIN EVERYTHING!

"RUIN"?

WHAT'S GOING *ON* HERE?

OH.

WERE YOU *EXPECTING* SOMEONE?

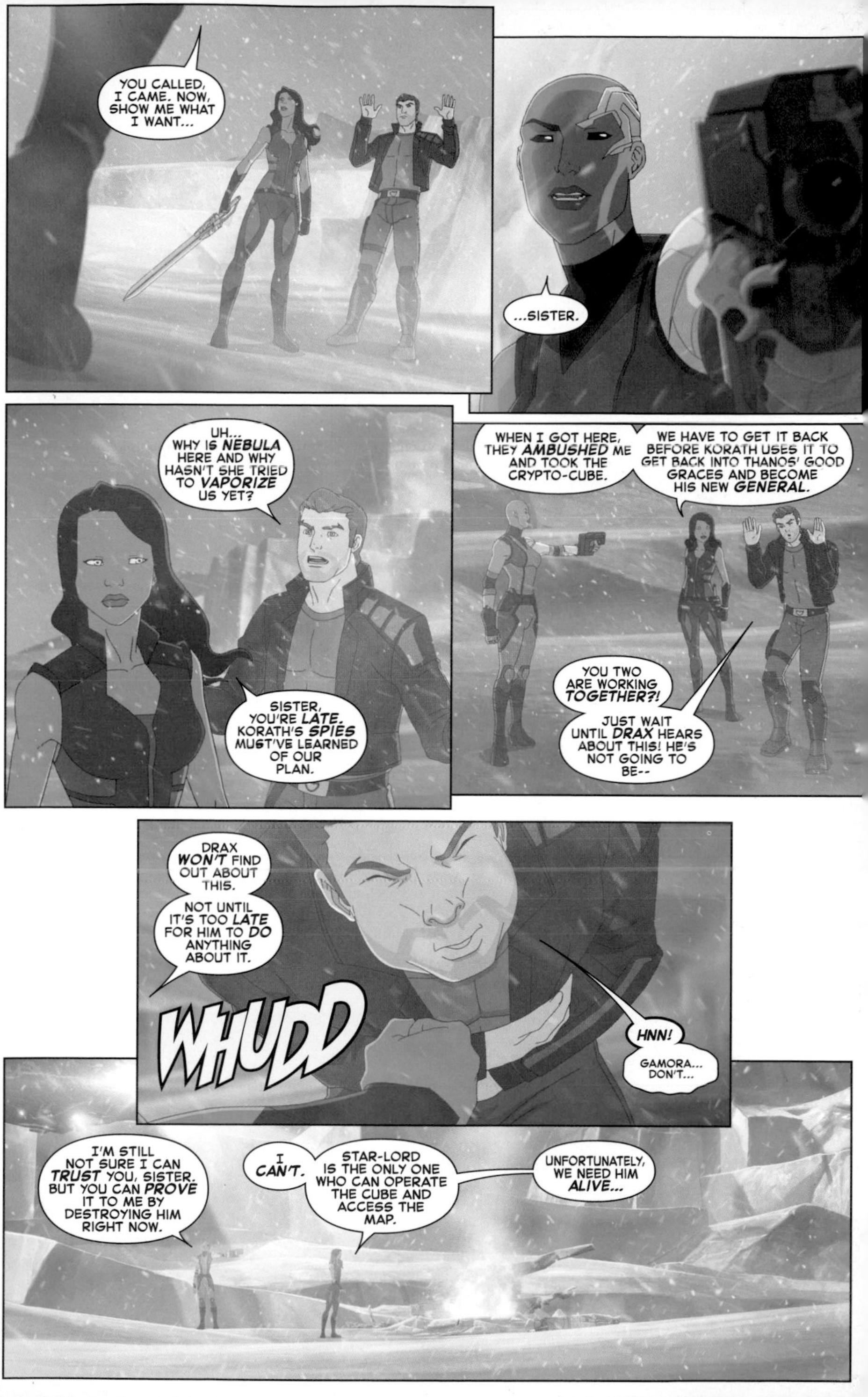
YOU CALLED, I CAME. NOW, SHOW ME WHAT I WANT...
...SISTER.
UH... WHY IS NEBULA HERE AND WHY HASN'T SHE TRIED TO VAPORIZE US YET?
SISTER, YOU'RE LATE. KORATH'S SPIES MUST'VE LEARNED OF OUR PLAN.
WHEN I GOT HERE, THEY AMBUSHED ME AND TOOK THE CRYPTO-CUBE.
WE HAVE TO GET IT BACK BEFORE KORATH USES IT TO GET BACK INTO THANOS' GOOD GRACES AND BECOME HIS NEW GENERAL.
YOU TWO ARE WORKING TOGETHER?!
JUST WAIT UNTIL DRAX HEARS ABOUT THIS! HE'S NOT GOING TO BE--
DRAX WON'T FIND OUT ABOUT THIS.
NOT UNTIL IT'S TOO LATE FOR HIM TO DO ANYTHING ABOUT IT.
WHUDD
HNN!
GAMORA... DON'T...
I'M STILL NOT SURE I CAN TRUST YOU, SISTER. BUT YOU CAN PROVE IT TO ME BY DESTROYING HIM RIGHT NOW.
I CAN'T.
STAR-LORD IS THE ONLY ONE WHO CAN OPERATE THE CUBE AND ACCESS THE MAP.
UNFORTUNATELY, WE NEED HIM ALIVE...

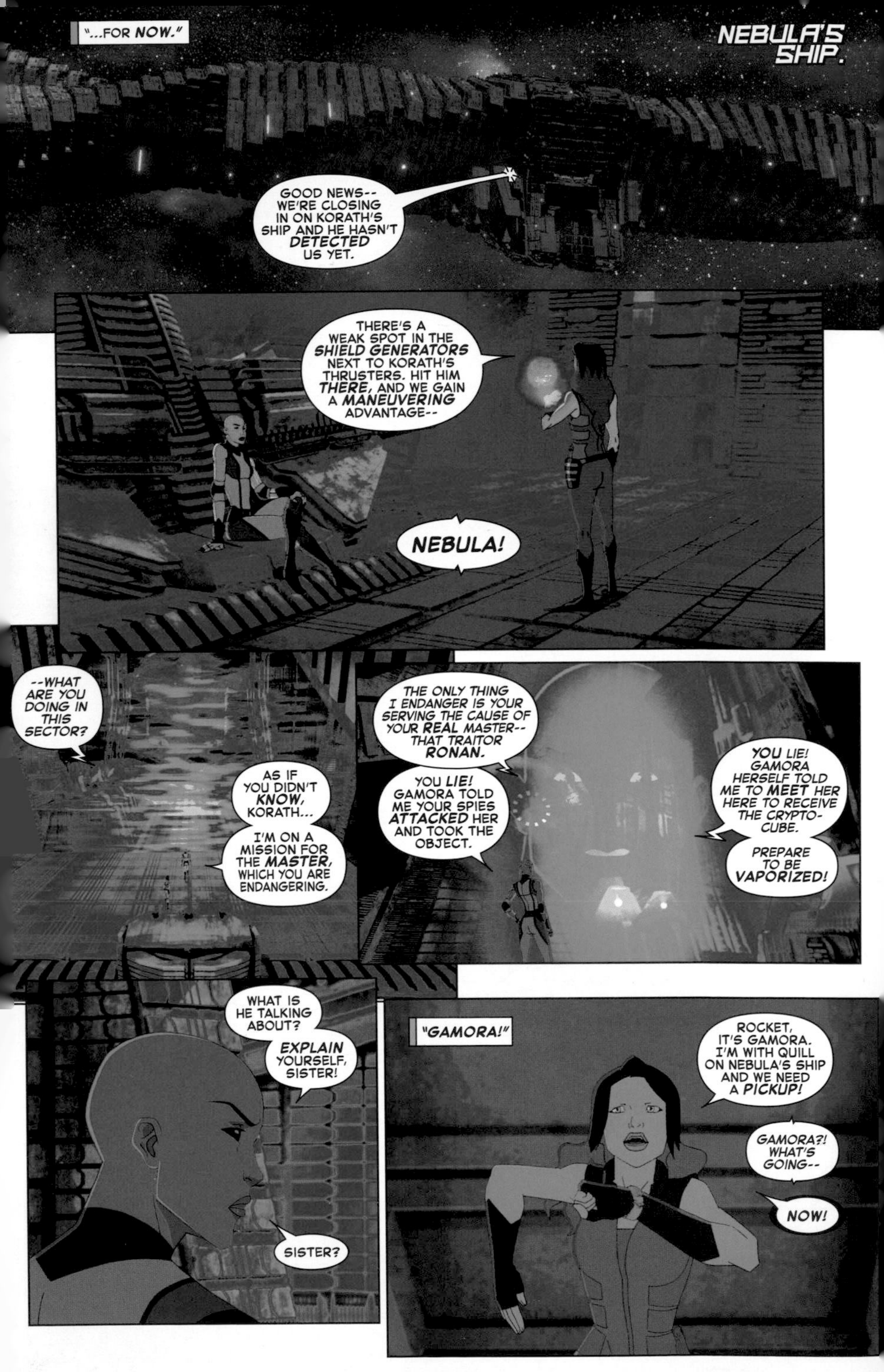
"...FOR NOW."
NEBULA'S SHIP.
GOOD NEWS-- WE'RE CLOSING IN ON KORATH'S SHIP AND HE HASN'T DETECTED US YET.
THERE'S A WEAK SPOT IN THE SHIELD GENERATORS NEXT TO KORATH'S THRUSTERS. HIT HIM THERE, AND WE GAIN A MANEUVERING ADVANTAGE--
NEBULA!
--WHAT ARE YOU DOING IN THIS SECTOR?
AS IF YOU DIDN'T KNOW, KORATH...
I'M ON A MISSION FOR THE MASTER, WHICH YOU ARE ENDANGERING.
THE ONLY THING I ENDANGER IS YOUR SERVING THE CAUSE OF YOUR REAL MASTER-- THAT TRAITOR RONAN.
YOU LIE! GAMORA TOLD ME YOUR SPIES ATTACKED HER AND TOOK THE OBJECT.
YOU LIE! GAMORA HERSELF TOLD ME TO MEET HER HERE TO RECEIVE THE CRYPTO-CUBE.
PREPARE TO BE VAPORIZED!
WHAT IS HE TALKING ABOUT?
EXPLAIN YOURSELF, SISTER!
SISTER?
"GAMORA!"
ROCKET, IT'S GAMORA. I'M WITH QUILL ON NEBULA'S SHIP AND WE NEED A PICKUP!
GAMORA?! WHAT'S GOING--
NOW!

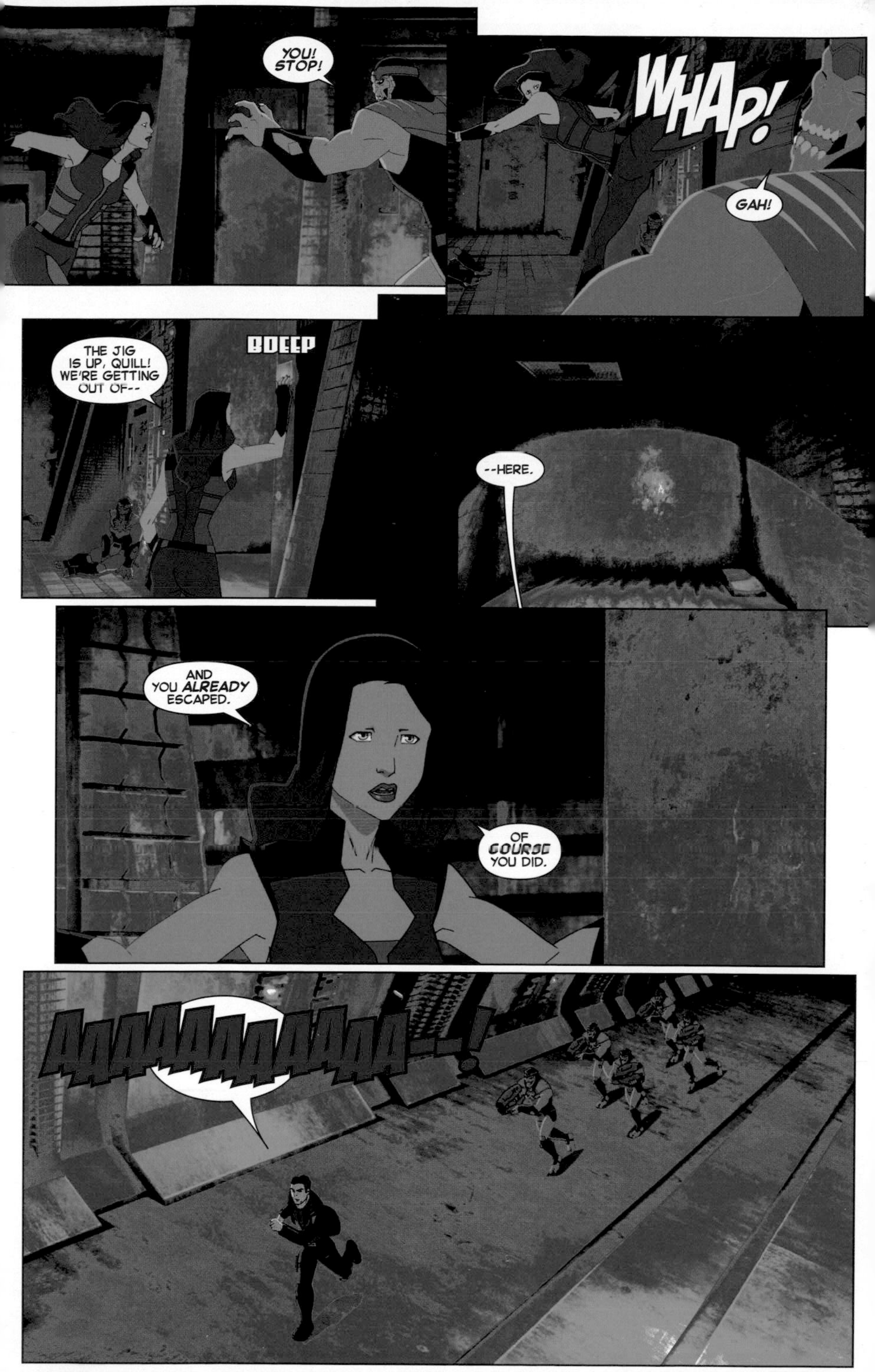
YOU! STOP!
WHAP!
GAH!
THE JIG IS UP, QUILL! WE'RE GETTING OUT OF--
BDEEP
--HERE.
AND YOU ALREADY ESCAPED.
OF COURSE YOU DID.
AAAAAAAAAAAA--!

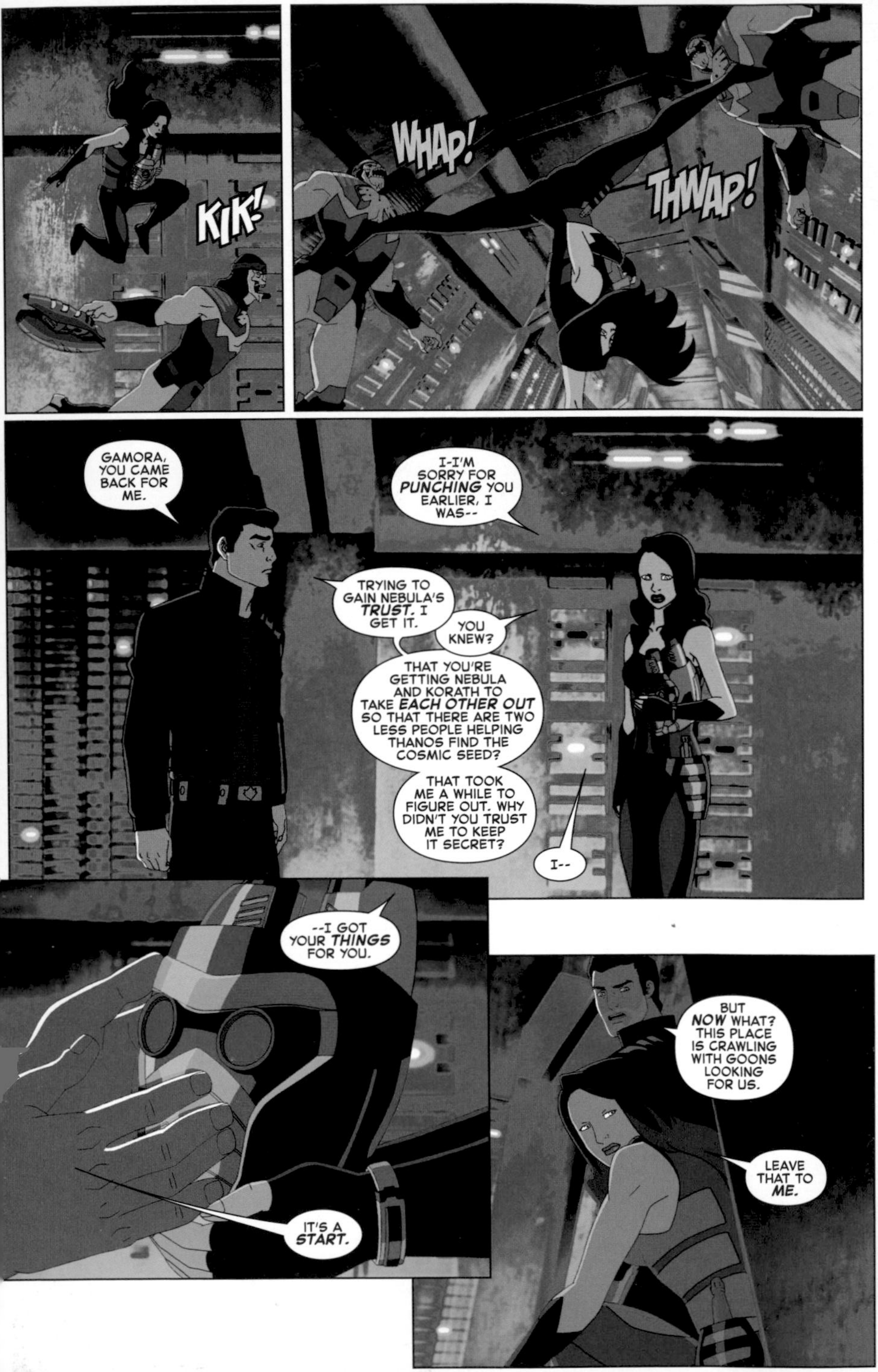
KIK!
WHAP!
THWAP!
GAMORA, YOU CAME BACK FOR ME.
I-I'M SORRY FOR PUNCHING YOU EARLIER, I WAS--
TRYING TO GAIN NEBULA'S TRUST. I GET IT.
YOU KNEW?
THAT YOU'RE GETTING NEBULA AND KORATH TO TAKE EACH OTHER OUT SO THAT THERE ARE TWO LESS PEOPLE HELPING THANOS FIND THE COSMIC SEED?
THAT TOOK ME A WHILE TO FIGURE OUT. WHY DIDN'T YOU TRUST ME TO KEEP IT SECRET?
I--
--I GOT YOUR THINGS FOR YOU.
IT'S A START.
BUT NOW WHAT? THIS PLACE IS CRAWLING WITH GOONS LOOKING FOR US.
LEAVE THAT TO ME.

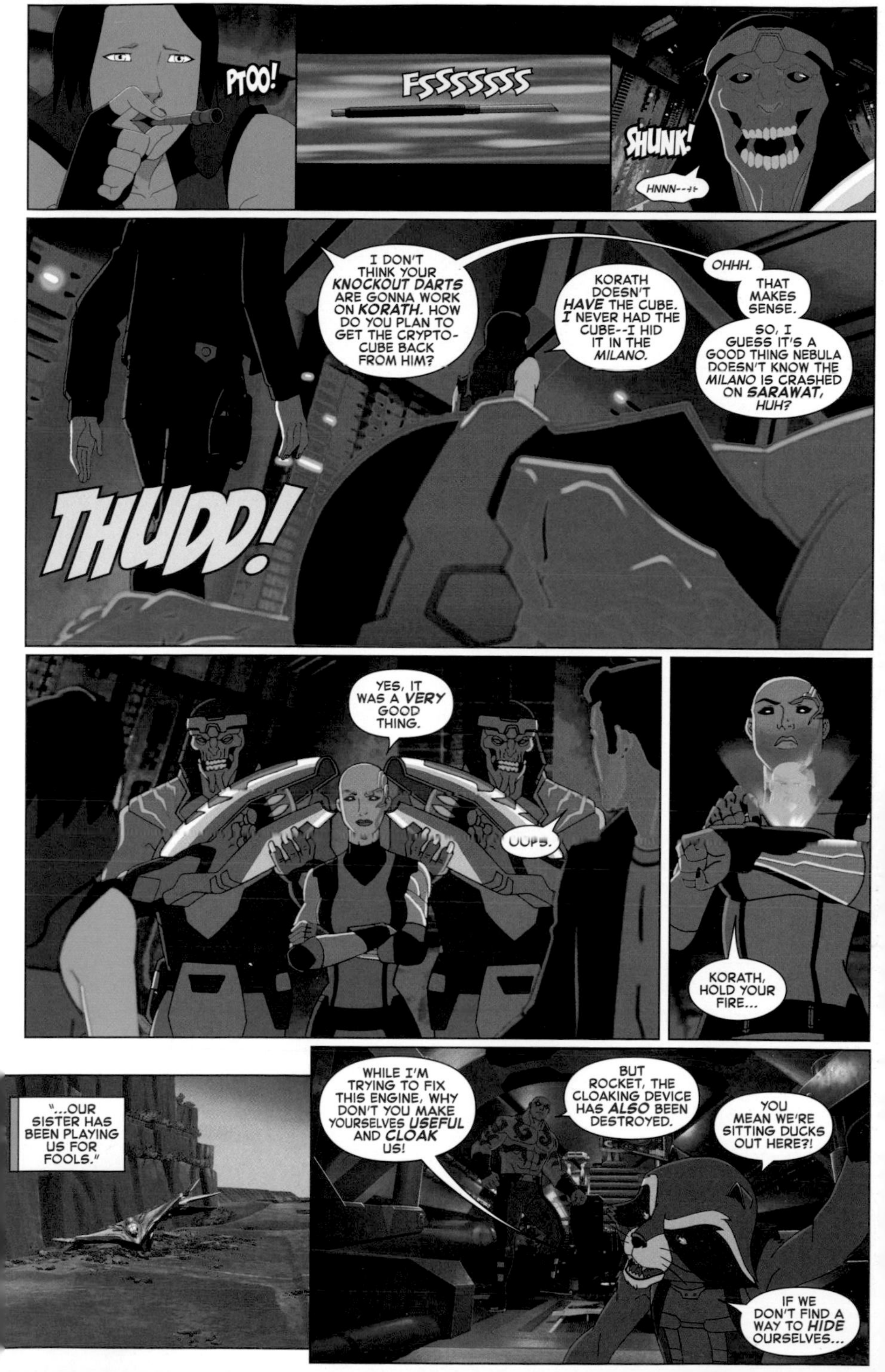
PTOO!
FSSSSSS
SHUNK!
HNNN--ff
I DON'T THINK YOUR KNOCKOUT DARTS ARE GONNA WORK ON KORATH. HOW DO YOU PLAN TO GET THE CRYPTO-CUBE BACK FROM HIM?
KORATH DOESN'T HAVE THE CUBE. I NEVER HAD THE CUBE--I HID IT IN THE MILANO.
OHHH.
THAT MAKES SENSE.
SO, I GUESS IT'S A GOOD THING NEBULA DOESN'T KNOW THE MILANO IS CRASHED ON SARAWAT, HUH?
THUDD!
YES, IT WAS A VERY GOOD THING.
OOPS.
KORATH, HOLD YOUR FIRE...
"...OUR SISTER HAS BEEN PLAYING US FOR FOOLS."
WHILE I'M TRYING TO FIX THIS ENGINE, WHY DON'T YOU MAKE YOURSELVES USEFUL AND CLOAK US!
BUT ROCKET, THE CLOAKING DEVICE HAS ALSO BEEN DESTROYED.
YOU MEAN WE'RE SITTING DUCKS OUT HERE?!
IF WE DON'T FIND A WAY TO HIDE OURSELVES...

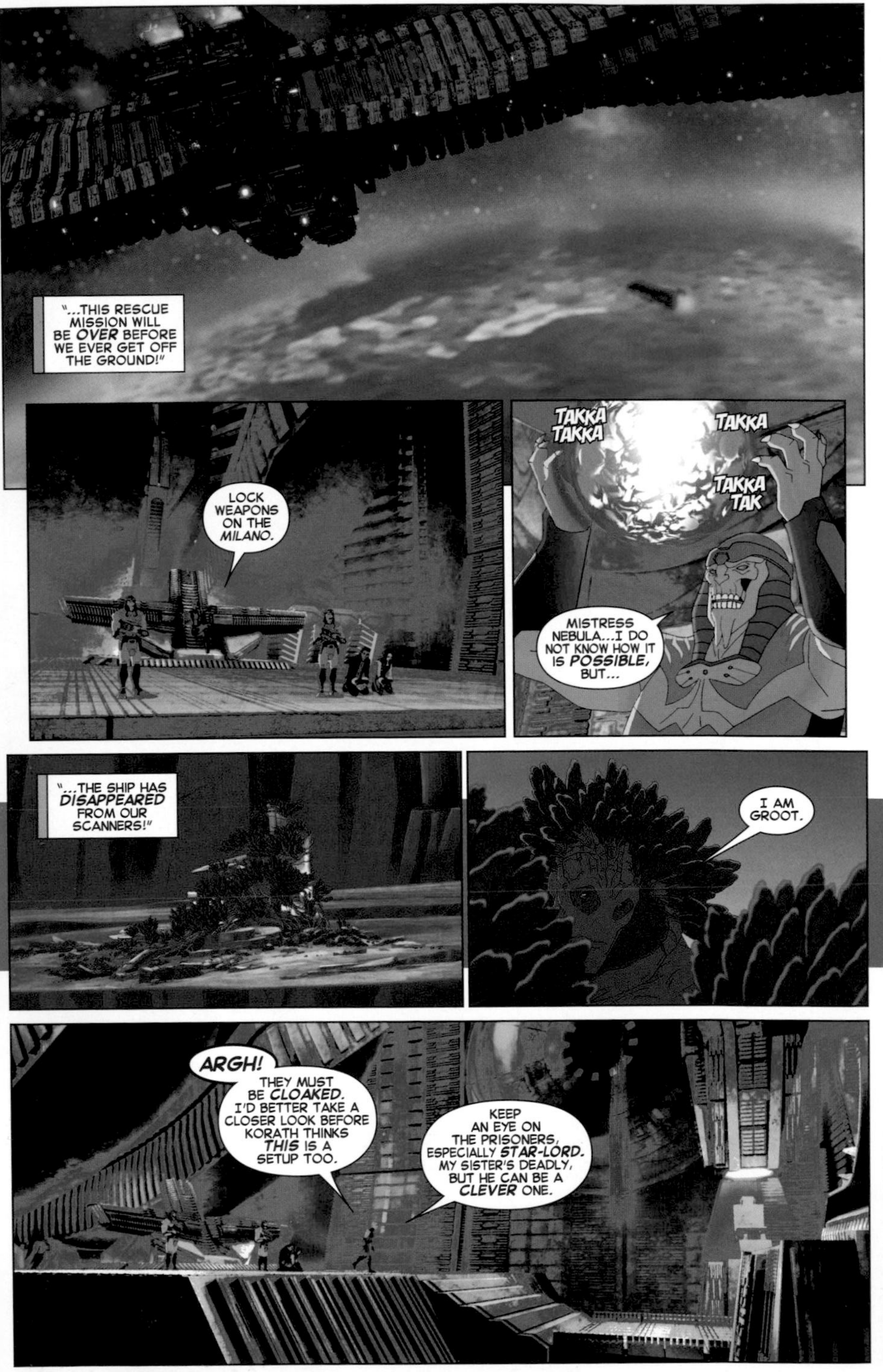
"...THIS RESCUE MISSION WILL BE OVER BEFORE WE EVER GET OFF THE GROUND!"
LOCK WEAPONS ON THE MILANO.
TAKKA TAKKA
TAKKA
TAKKA TAK
MISTRESS NEBULA...I DO NOT KNOW HOW IT IS POSSIBLE, BUT...
"...THE SHIP HAS DISAPPEARED FROM OUR SCANNERS!"
I AM GROOT.
ARGH!
THEY MUST BE CLOAKED. I'D BETTER TAKE A CLOSER LOOK BEFORE KORATH THINKS THIS IS A SETUP TOO.
KEEP AN EYE ON THE PRISONERS, ESPECIALLY STAR-LORD. MY SISTER'S DEADLY, BUT HE CAN BE A CLEVER ONE.

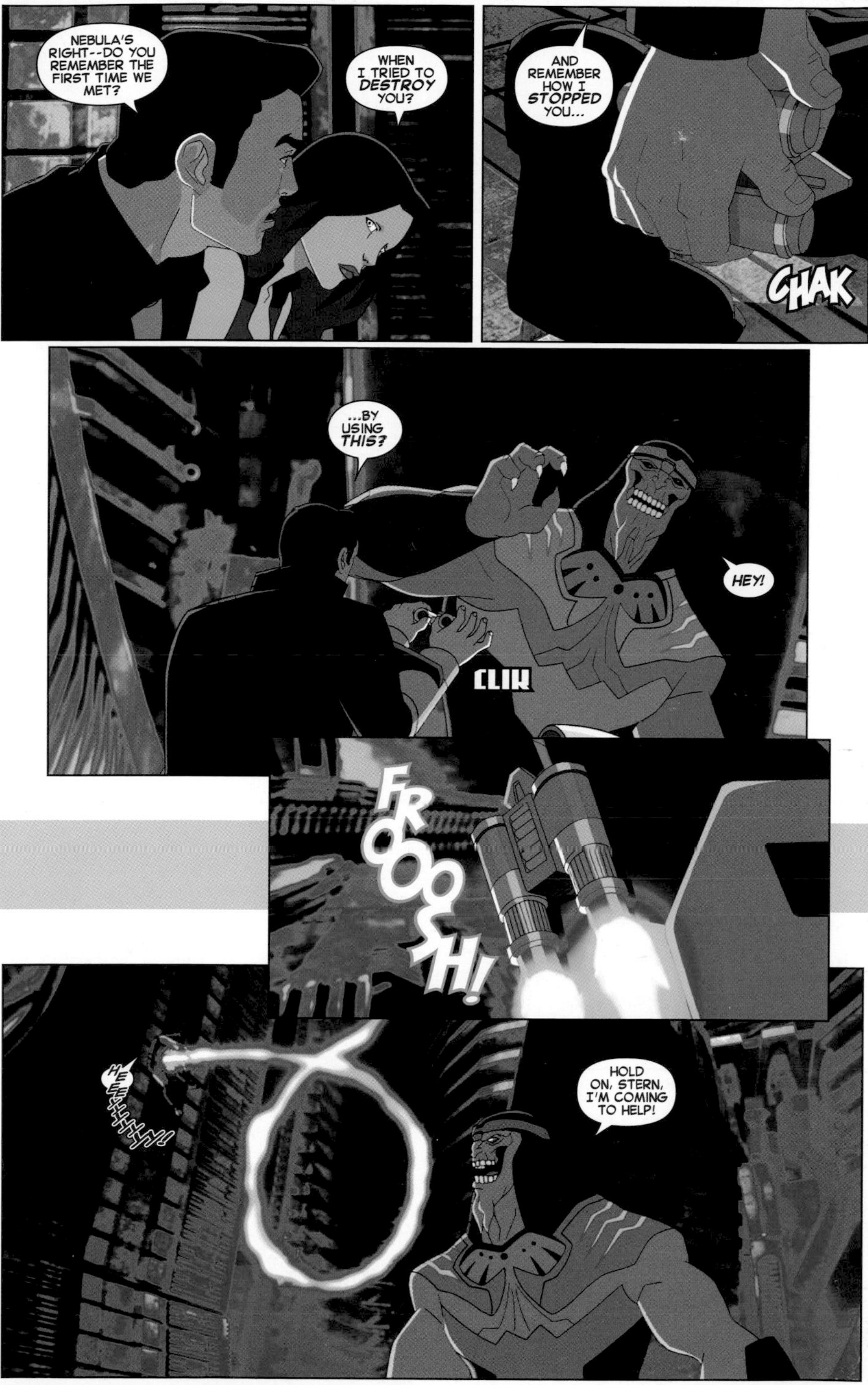
NEBULA'S RIGHT--DO YOU REMEMBER THE FIRST TIME WE MET?
WHEN I TRIED TO *DESTROY* YOU?
AND REMEMBER HOW I *STOPPED* YOU...
CHAK
...BY USING *THIS?*
HEY!
CLIK
FROOOOSH!
HEEEYYYYY!
HOLD ON, STERN, I'M COMING TO HELP!

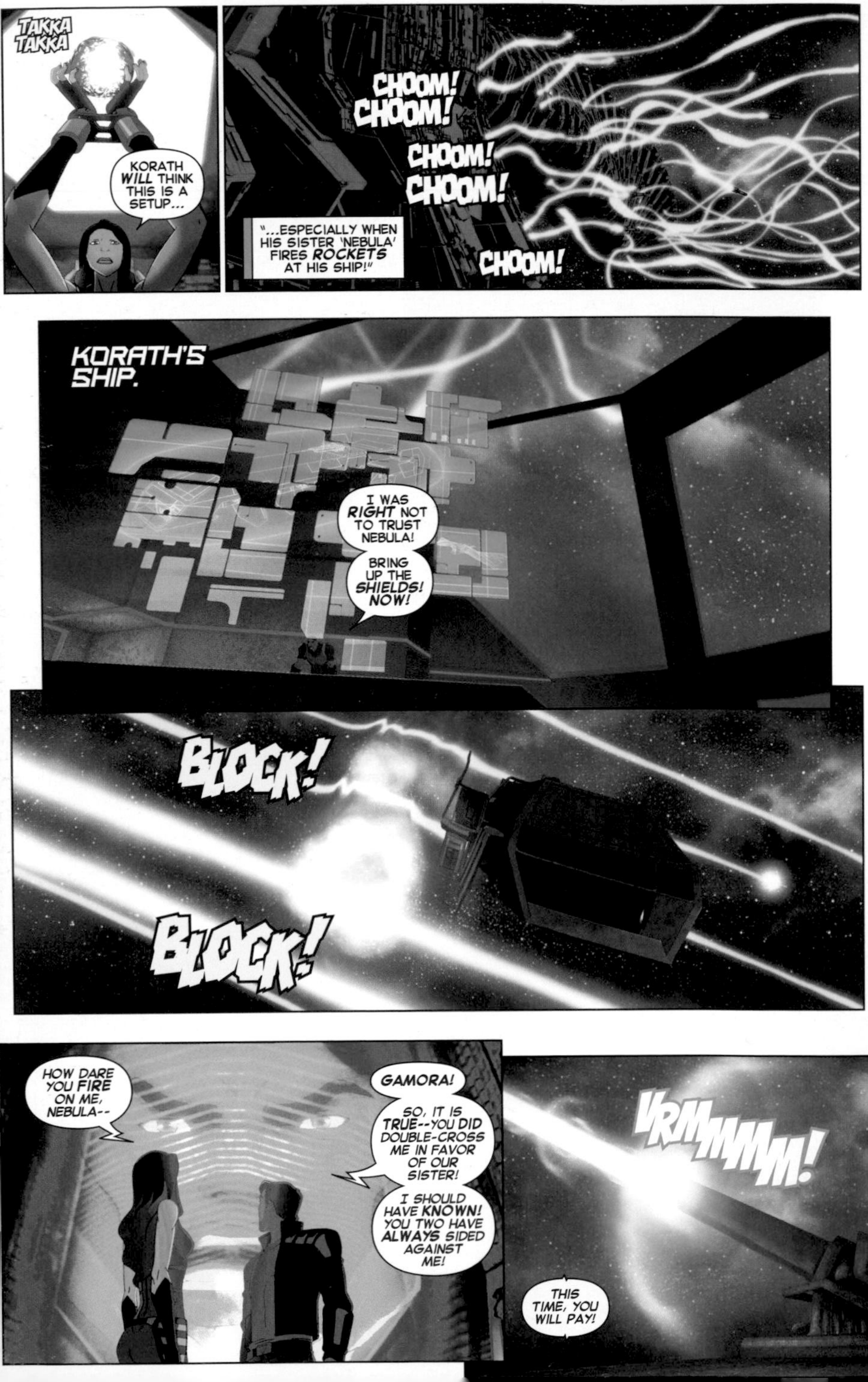
TAKKA TAKKA
KORATH WILL THINK THIS IS A SETUP...
"...ESPECIALLY WHEN HIS SISTER 'NEBULA' FIRES ROCKETS AT HIS SHIP!"
CHOOM! CHOOM!
CHOOM! CHOOM!
CHOOM!
KORATH'S SHIP.
I WAS RIGHT NOT TO TRUST NEBULA!
BRING UP THE SHIELDS! NOW!
BLOCK!
BLOCK!
HOW DARE YOU FIRE ON ME, NEBULA--
GAMORA!
SO, IT IS TRUE--YOU DID DOUBLE-CROSS ME IN FAVOR OF OUR SISTER!
I SHOULD HAVE KNOWN! YOU TWO HAVE ALWAYS SIDED AGAINST ME!
VRMMMM!
THIS TIME, YOU WILL PAY!

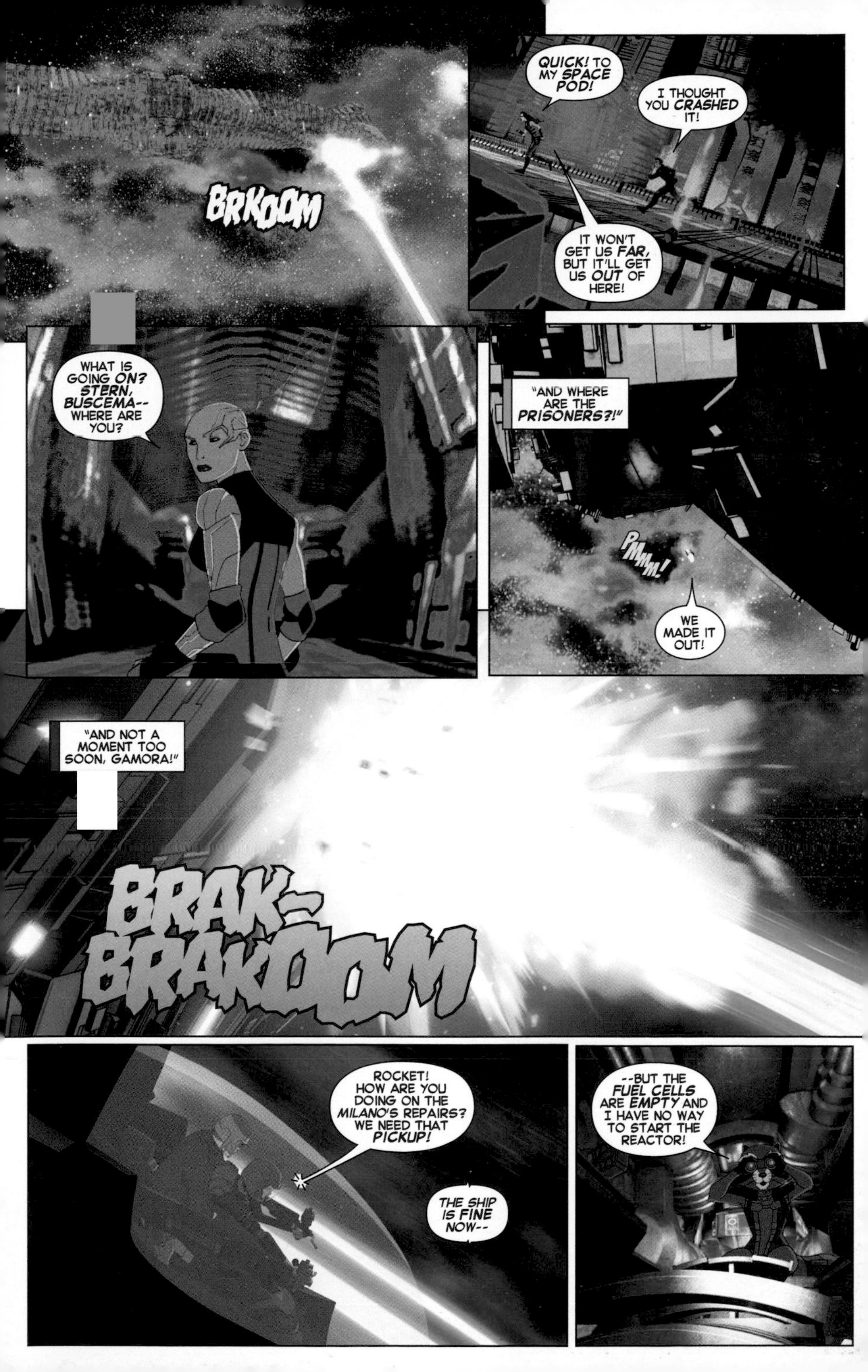
BRKOOM
QUICK! TO MY SPACE POD!
I THOUGHT YOU CRASHED IT!
IT WON'T GET US FAR, BUT IT'LL GET US OUT OF HERE!
WHAT IS GOING ON? STERN, BUSCEMA-- WHERE ARE YOU?
"AND WHERE ARE THE PRISONERS?!"
PMMM!
WE MADE IT OUT!
"AND NOT A MOMENT TOO SOON, GAMORA!"
BRAK-BRAKOOM
ROCKET! HOW ARE YOU DOING ON THE MILANO'S REPAIRS? WE NEED THAT PICKUP!
THE SHIP IS FINE NOW--
--BUT THE FUEL CELLS ARE EMPTY AND I HAVE NO WAY TO START THE REACTOR!

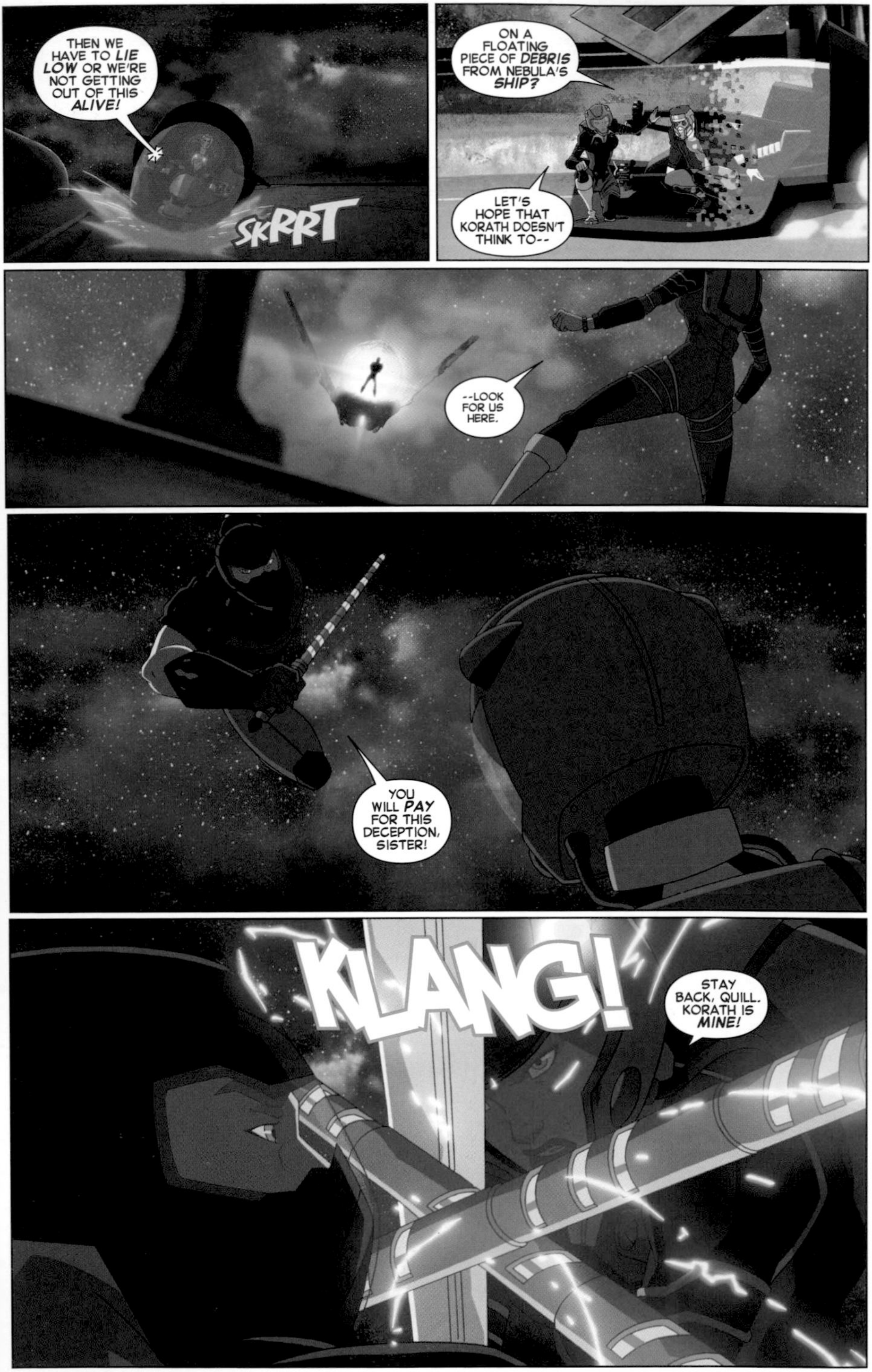
THEN WE HAVE TO LIE LOW OR WE'RE NOT GETTING OUT OF THIS ALIVE!
SKRRT
ON A FLOATING PIECE OF DEBRIS FROM NEBULA'S SHIP?
LET'S HOPE THAT KORATH DOESN'T THINK TO--
--LOOK FOR US HERE.
YOU WILL PAY FOR THIS DECEPTION, SISTER!
KLANG!
STAY BACK, QUILL. KORATH IS MINE!

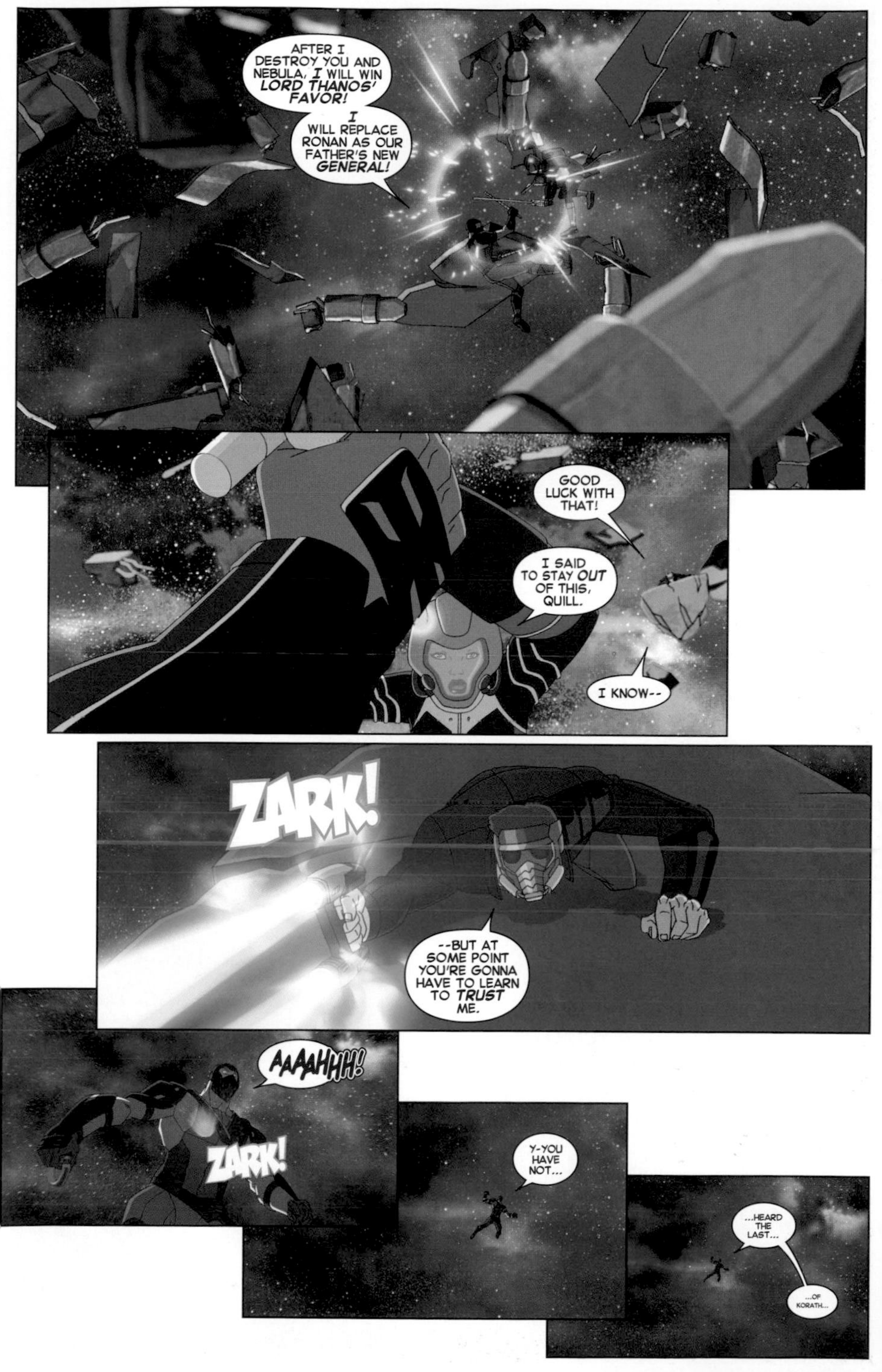
AFTER I DESTROY YOU AND NEBULA, I WILL WIN LORD THANOS' FAVOR!
I WILL REPLACE RONAN AS OUR FATHER'S NEW GENERAL!
GOOD LUCK WITH THAT!
I SAID TO STAY OUT OF THIS, QUILL.
I KNOW--
ZARK!
--BUT AT SOME POINT YOU'RE GONNA HAVE TO LEARN TO TRUST ME.
AAAAHHH!
ZARK!
Y-YOU HAVE NOT...
...HEARD THE LAST...
...OF KORATH...

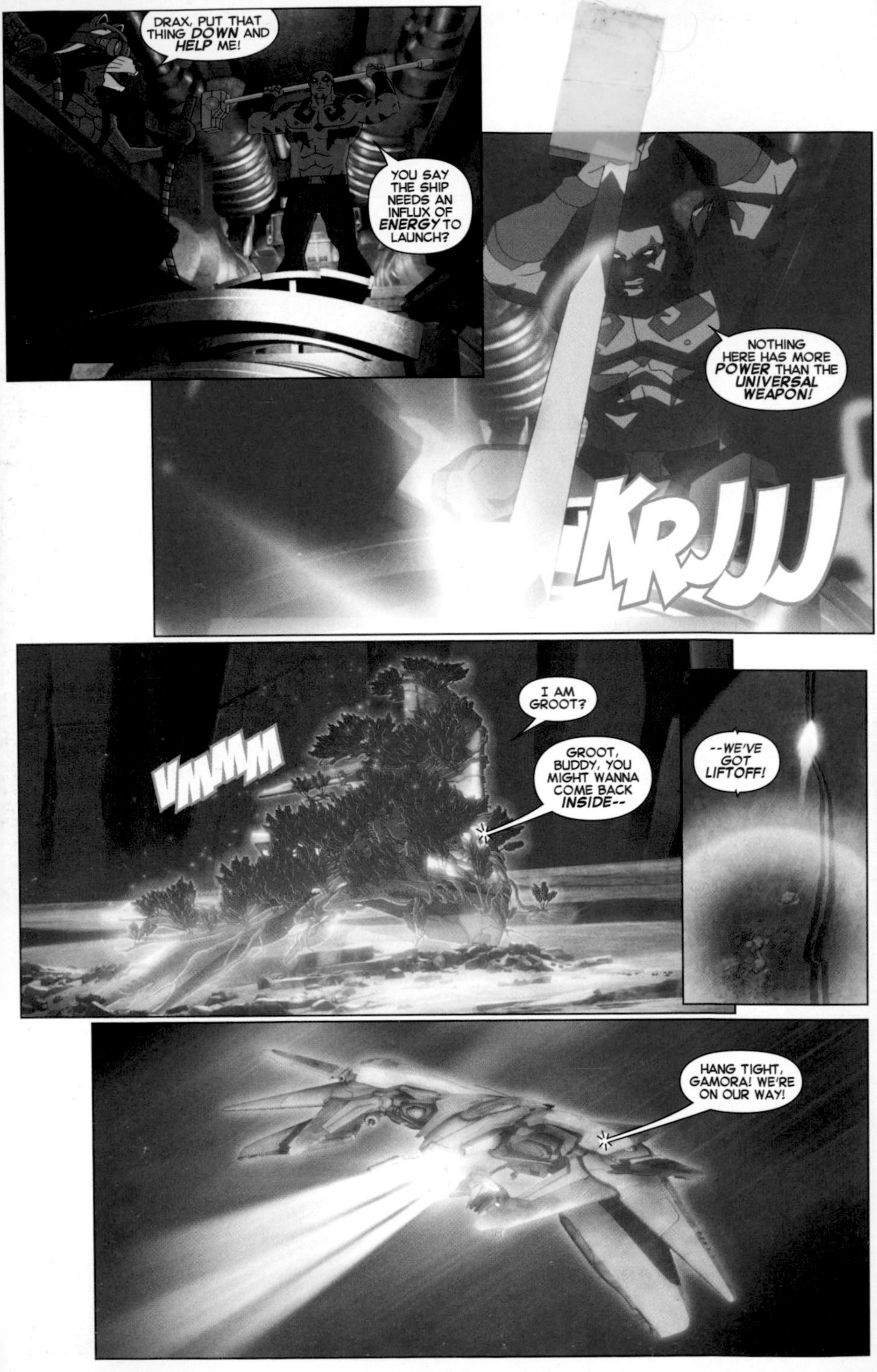

DRAX, PUT THAT THING DOWN AND HELP ME!
YOU SAY THE SHIP NEEDS AN INFLUX OF ENERGY TO LAUNCH?
NOTHING HERE HAS MORE POWER THAN THE UNIVERSAL WEAPON!
KRJJJ
VMMM
I AM GROOT?
GROOT, BUDDY, YOU MIGHT WANNA COME BACK INSIDE--
--WE'VE GOT LIFTOFF!
HANG TIGHT, GAMORA! WE'RE ON OUR WAY!

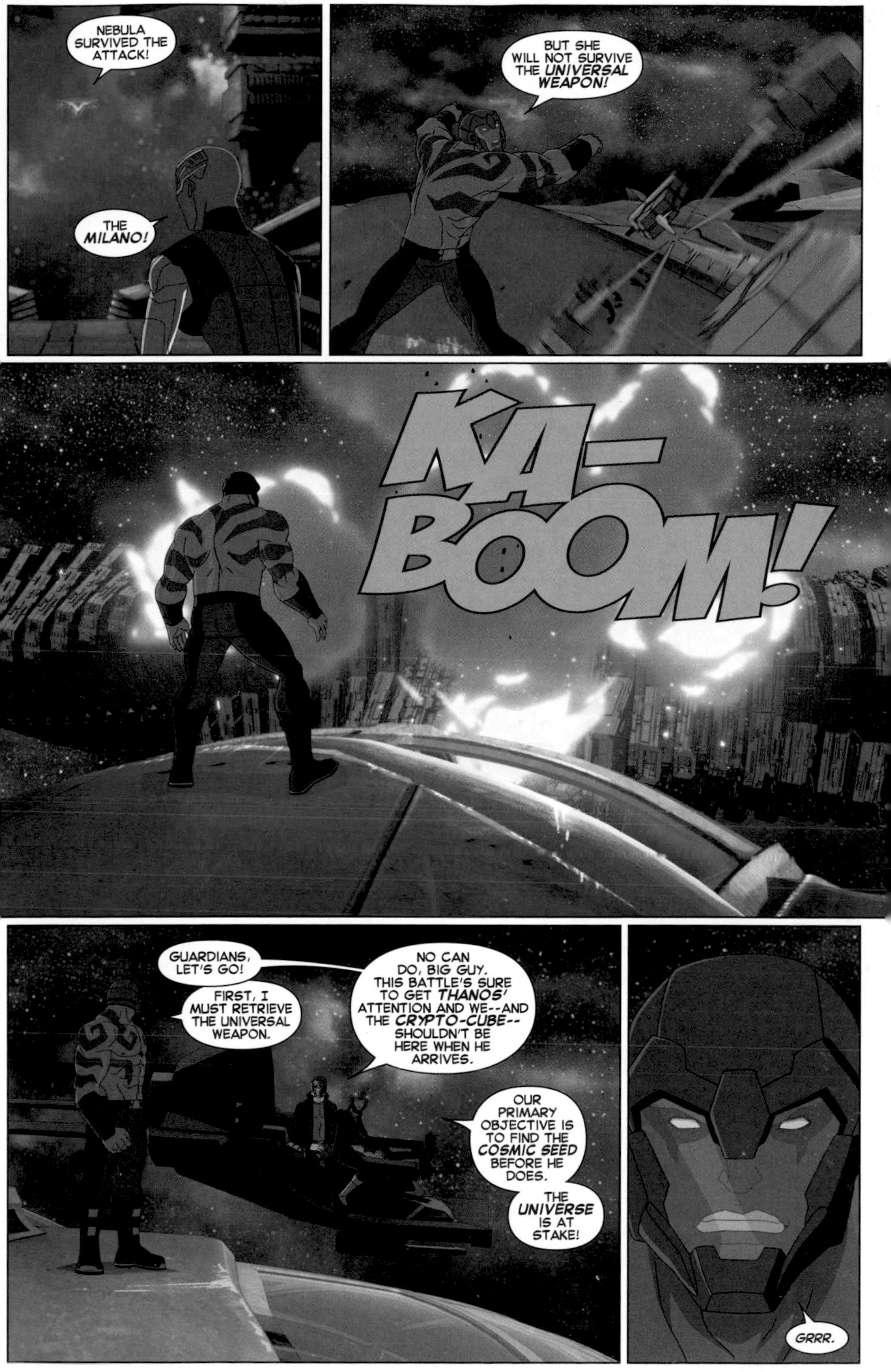
NEBULA SURVIVED THE ATTACK!
THE MILANO!
BUT SHE WILL NOT SURVIVE THE UNIVERSAL WEAPON!
KA-BOOM!
GUARDIANS, LET'S GO!
FIRST, I MUST RETRIEVE THE UNIVERSAL WEAPON.
NO CAN DO, BIG GUY. THIS BATTLE'S SURE TO GET THANOS' ATTENTION AND WE--AND THE CRYPTO-CUBE--SHOULDN'T BE HERE WHEN HE ARRIVES.
OUR PRIMARY OBJECTIVE IS TO FIND THE COSMIC SEED BEFORE HE DOES.
THE UNIVERSE IS AT STAKE!
GRRR.

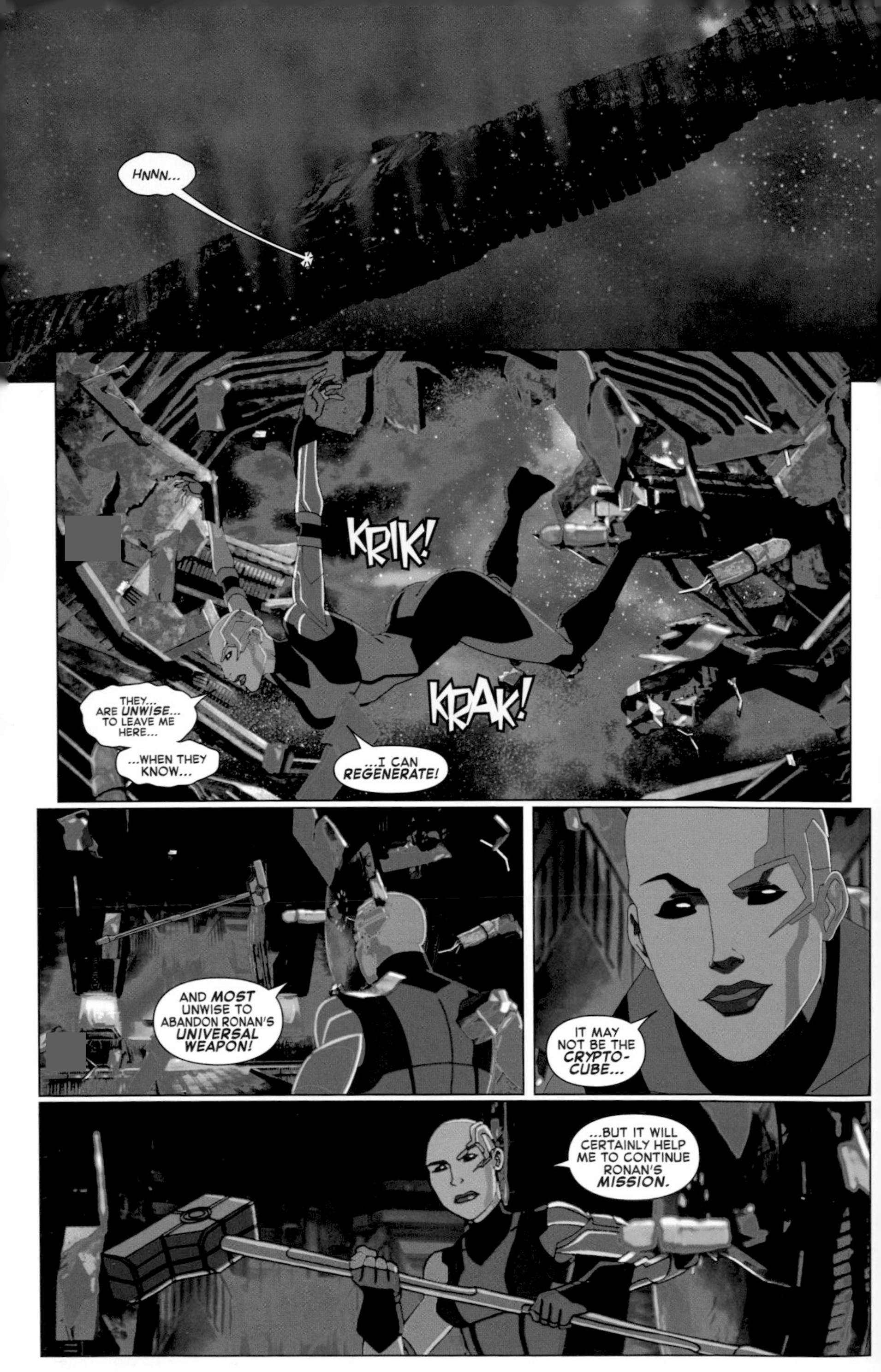
HNNN...
KRIK!
KRAK!
THEY... ARE UNWISE... TO LEAVE ME HERE...
...WHEN THEY KNOW...
...I CAN REGENERATE!
AND MOST UNWISE TO ABANDON RONAN'S UNIVERSAL WEAPON!
IT MAY NOT BE THE CRYPTO-CUBE...
...BUT IT WILL CERTAINLY HELP ME TO CONTINUE RONAN'S MISSION.

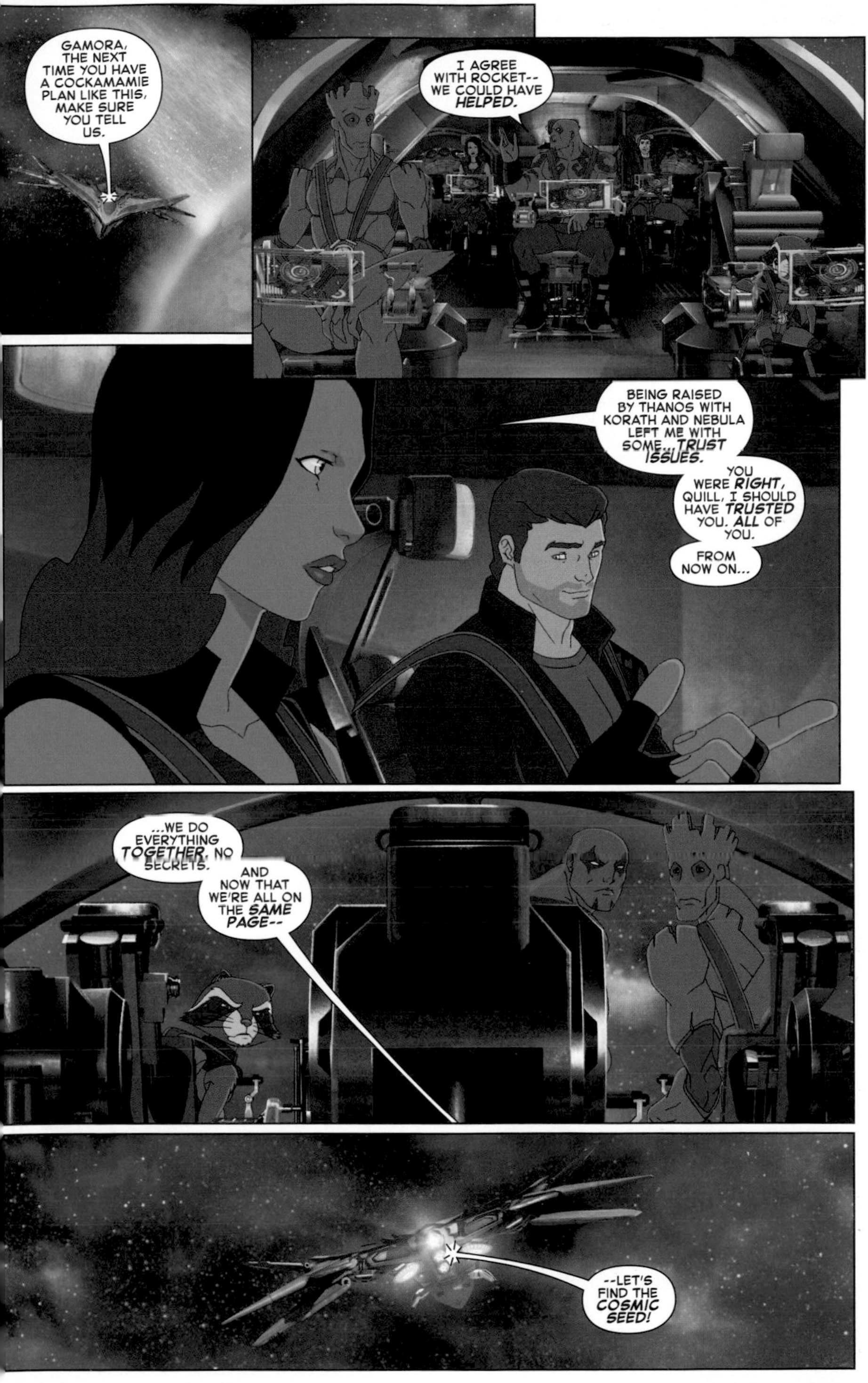
GAMORA, THE NEXT TIME YOU HAVE A COCKAMAMIE PLAN LIKE THIS, MAKE SURE YOU TELL US.
I AGREE WITH ROCKET-- WE COULD HAVE HELPED.
BEING RAISED BY THANOS WITH KORATH AND NEBULA LEFT ME WITH SOME... TRUST ISSUES.
YOU WERE RIGHT, QUILL, I SHOULD HAVE TRUSTED YOU. ALL OF YOU.
FROM NOW ON...
...WE DO EVERYTHING TOGETHER. NO SECRETS.
AND NOW THAT WE'RE ALL ON THE SAME PAGE--
--LET'S FIND THE COSMIC SEED!

TO SAVE THE GUARDIANS FROM AN ALIEN SYMBIOTE...

...WILL ROCKET DESTROY GROOT?

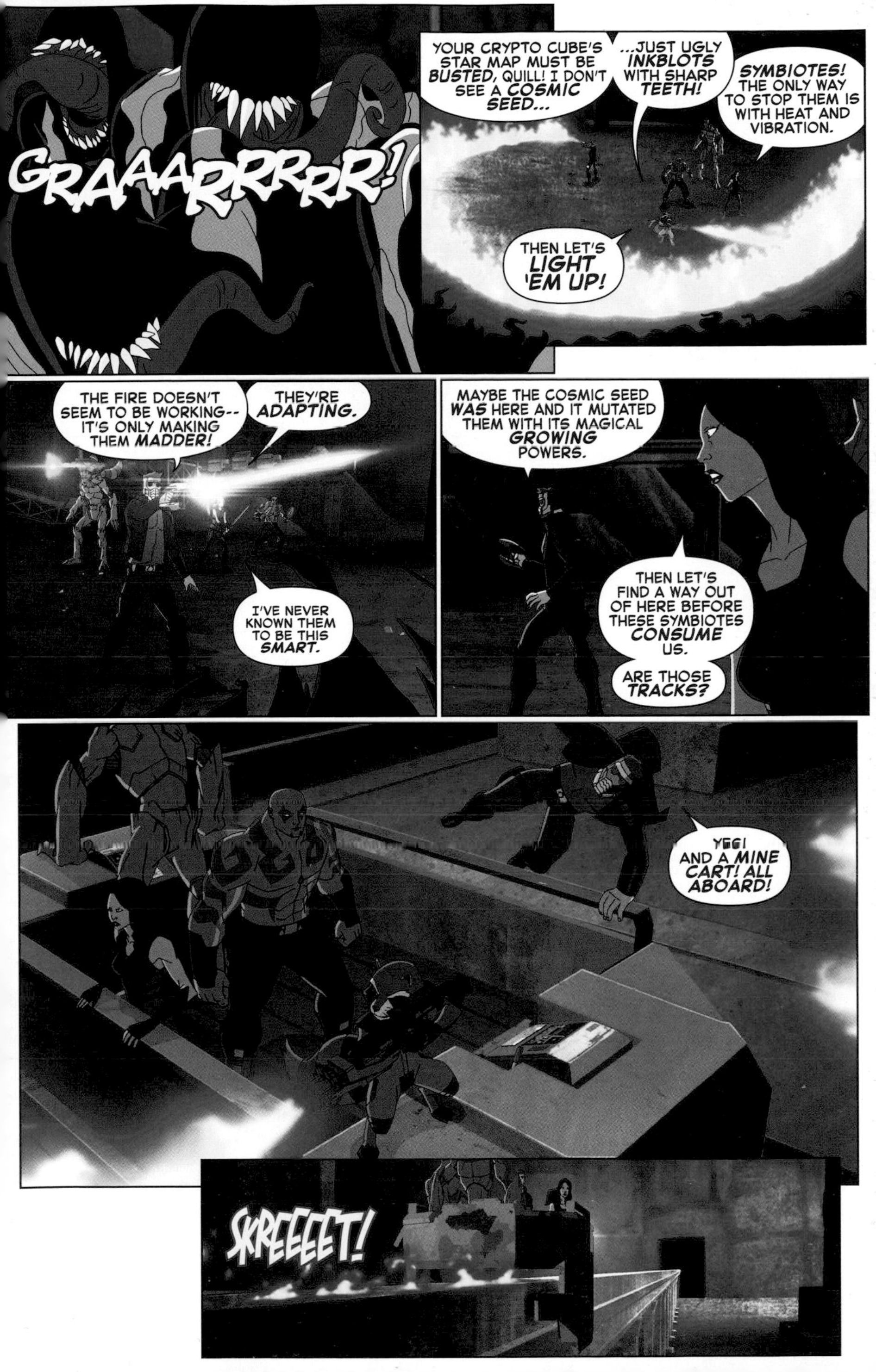
GRAAAARRRRR!
YOUR CRYPTO CUBE'S STAR MAP MUST BE BUSTED, QUILL! I DON'T SEE A COSMIC SEED...
...JUST UGLY INKBLOTS WITH SHARP TEETH!
SYMBIOTES! THE ONLY WAY TO STOP THEM IS WITH HEAT AND VIBRATION.
THEN LET'S LIGHT 'EM UP!
THE FIRE DOESN'T SEEM TO BE WORKING-- IT'S ONLY MAKING THEM MADDER!
THEY'RE ADAPTING.
I'VE NEVER KNOWN THEM TO BE THIS SMART.
MAYBE THE COSMIC SEED WAS HERE AND IT MUTATED THEM WITH ITS MAGICAL GROWING POWERS.
THEN LET'S FIND A WAY OUT OF HERE BEFORE THESE SYMBIOTES CONSUME US.
ARE THOSE TRACKS?
AND A MINE CART! ALL ABOARD!
SKREEEEET!

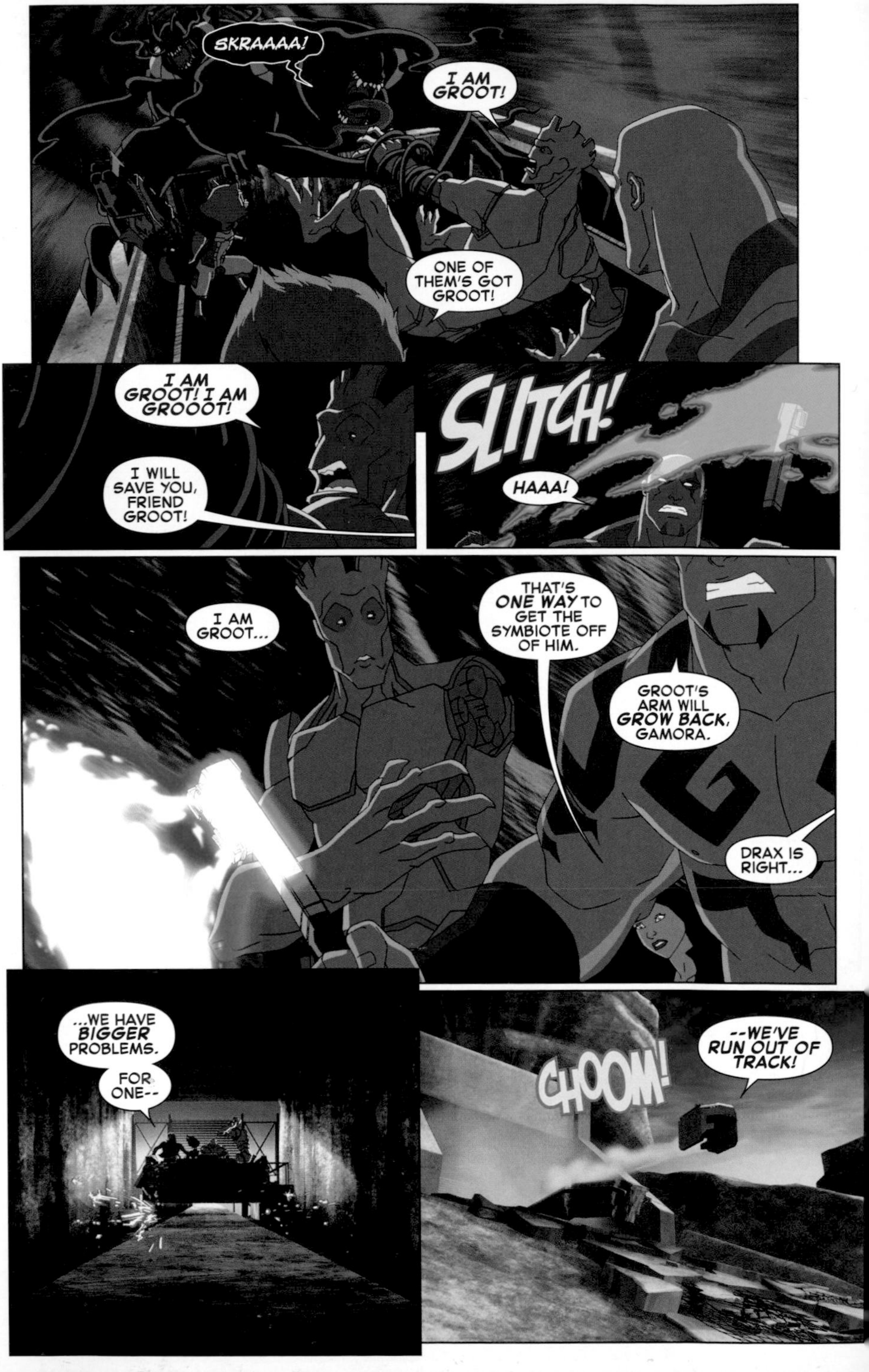
SKRAAAA!
I AM GROOT!
ONE OF THEM'S GOT GROOT!
I AM GROOT! I AM GROOOT!
I WILL SAVE YOU, FRIEND GROOT!
SLITCH!
HAAA!
I AM GROOT...
THAT'S ONE WAY TO GET THE SYMBIOTE OFF OF HIM.
GROOT'S ARM WILL GROW BACK, GAMORA.
DRAX IS RIGHT...
...WE HAVE BIGGER PROBLEMS.
FOR ONE--
CHOOM!
--WE'VE RUN OUT OF TRACK!

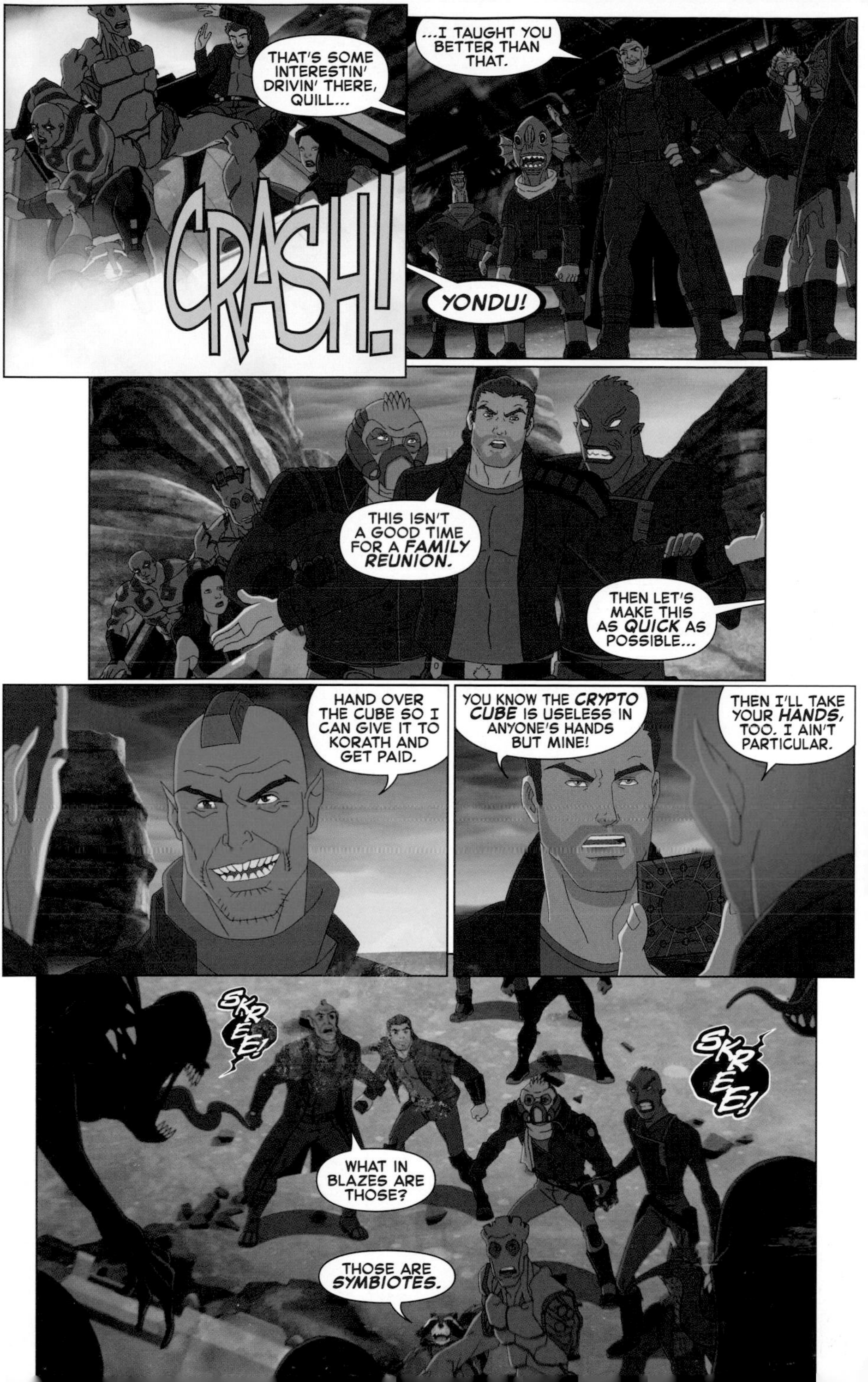

THAT'S SOME INTERESTIN' DRIVIN' THERE, QUILL...
CRASH!
...I TAUGHT YOU BETTER THAN THAT.
YONDU!
THIS ISN'T A GOOD TIME FOR A FAMILY REUNION.
THEN LET'S MAKE THIS AS QUICK AS POSSIBLE...
HAND OVER THE CUBE SO I CAN GIVE IT TO KORATH AND GET PAID.
YOU KNOW THE CRYPTO CUBE IS USELESS IN ANYONE'S HANDS BUT MINE!
THEN I'LL TAKE YOUR HANDS, TOO. I AIN'T PARTICULAR.
SKREE!
SKREE!
WHAT IN BLAZES ARE THOSE?
THOSE ARE SYMBIOTES.

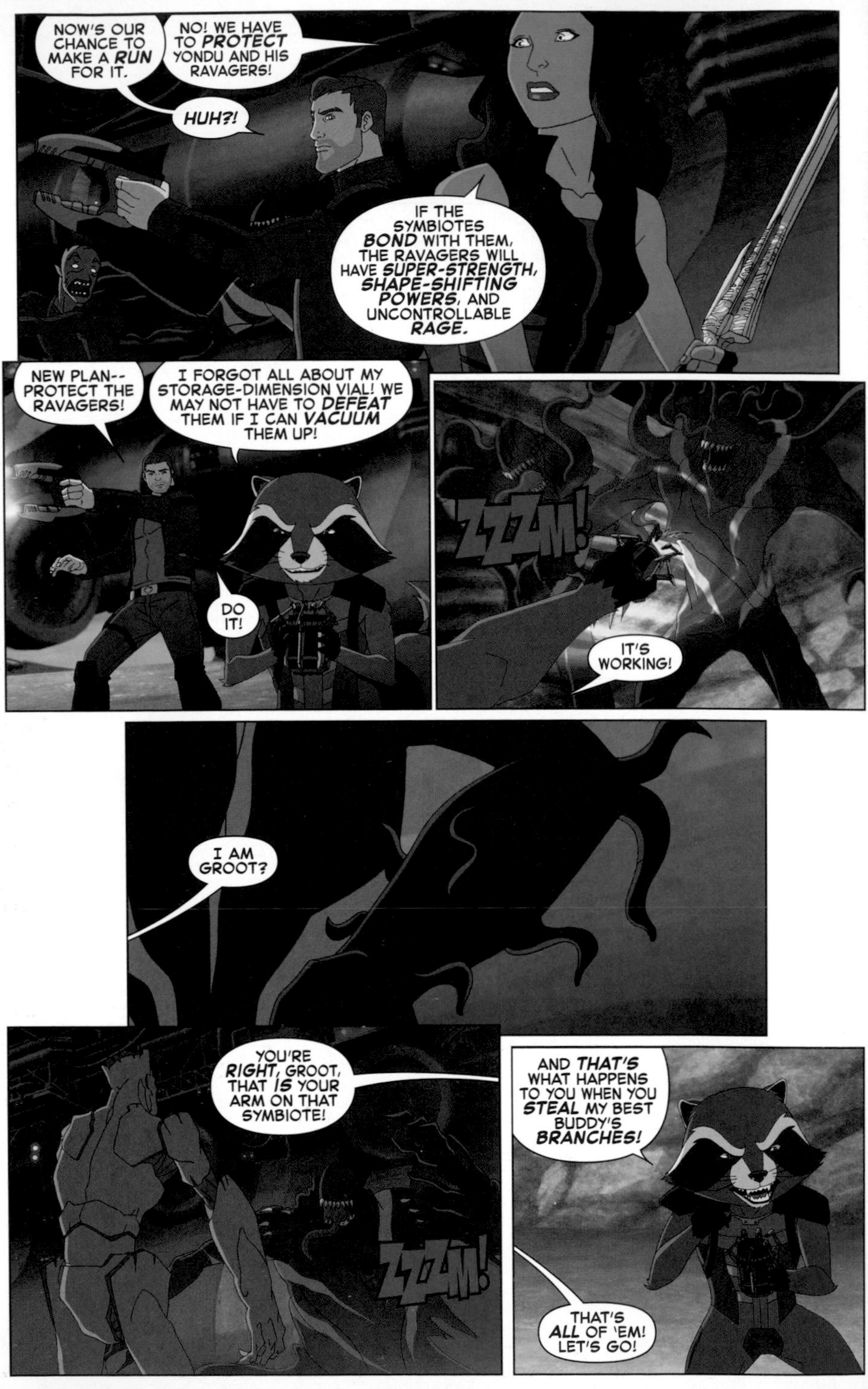
NOW'S OUR CHANCE TO MAKE A RUN FOR IT.
NO! WE HAVE TO PROTECT YONDU AND HIS RAVAGERS!
HUH?!
IF THE SYMBIOTES BOND WITH THEM, THE RAVAGERS WILL HAVE SUPER-STRENGTH, SHAPE-SHIFTING POWERS, AND UNCONTROLLABLE RAGE.
NEW PLAN-- PROTECT THE RAVAGERS!
I FORGOT ALL ABOUT MY STORAGE-DIMENSION VIAL! WE MAY NOT HAVE TO DEFEAT THEM IF I CAN VACUUM THEM UP!
DO IT!
ZZZM!
IT'S WORKING!
I AM GROOT?
YOU'RE RIGHT, GROOT, THAT IS YOUR ARM ON THAT SYMBIOTE!
ZZZM!
AND THAT'S WHAT HAPPENS TO YOU WHEN YOU STEAL MY BEST BUDDY'S BRANCHES!
THAT'S ALL OF 'EM! LET'S GO!

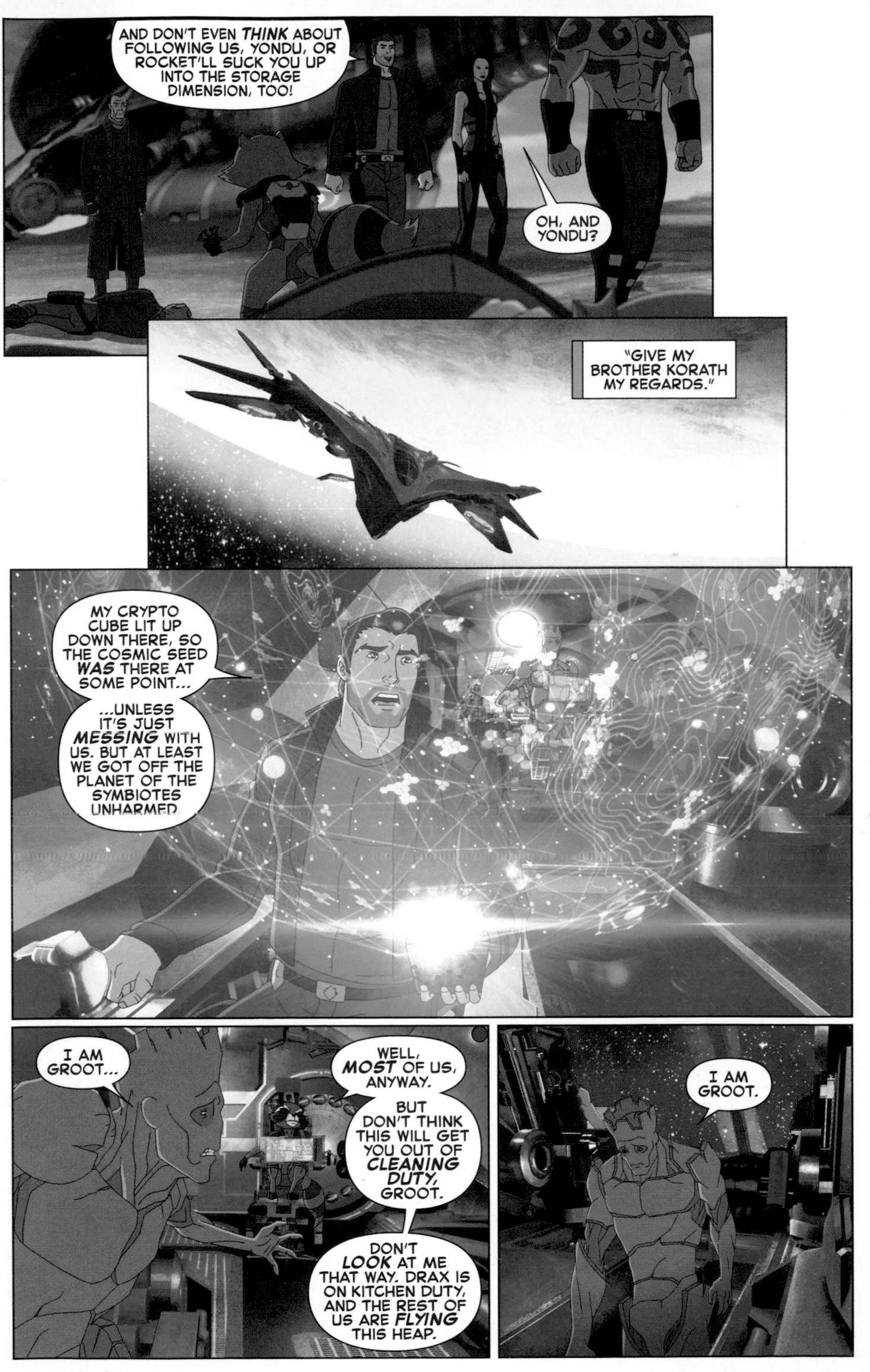

AND DON'T EVEN THINK ABOUT FOLLOWING US, YONDU, OR ROCKET'LL SUCK YOU UP INTO THE STORAGE DIMENSION, TOO!
OH, AND YONDU?
"GIVE MY BROTHER KORATH MY REGARDS."
MY CRYPTO CUBE LIT UP DOWN THERE, SO THE COSMIC SEED WAS THERE AT SOME POINT...
...UNLESS IT'S JUST MESSING WITH US. BUT AT LEAST WE GOT OFF THE PLANET OF THE SYMBIOTES UNHARMED.
I AM GROOT...
WELL, MOST OF US, ANYWAY.
BUT DON'T THINK THIS WILL GET YOU OUT OF CLEANING DUTY, GROOT.
DON'T LOOK AT ME THAT WAY. DRAX IS ON KITCHEN DUTY, AND THE REST OF US ARE FLYING THIS HEAP.
I AM GROOT.

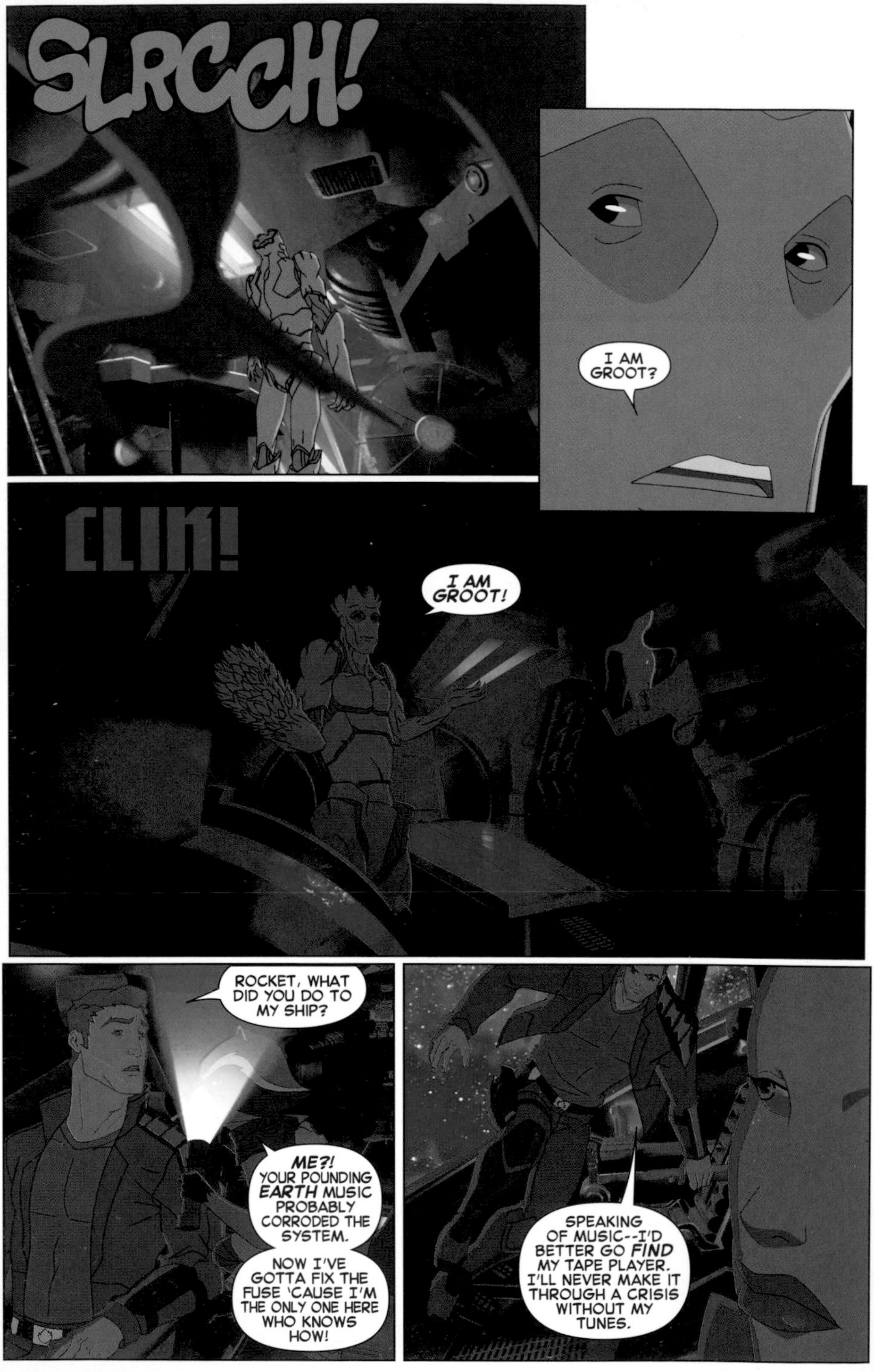
SLRCCH!
I AM GROOT?
CLIK!
I AM GROOT!
ROCKET, WHAT DID YOU DO TO MY SHIP?
ME?! YOUR POUNDING EARTH MUSIC PROBABLY CORRODED THE SYSTEM.
NOW I'VE GOTTA FIX THE FUSE 'CAUSE I'M THE ONLY ONE HERE WHO KNOWS HOW!
SPEAKING OF MUSIC--I'D BETTER GO FIND MY TAPE PLAYER. I'LL NEVER MAKE IT THROUGH A CRISIS WITHOUT MY TUNES.

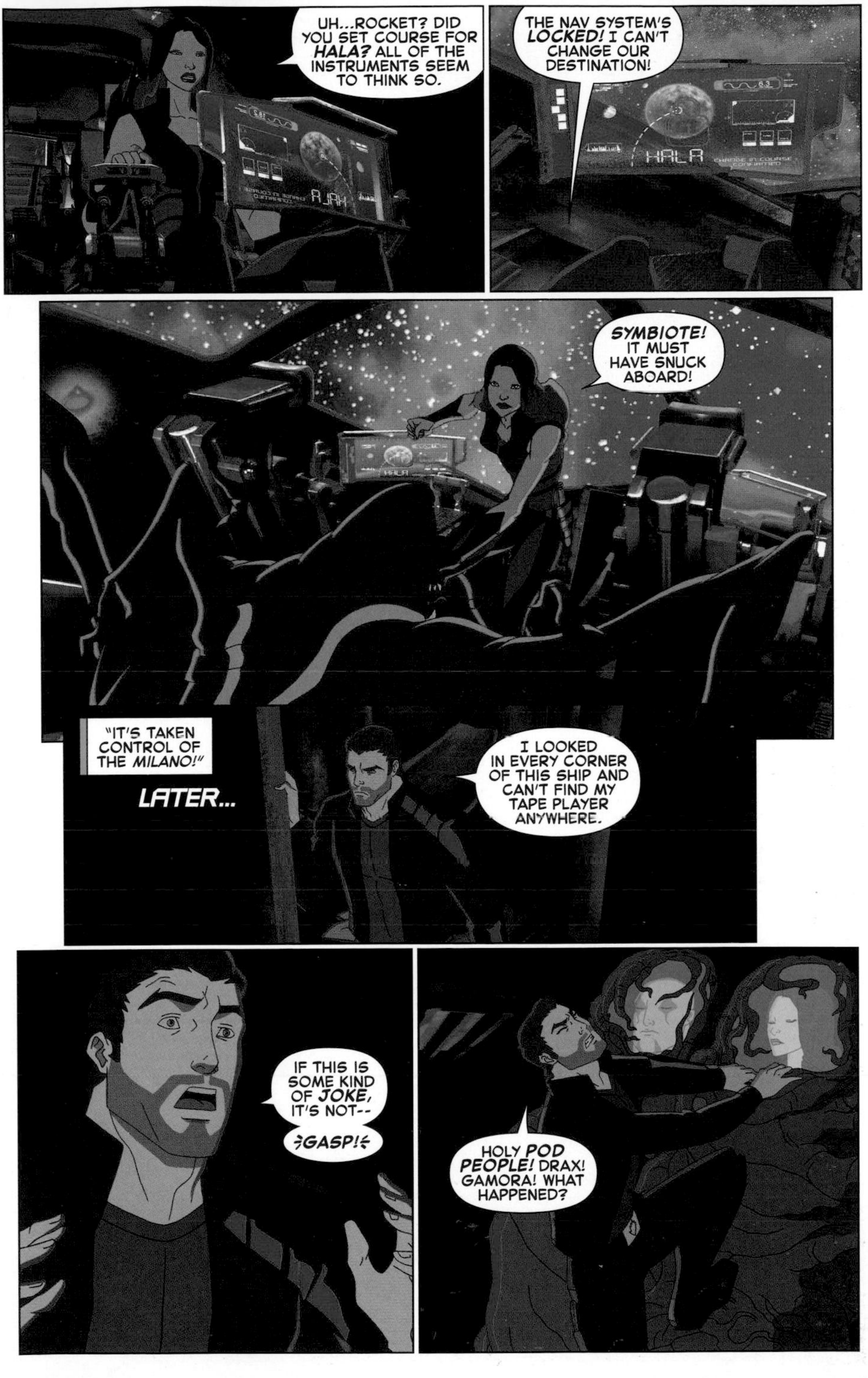
UH...ROCKET? DID YOU SET COURSE FOR HALA? ALL OF THE INSTRUMENTS SEEM TO THINK SO.
THE NAV SYSTEM'S LOCKED! I CAN'T CHANGE OUR DESTINATION!
HALA
SYMBIOTE! IT MUST HAVE SNUCK ABOARD!
"IT'S TAKEN CONTROL OF THE MILANO!"
LATER...
I LOOKED IN EVERY CORNER OF THIS SHIP AND CAN'T FIND MY TAPE PLAYER ANYWHERE.
IF THIS IS SOME KIND OF JOKE, IT'S NOT--
GASP!
HOLY POD PEOPLE! DRAX! GAMORA! WHAT HAPPENED?

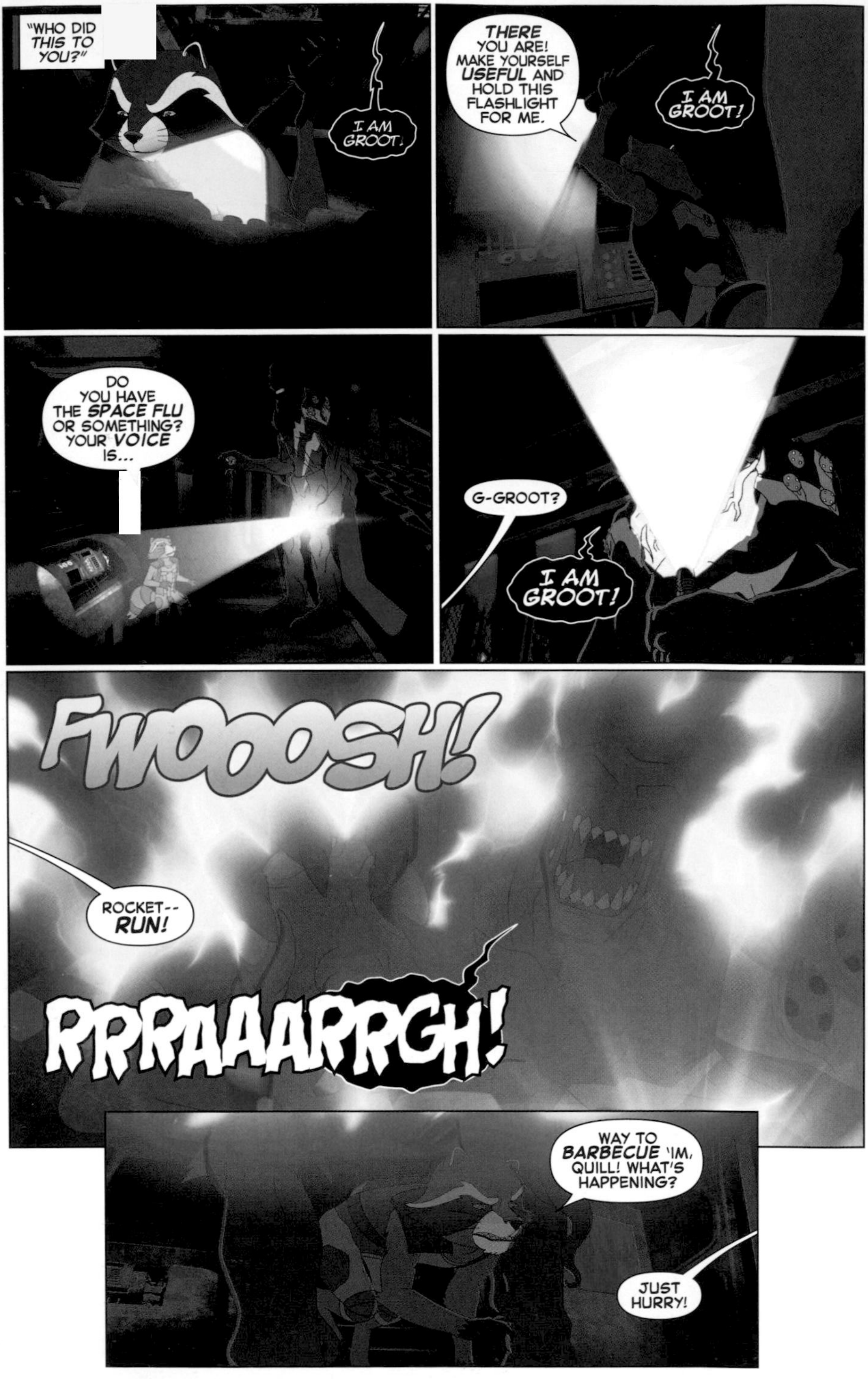
"WHO DID THIS TO YOU?"
I AM GROOT!
THERE YOU ARE! MAKE YOURSELF USEFUL AND HOLD THIS FLASHLIGHT FOR ME.
I AM GROOT!
DO YOU HAVE THE SPACE FLU OR SOMETHING? YOUR VOICE IS...
G-GROOT?
I AM GROOT!
FWOOOSH!
ROCKET-- RUN!
RRRAAARRGH!
WAY TO BARBECUE 'IM, QUILL! WHAT'S HAPPENING?
JUST HURRY!

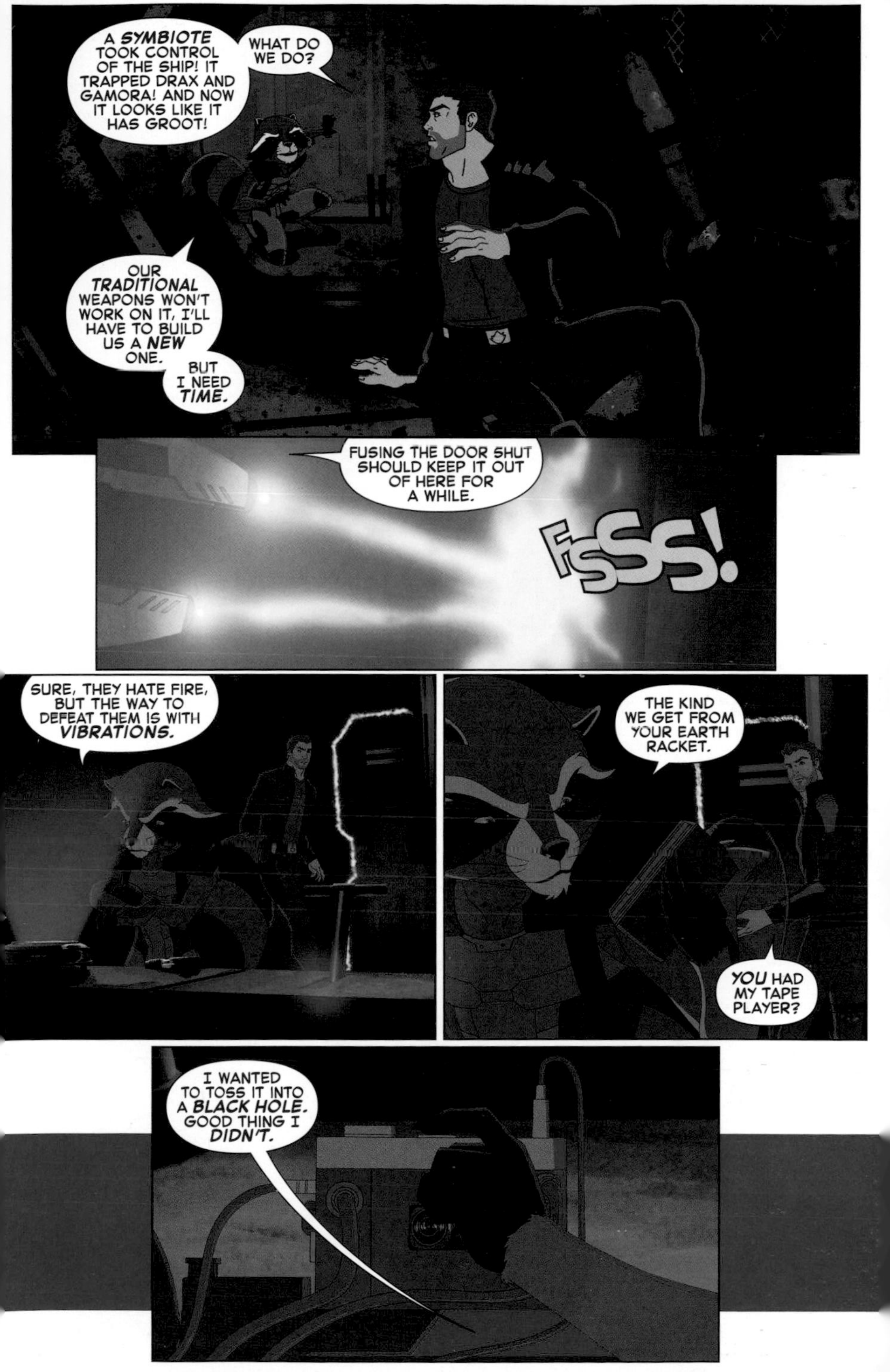
A SYMBIOTE TOOK CONTROL OF THE SHIP! IT TRAPPED DRAX AND GAMORA! AND NOW IT LOOKS LIKE IT HAS GROOT!
WHAT DO WE DO?
OUR TRADITIONAL WEAPONS WON'T WORK ON IT, I'LL HAVE TO BUILD US A NEW ONE.
BUT I NEED TIME.
FUSING THE DOOR SHUT SHOULD KEEP IT OUT OF HERE FOR A WHILE.
FSSS!
SURE, THEY HATE FIRE, BUT THE WAY TO DEFEAT THEM IS WITH VIBRATIONS.
THE KIND WE GET FROM YOUR EARTH RACKET.
YOU HAD MY TAPE PLAYER?
I WANTED TO TOSS IT INTO A BLACK HOLE. GOOD THING I DIDN'T.

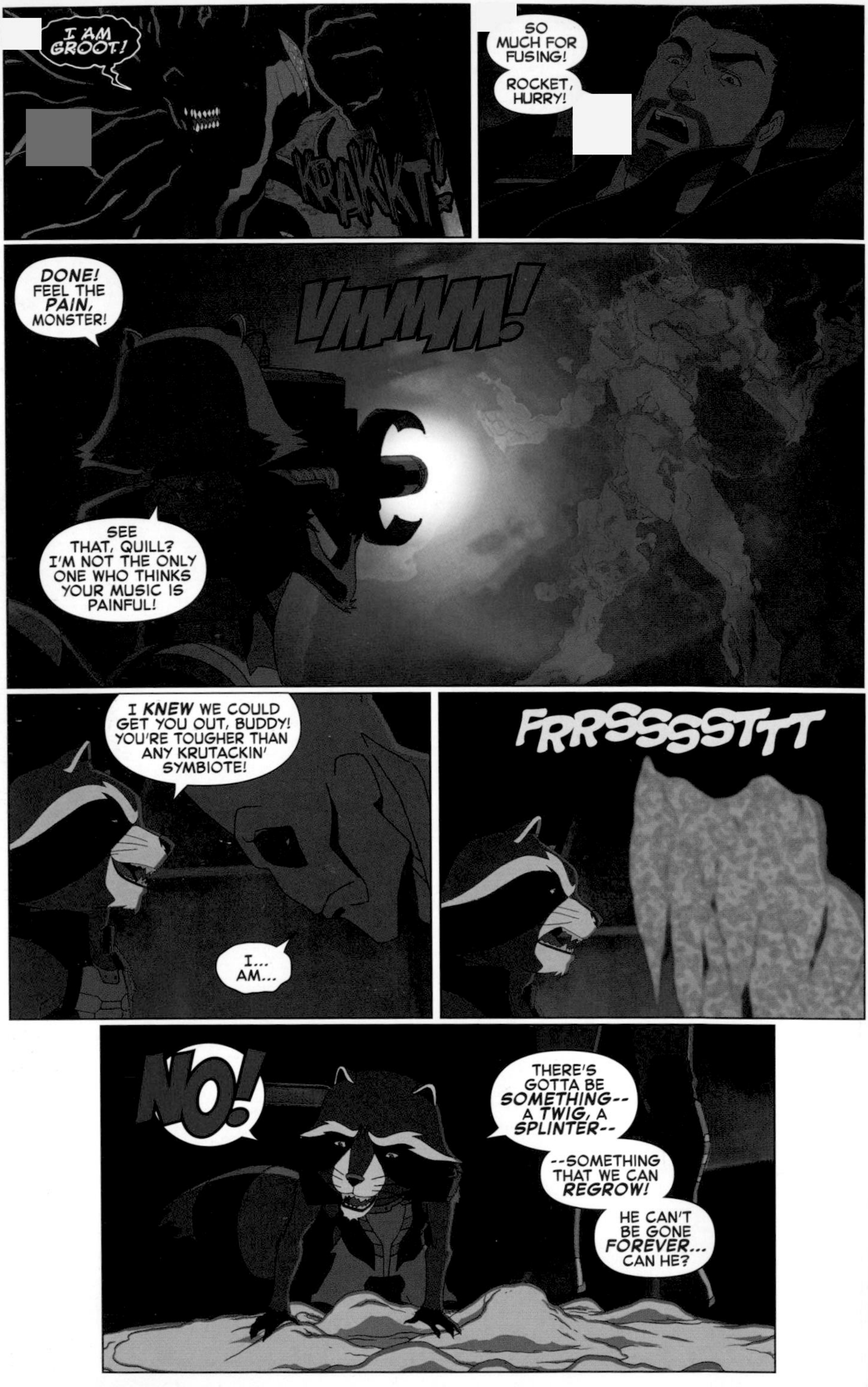
I AM GROOT!
KRAKKT!
SO MUCH FOR FUSING!
ROCKET, HURRY!
DONE! FEEL THE PAIN, MONSTER!
VMMMM!
SEE THAT, QUILL? I'M NOT THE ONLY ONE WHO THINKS YOUR MUSIC IS PAINFUL!
I KNEW WE COULD GET YOU OUT, BUDDY! YOU'RE TOUGHER THAN ANY KRUTACKIN' SYMBIOTE!
I... AM...
FRRSSSSSTTT
NO!
THERE'S GOTTA BE SOMETHING-- A TWIG, A SPLINTER--
--SOMETHING THAT WE CAN REGROW!
HE CAN'T BE GONE FOREVER... CAN HE?

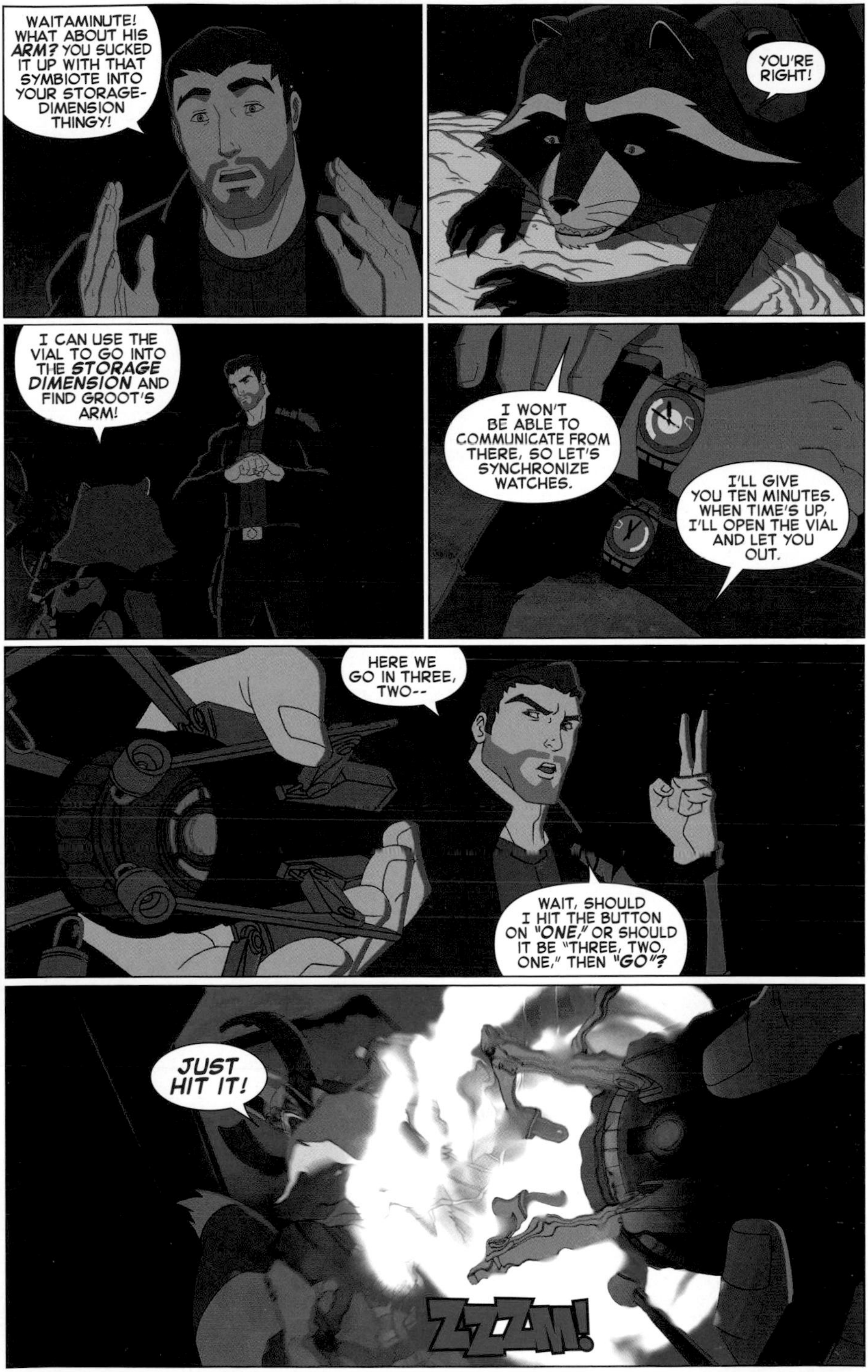

WAITAMINUTE! WHAT ABOUT HIS ARM? YOU SUCKED IT UP WITH THAT SYMBIOTE INTO YOUR STORAGE-DIMENSION THINGY!
YOU'RE RIGHT!
I CAN USE THE VIAL TO GO INTO THE STORAGE DIMENSION AND FIND GROOT'S ARM!
I WON'T BE ABLE TO COMMUNICATE FROM THERE, SO LET'S SYNCHRONIZE WATCHES.
I'LL GIVE YOU TEN MINUTES. WHEN TIME'S UP, I'LL OPEN THE VIAL AND LET YOU OUT.
HERE WE GO IN THREE, TWO--
WAIT, SHOULD I HIT THE BUTTON ON "ONE," OR SHOULD IT BE "THREE, TWO, ONE," THEN "GO"?
JUST HIT IT!
ZZZZM!

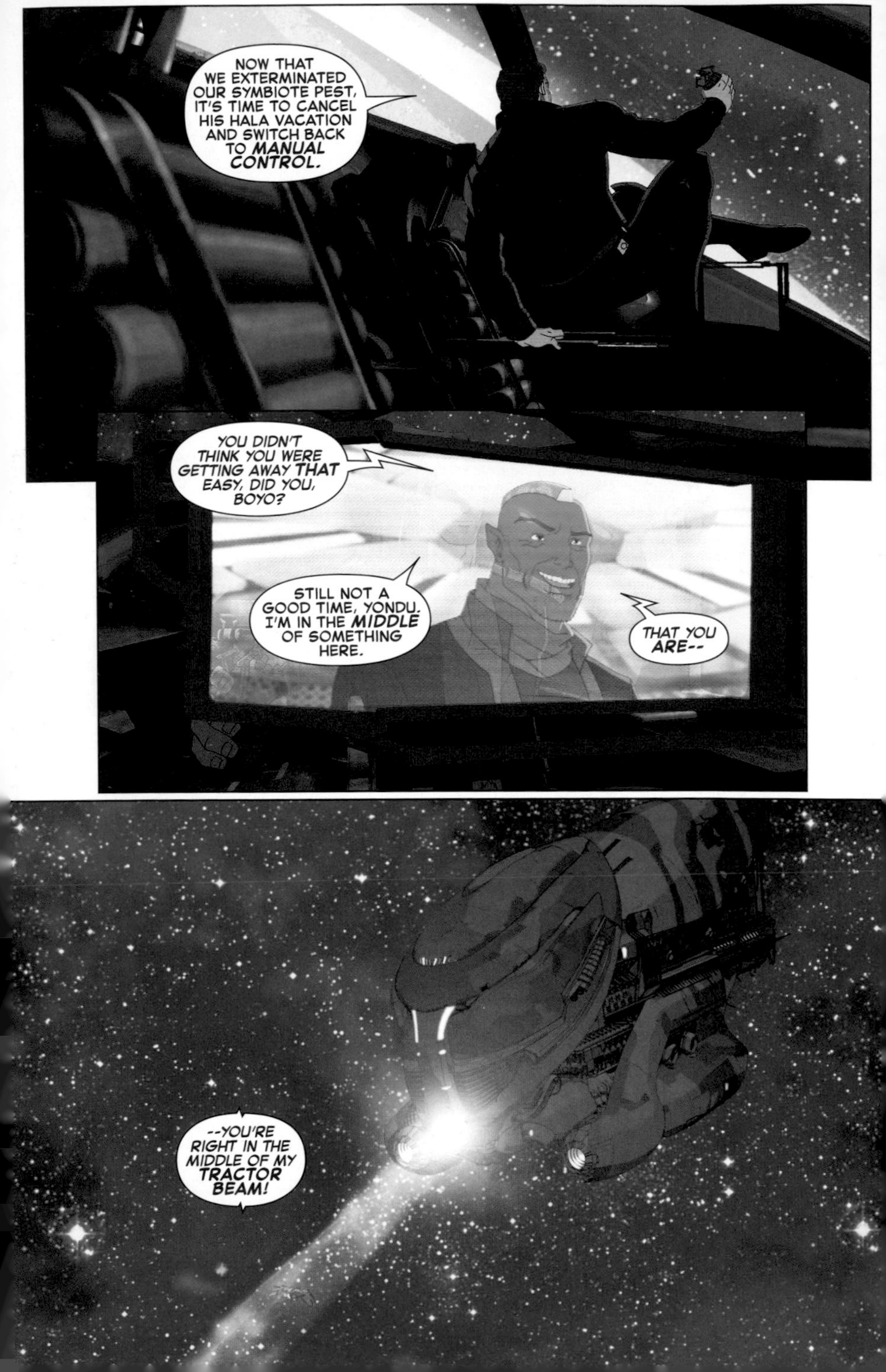
NOW THAT WE EXTERMINATED OUR SYMBIOTE PEST, IT'S TIME TO CANCEL HIS HALA VACATION AND SWITCH BACK TO MANUAL CONTROL.
YOU DIDN'T THINK YOU WERE GETTING AWAY THAT EASY, DID YOU, BOYO?
STILL NOT A GOOD TIME, YONDU. I'M IN THE MIDDLE OF SOMETHING HERE.
THAT YOU ARE--
--YOU'RE RIGHT IN THE MIDDLE OF MY TRACTOR BEAM!

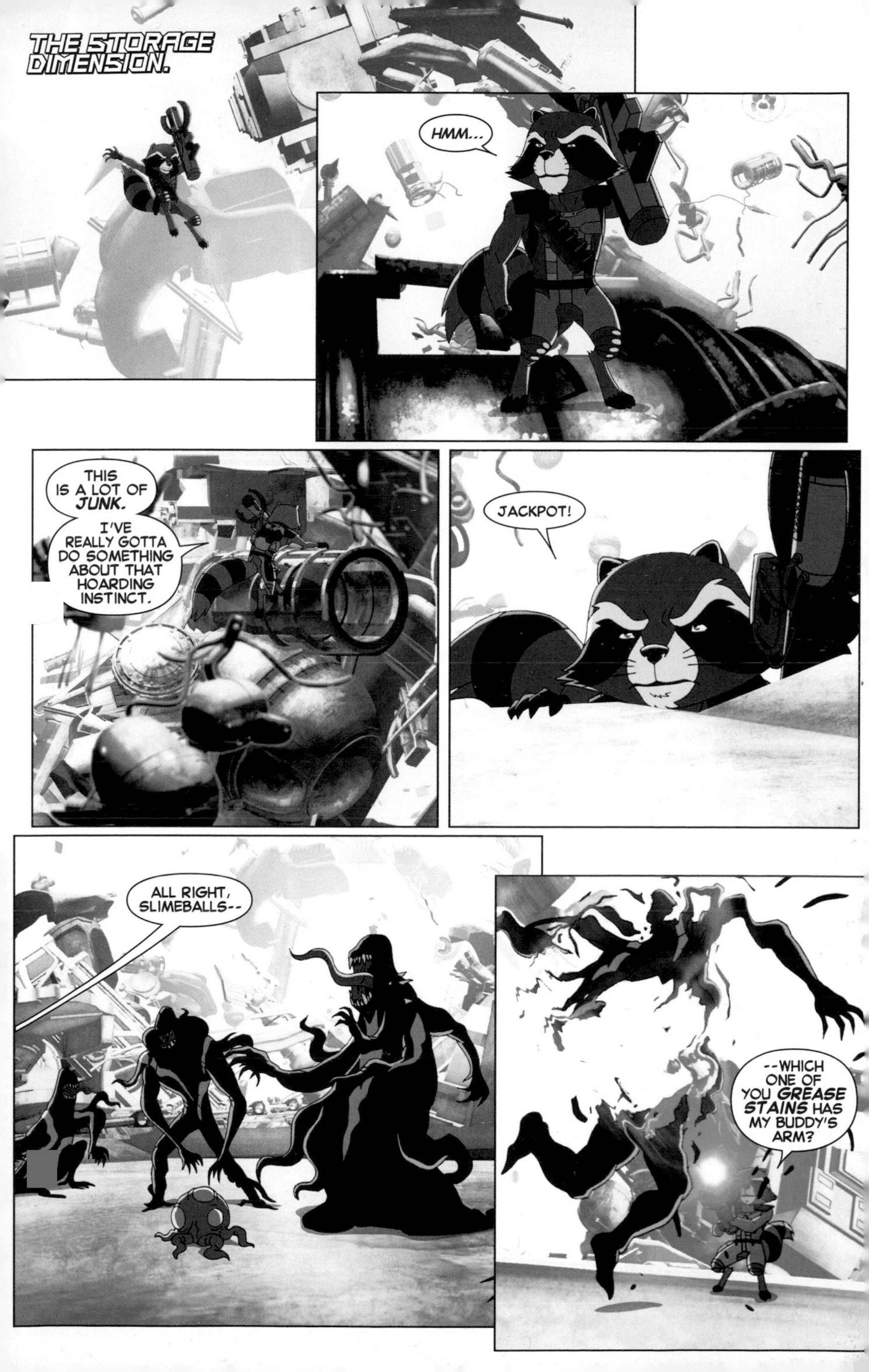
THE STORAGE DIMENSION.
HMM...
THIS IS A LOT OF JUNK.
I'VE REALLY GOTTA DO SOMETHING ABOUT THAT HOARDING INSTINCT.
JACKPOT!
ALL RIGHT, SLIMEBALLS--
--WHICH ONE OF YOU GREASE STAINS HAS MY BUDDY'S ARM?

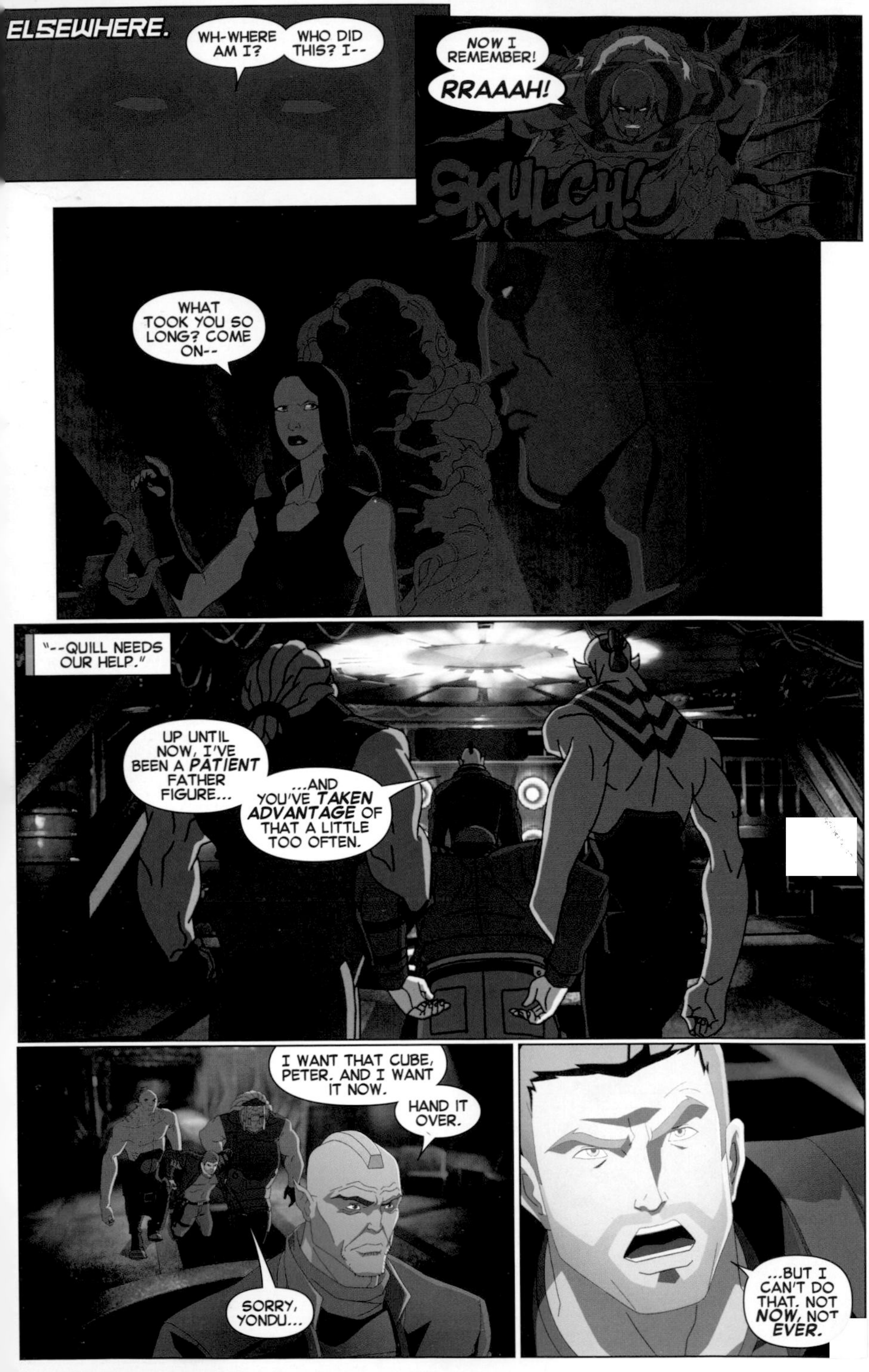
ELSEWHERE.
WH-WHERE AM I?
WHO DID THIS? I--
NOW I REMEMBER!
RRAAAH!
SKULCH!
WHAT TOOK YOU SO LONG? COME ON--
"--QUILL NEEDS OUR HELP."
UP UNTIL NOW, I'VE BEEN A PATIENT FATHER FIGURE...
...AND YOU'VE TAKEN ADVANTAGE OF THAT A LITTLE TOO OFTEN.
I WANT THAT CUBE, PETER. AND I WANT IT NOW.
HAND IT OVER.
SORRY, YONDU...
...BUT I CAN'T DO THAT. NOT NOW, NOT EVER.

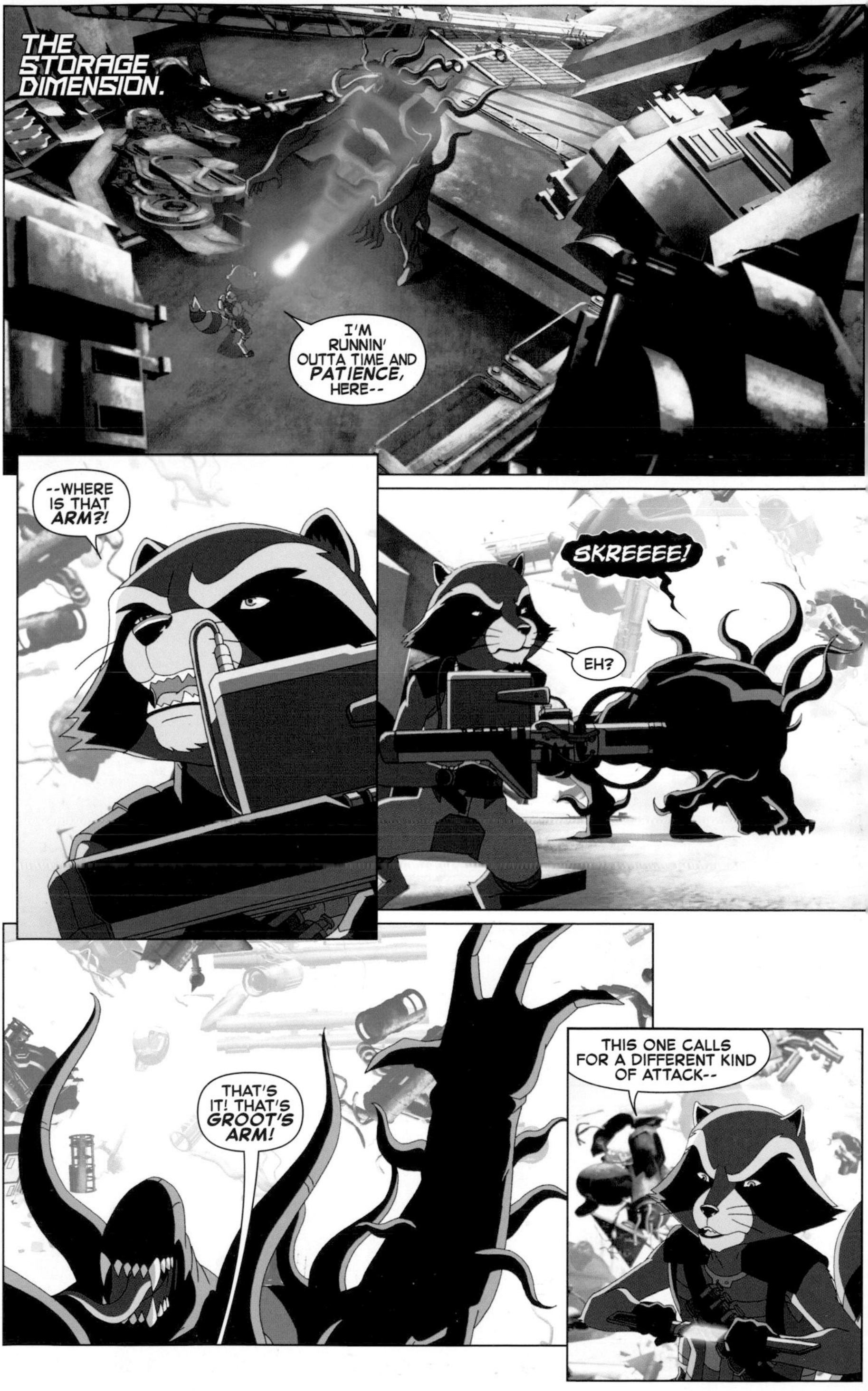
THE STORAGE DIMENSION.
I'M RUNNIN' OUTTA TIME AND PATIENCE, HERE--
--WHERE IS THAT ARM?!
SKREEEEE!
EH?
THAT'S IT! THAT'S GROOT'S ARM!
THIS ONE CALLS FOR A DIFFERENT KIND OF ATTACK--

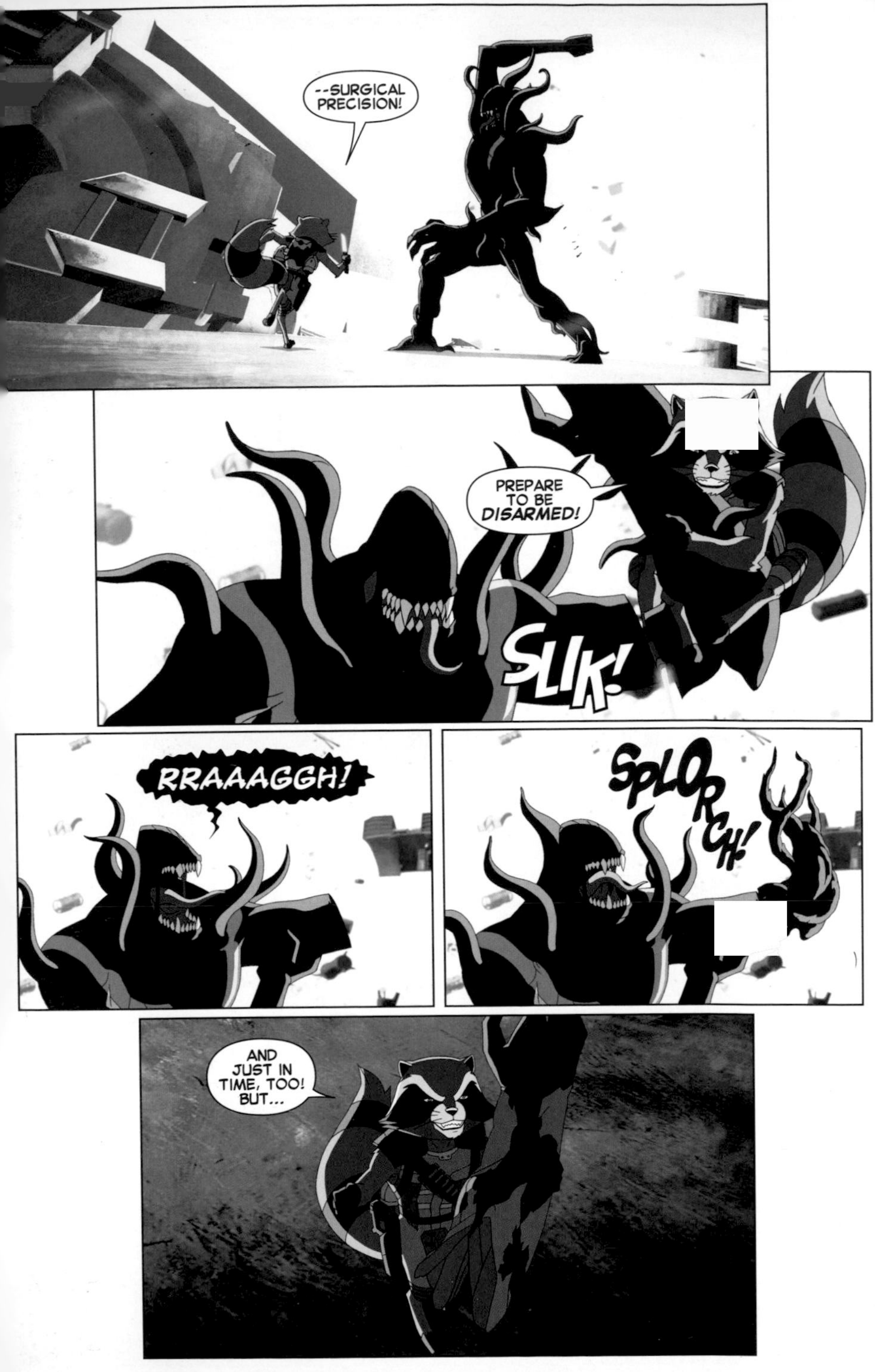
--SURGICAL PRECISION!
PREPARE TO BE DISARMED!
SLIK!
RRAAAGGH!
SPLORCH!
AND JUST IN TIME, TOO! BUT...

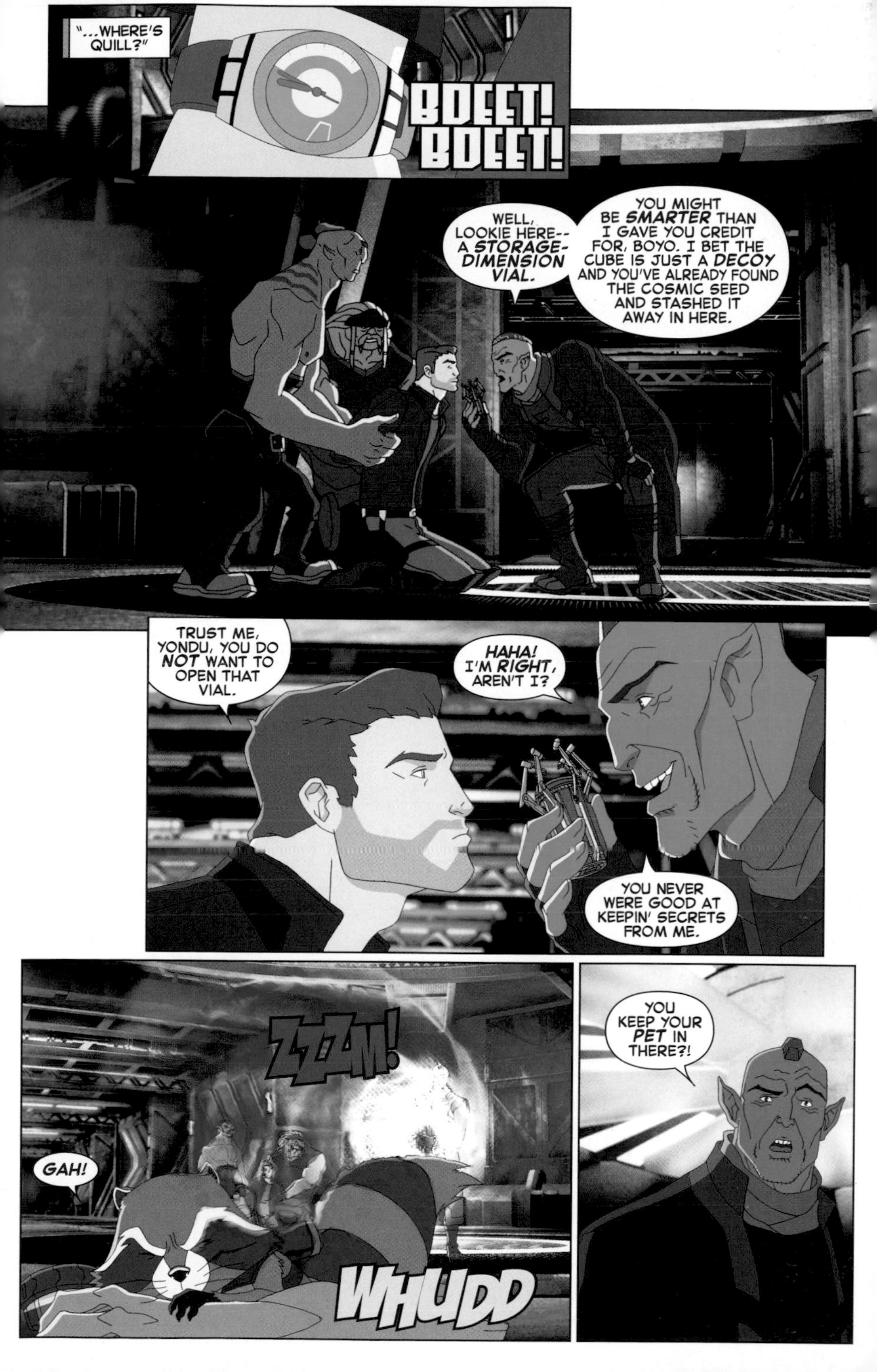
"...WHERE'S QUILL?"
BDEET! BDEET!
WELL, LOOKIE HERE-- A STORAGE-DIMENSION VIAL.
YOU MIGHT BE SMARTER THAN I GAVE YOU CREDIT FOR, BOYO. I BET THE CUBE IS JUST A DECOY AND YOU'VE ALREADY FOUND THE COSMIC SEED AND STASHED IT AWAY IN HERE.
TRUST ME, YONDU, YOU DO NOT WANT TO OPEN THAT VIAL.
HAHA! I'M RIGHT, AREN'T I?
YOU NEVER WERE GOOD AT KEEPIN' SECRETS FROM ME.
ZZZM!
GAH!
WHUDD
YOU KEEP YOUR PET IN THERE?!

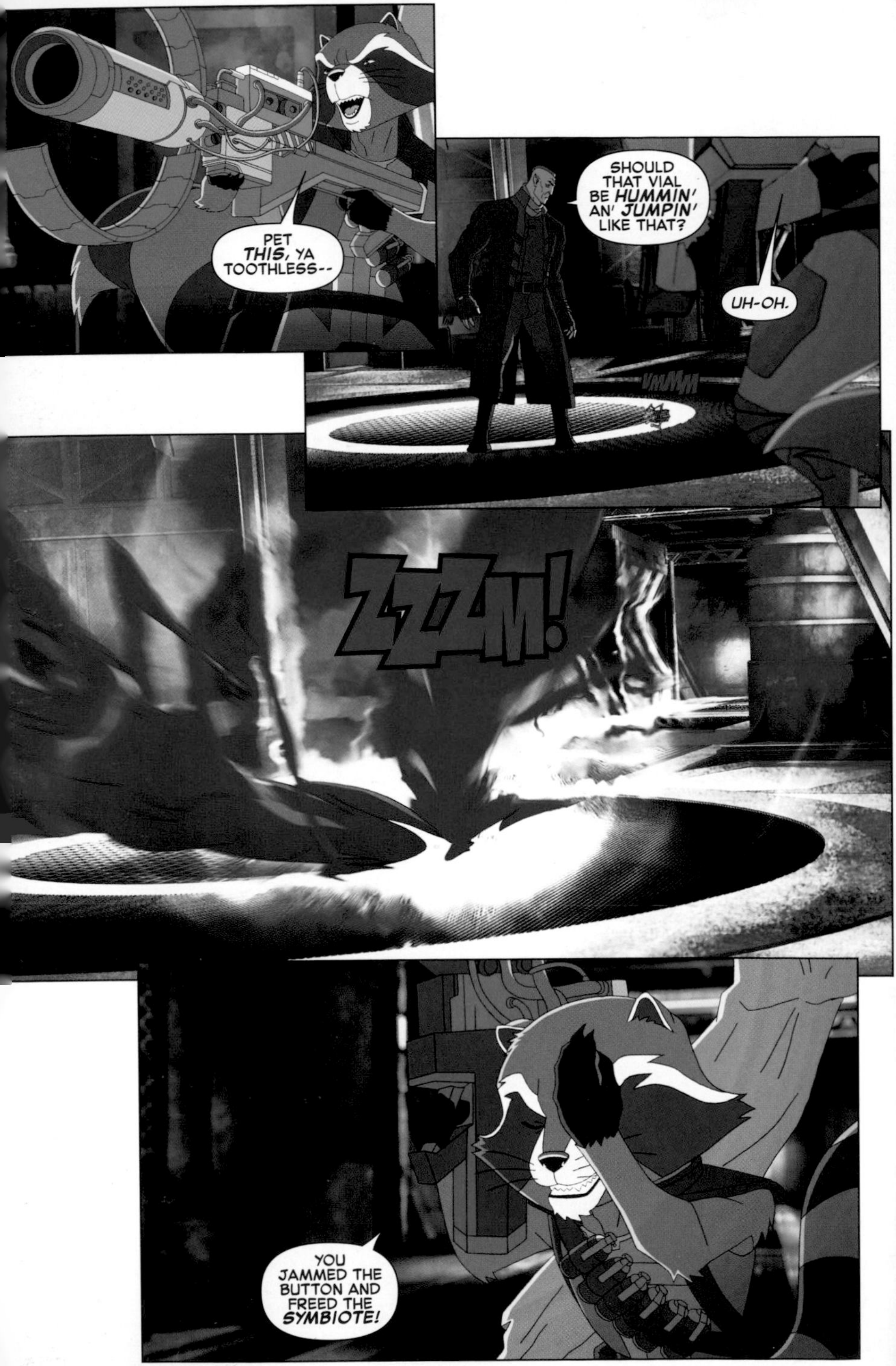
PET *THIS*, YA TOOTHLESS--
SHOULD THAT VIAL BE *HUMMIN'* AN' *JUMPIN'* LIKE THAT?
UH-OH.
VMMMM
ZZZZM!
YOU JAMMED THE BUTTON AND FREED THE *SYMBIOTE*!

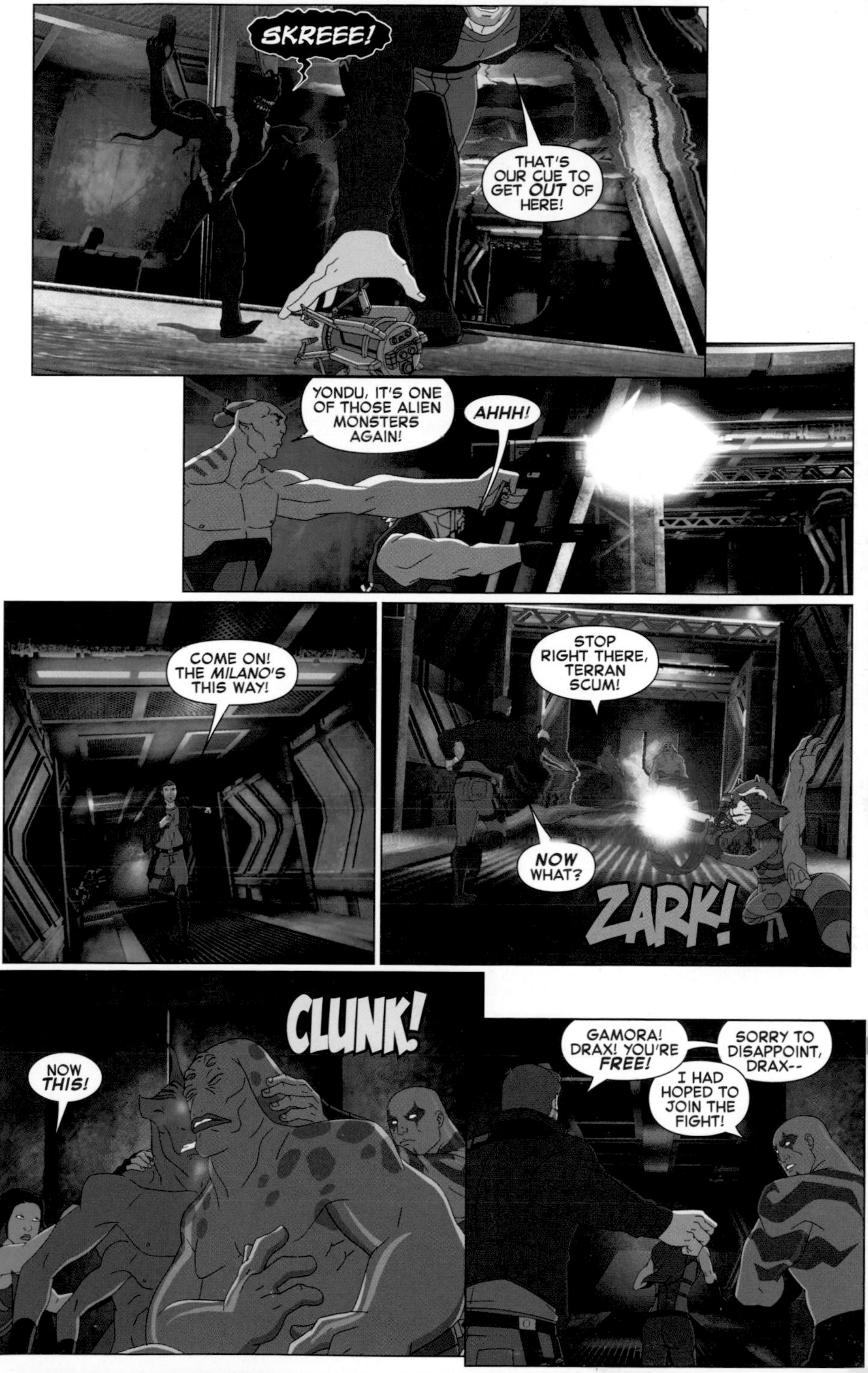
SKREEE!
THAT'S OUR CUE TO GET OUT OF HERE!
YONDU, IT'S ONE OF THOSE ALIEN MONSTERS AGAIN!
AHHH!
COME ON! THE MILANO'S THIS WAY!
STOP RIGHT THERE, TERRAN SCUM!
NOW WHAT?
ZARK!
CLUNK!
NOW THIS!
GAMORA! DRAX! YOU'RE FREE!
SORRY TO DISAPPOINT, DRAX--
I HAD HOPED TO JOIN THE FIGHT!

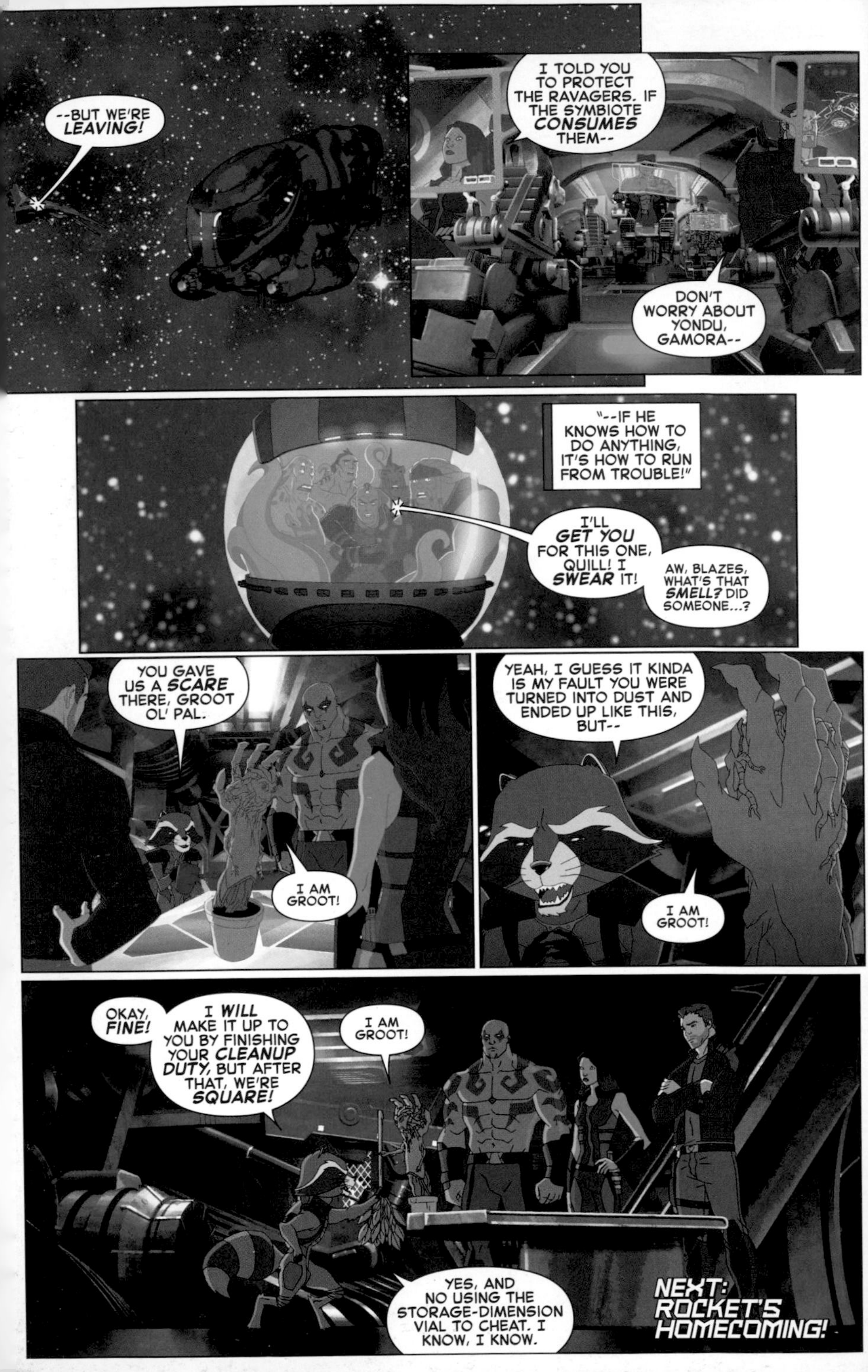

--BUT WE'RE LEAVING!
I TOLD YOU TO PROTECT THE RAVAGERS. IF THE SYMBIOTE CONSUMES THEM--
DON'T WORRY ABOUT YONDU, GAMORA--
"--IF HE KNOWS HOW TO DO ANYTHING, IT'S HOW TO RUN FROM TROUBLE!"
I'LL GET YOU FOR THIS ONE, QUILL! I SWEAR IT!
AW, BLAZES, WHAT'S THAT SMELL? DID SOMEONE...?
YOU GAVE US A SCARE THERE, GROOT OL' PAL.
I AM GROOT!
YEAH, I GUESS IT KINDA IS MY FAULT YOU WERE TURNED INTO DUST AND ENDED UP LIKE THIS, BUT--
I AM GROOT!
OKAY, FINE!
I WILL MAKE IT UP TO YOU BY FINISHING YOUR CLEANUP DUTY, BUT AFTER THAT, WE'RE SQUARE!
I AM GROOT!
YES, AND NO USING THE STORAGE-DIMENSION VIAL TO CHEAT. I KNOW, I KNOW.
NEXT: ROCKET'S HOMECOMING!

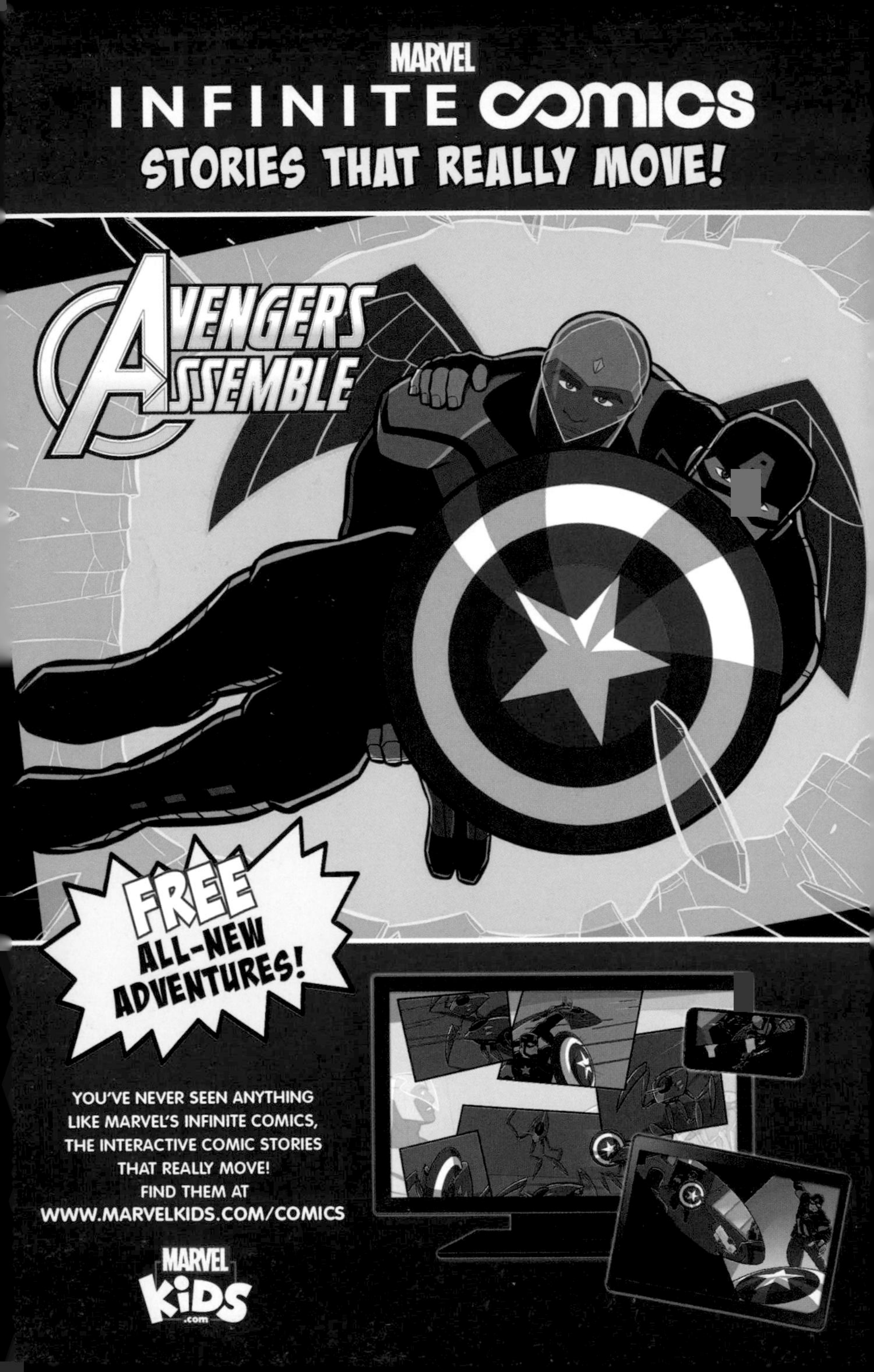

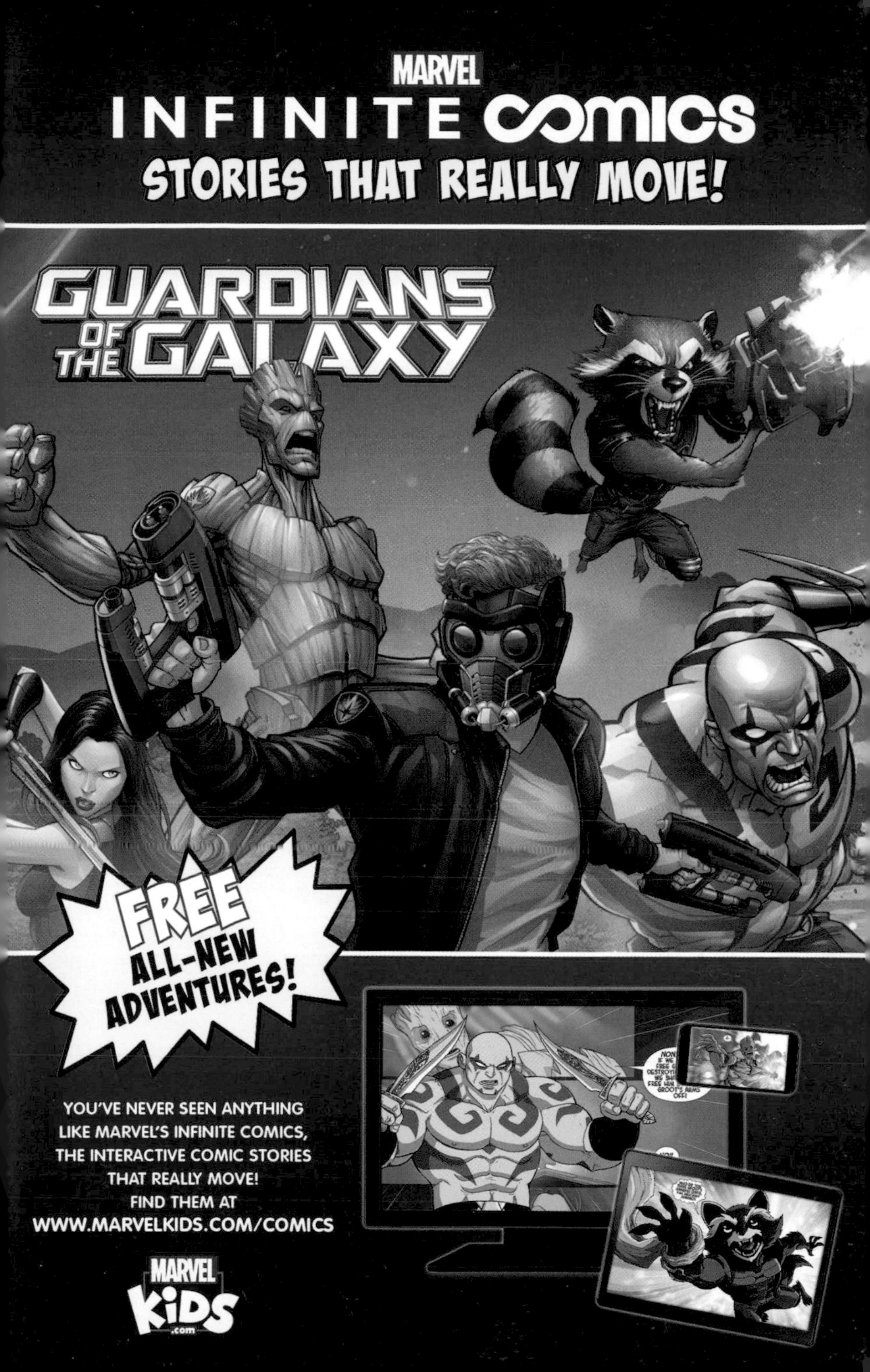
MARVEL
INFINITE COMICS
STORIES THAT REALLY MOVE!
GUARDIANS OF THE GALAXY
FREE ALL-NEW ADVENTURES!
YOU'VE NEVER SEEN ANYTHING
LIKE MARVEL'S INFINITE COMICS,
THE INTERACTIVE COMIC STORIES
THAT REALLY MOVE!
FIND THEM AT
WWW.MARVELKIDS.COM/COMICS
MARVEL KIDS .com

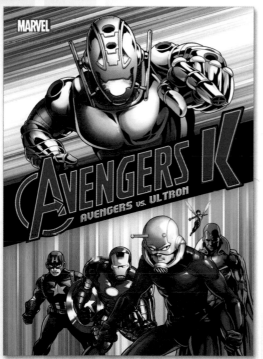

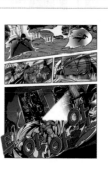

DEADPOOL AND WOLVERINE.
WHAT'S THE WORST THAT CAN HAPPEN?